PRAISE FOR *BLACK SUNDAY*

FINALIST FOR THE KIRKUS PRIZE IN FICTION

"Ms. Abraham's debut is fierce, deeply intimate, and shares with vivid detail a time and place I had never known . . . I am left reeling and in awe of her beautiful writing." —SARAH JESSICA PARKER

"Tola Rotimi Abraham's *Black Sunday* will destroy you . . . Abraham creates believable characters whose stories could easily have come from real life, stories full of mistakes, rejection, and poverty that mirror some of the things we've all lived through. That makes them simultaneously unique and universal, and it makes it easy to understand the way they see the world, even if their lens is ugly . . . *Black Sunday* is a literary wound that bleeds pain for a while, but you should stay the course, because that's followed by lots of love, beauty, and hope." —GABINO IGLESIAS, NPR

"A searing debut novel about Nigerian twin sisters whose childhood bond is shattered by the political and social strife that impoverishes their family . . . Abraham explores deeply felt themes of violence, kinship, and self-reliance." —ADRIENNE WESTENFELD, *Esquire*

"Set in Lagos over a period of decades, this absorbing debut follows twin sisters Bibike and Ariyike from the inseparable bonds of relative comfort to the challenges and independence of poverty." —KARLA STRAND, *Ms.*

"[A] piercing, supple debut . . . Abraham stuffs her novel past brimming, but its sophisticated structure and propulsive narration allow her to tuck in a biting critique of corrupt colonial religion and universally exploitative men . . . Twin sisters cut adrift in a perilous, duplicitous world learn that 'only the wise survive.' A formidable debut."   —*Kirkus Reviews* (starred review)

"Abraham's gift as a writer is her ability to simultaneously see people's lives as both stories and as something more than narrative . . . Although Abraham's novel can be described as an exercise in confronting pain, her narrative is also an exercise in emboldening the 'female spirit.'"   —KEITH CONTORNO, *Chicago Review of Books*

"Arresting . . . Abraham writes with a fluid yet deliberate moral compass . . . Gripping . . . Exploring themes that delve into the power of storytelling, the fragility of identity, the nature of regret, and the power of redemption, Abraham writes with a grace and sophistication that belie this novel's debut status. Hers is a voice and a vision to be recognized and watched."   —CAROL HAGGAS, *Another Chicago Magazine*

"This may be her first book, but Tola Abraham's storytelling power is immediately apparent—lush, sharp, and shot through with hope!"   —*Well-Read Black Girl*

"A poignant debut."   —*Bustle*

"There are some novels that stay with you, imparting a lasting message and leaving an intangible impact. *Black Sunday*, a debut novel from author Tola Rotimi Abraham, is one of them . . . A profound narrative." *—Zora*

"This novel explores kinship, exploitation and making ends meet, love and loss, and what it means to be all alone even with siblings by your side." —ARRIEL VINSON, *Electric Literature*

"Abraham's fierce debut follows four Nigerian siblings living in Lagos from childhood in 1996 through early adulthood in 2015 . . . The novel's strength lies in its lush, unflinching scenes, as when a seemingly simple infection leads gradually but inexorably to a life-threatening condition, revealing the dynamics of the family and community along the way. Abraham mightily captures a sense of the stresses of daily life in a family, city, and culture that always seems on the edge of self-destruction." *—Publishers Weekly*

"Abraham's debut novel tackles weighty topics like rape, self-discovery, and the mischief of prominent religious figures with a refreshing elegance. Bibike and Ariyike are nuanced characters who often make decisions with a jarred moral compass. Abraham gently ushers readers into both sisters' perspectives, inviting us into their journey to autonomous peace." *—Booklist*

"With stunning beauty and painful wisdom, Tola Rotimi Abraham's *Black Sunday* lays bare her characters' deepest aches and desires in a voice that is as haunting as it is addictive."

—MARGARET WILKERSON SEXTON,
author of *A Kind of Freedom* and *The Revisioners*

BLACK SUNDAY

A Novel

....

TOLA ROTIMI ABRAHAM

CATAPULT

NEW YORK

Copyright © 2020 by Tola Rotimi Abraham

Hardcover ISBN: 978-1-948226-56-1
Paperback ISBN: 978-1-64622-052-6

Cover design by Nicole Caputo
Book design by Wah-Ming Chang
Illustration by Nicole Caputo

Library of Congress Control Number: 2019944287

Printed in the United States of America
1 3 5 7 9 10 8 6 4 2

For Afolarori, Oluwatomi, Akinloluwa, and Oluwaseye

Iya ni wura, Baba ni dingi.
YORUBA PROVERB

Mother is gold, Father is a mirror.

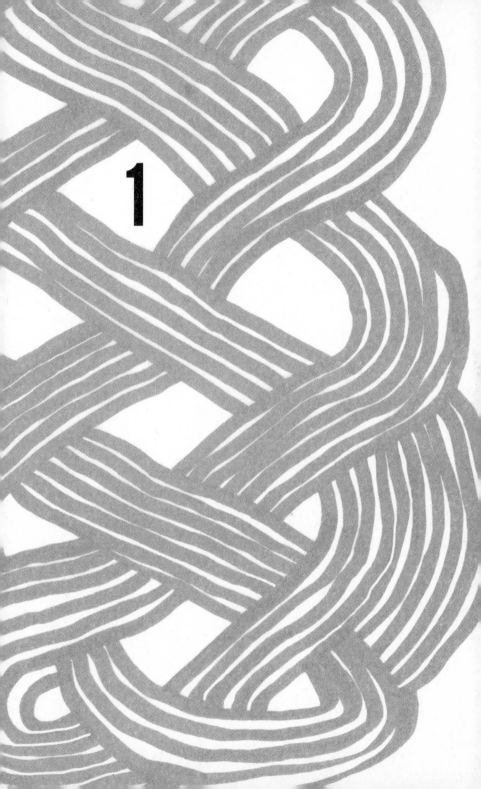

HOW TO BE A STUPID GIRL
IN LAGOS

BIBIKE

1996

THERE WERE MANY easy ways to be a stupid girl in Lagos. We were not stupid girls. We were bright with borrowed wisdom. We never paid full fare to drivers of yellow
city cabs before we arrived at the final stop. We did not wear
any kind of visible jewelry walking around busy streets like
Balogun. When we went to Tejuosho market and a stranger
shouted, "Hey. Fine girl. Stop, see your money for ground,"
we never stopped to look.

When many of the ECOMOG soldiers were return-
ing from peacekeeping in Liberia, flush with UN dollars,
we were still protected prepubescent girls, yet we knew to
avoid the one we called Uncle Timo, the one who gave all

the little girls Mills & Boon paperbacks wrapped in old newspapers.

MY TWIN SISTER and I were almost stupid girls once, and this is how it begins, with Ariyike and me lost on our way home from school. I am holding on to her out of habit; she is pulling away, walking up to and talking to every stranger we meet, asking over and over, "Uncle, please, where can we get a bus to Fadeyi?"

We are walking home from secondary school. Today is the first time we have been allowed to come home by ourselves. Our younger brothers, Andrew and Peter, attend Holy Child Academy, the primary school that shares a fence with the military cemetery where all the agbalumo trees grow. They don't need to be picked up. The church bus drops them off every day at half past four.

I am thinking of school and today's government studies class and *gerrymandering*, how I like the way that word sounds, well calculated and important, like *meandering*, only with purpose. Everything is better with purpose.

I am also thinking of Father, who likes to say our government studies teacher is verbose:

"Mr. Agbo fancies himself a university lecturer, he is always going off tangent, completely missing the point."

And of Mother, who likes to say: "We pay a lot of money for you girls to go to that school." Or: "You girls should listen to Mr. Agbo. He is a brilliant man."

We have walked for almost twenty minutes, and now we make our first stop, to buy roast plantains and groundnuts from the woman who is selling them under a 7 Up canopy. She is amused when we ask if she has any cold drinks for sale.

"Can you see any fridge here?" she asks. "Will I keep the drinks in my brassiere?" We are waiting for our plantains when Ariyike stops a stranger on a motorcycle. He is a tall man wearing combat shorts and a black T-shirt that says GOT MILK? in bold white print. They take a few steps together, her listening, him pointing. When she is done, she comes back under the canopy. I clench my right fist and put it under her chin.

"Here, take this microphone. Announce to all the world that we are two girls who don't know the way home," I say.

The woman selling plantains laughs. She says Ariyike is being stupid, walking up to strange men. She tells us that just last week three girls got kidnapped in Mushin. They were found dismembered in a roadside heap.

Ariyike looks at me like she is about to say something but changes her mind.

"So, what did that motorcycle man say?" I ask.

"He says we should come with him, he'd take us home," she says.

"Really?" I ask.

"No. He said keep walking straight down, the buses are waiting under the pedestrian bridge," she says.

Our plantains are soon ready. The woman gives us extra groundnuts.

"Pray for me o," she says. "I want fine ibeji twins like you two."

Ariyike assures her that we will pray every day. She is the friendly one. The *friendlier* one. My sister talks to strangers because she likes people, she likes to hear their stories, she likes to make people feel comfortable, welcome. I do not think that I am mean, I just let her be the nice and welcoming one. We work better that way.

I learned when I was a little girl that people always lie. I am not sure everyone means to lie. It is just that they have in their hearts ideas of who they should be, and they are trying to convince themselves that they are who they insist on being. It is tiring. I learn a lot more about people, about who they are and what they care about, by observing in quiet.

There are many buses and hundreds of people waiting at the bus stop. There are many young men hanging at the sides of the buses shouting their destinations—"Maryland," "CMS," "Obalende." There is no bus going to Fadeyi. We stand next to a row of older women with woven baskets and trays in front of them selling all types of things, fruits, vegetables, tiny toys.

I watch a young woman haggle with almost every seller. Finally, she buys smoked fish, okra, tomatoes, habaneros, and red bell peppers. She will go home to her tiny, sufficient apartment with one soot-stained kerosene stove in a corner and make food just enough for herself and eat less than half of it and fall asleep on her bed and be glad to be alone and unbothered.

The first bus going to Fadeyi is a danfo, a 1988 Volkswagen bus. Its wooden, cushionless seats are filled with people before we get a chance to go in. We are part of the small crowd of people who fail to make it in. We murmur one to another, we hope more buses come quickly. Two curly-haired girls come to stand next to the group. They hold out cracked plastic bowls and begin singing in Yoruba.

"Brother, God bless you.

Sister, God bless you.

Give me money and I pray for you.

A setup,

A trap,

May God prevent its occurrence."

The woman who bought her dinner now drops five naira in one bowl, then five naira in the other. I plan to give them money, but they do not come close to us, and no one else gives them money, so they move away, singing to other adults.

There is a group of kids from the public school talking in a corner. The beggar children attempt to avoid them as they go past. One of the kids tugs at the wrapper of the older girl as she walks past him. She does not notice. After walking a couple of steps, her wrapper unravels. It's then I see that she isn't wearing any underwear. She drops her bowl and wraps the cloth back around herself in a quick second. She walks on without looking back. I make Ariyike turn around to look but it is too late for her to see anything. The public school kids laugh and laugh. Stupid children laughing out loud with their torn rubber sandals and dirty shirts and books in black shopping bags and yellowing teeth and rusty fake gold earrings and matted braids. Stupid children.

When we were in primary school at St. Catherine's, there

was another set of identical twins. They were short, bow-legged boys who got into fights with everyone. We hated that because they were also Yoruba twins, we had the same traditional names. Ariyike and I therefore became "Girl Taiwo" and "Girl Kehinde." The most annoying people were the ones who called me "Girl Kenny." Kenny is a totally different name, it is not short for Kehinde no matter how hard Yoruba people try. These public school kids make me think of Boy Kehinde and Boy Taiwo. I wonder what they are like now. Still stupid, I bet.

Once we got to secondary school, we insisted on being called by our middle names, and even though Ariyike and Bibike have the exact same meaning and everywhere we go people still ask, "Who is Kehinde, who is Taiwo?" I like our new names.

Ariyike was born first, so she is Taiwo. Our grandmother, Father's mother, says that Kehinde is the elder twin because Orisa ibeji, the god of twin births, is Kehinde. He was the one who sent his younger one to be born first to confirm by loud crying that the world was fit for him.

Father's mother believes all these things with her whole heart. Mother says her stories are tales of demons. She says if we listen to her too closely, we invite evil beings into our destinies and we will end up poor and alone.

I think everything is a story unless you live in it. I like the idea of a god who knows what it's like to be a twin. To have no memory of ever being alone. To be happy you are different from your twin but also to be sad about it. To know almost everything about your twin and sometimes want to stop knowing so much. To know you were born with everything you will ever need for love but to be afraid that this one person is too important. Or that this person will never be enough. To pray to a god like that, all I would ever have to say is Help me.

There are many more people at the bus stop now. We are all standing so close to one another. Ariyike and I have our backpacks turned to the front of us, protecting them like little babies. We have eaten all our plantains and groundnuts. She tells me she is going to look for drinking water to buy, but just as she is about to leave, a molue bus arrives, its rusty croaking like an old man's cough. I call out her name but there are already seven people between us. I push through and get in the bus, hoping I can save her a seat; the bus is already filled up with many standing people, holding on to the metal poles. I find a seat in the back of the bus and shout for my sister as loud as I can. She finds me and sits on my thighs. The public school kids are sitting close to us, three on a single seat. I have no idea how they plan to sit like that for so long.

Across from me is a lady I did not see at the bus stop. I wonder how long she has been on the bus. She looks like she just got out of university, or maybe she still is in university. She is wearing jeans, and only university girls wear jeans outside the house. Her shoulder-length auburn braids with burnt ends are tucked behind her ears, kajal eyeliner spilling under her eyes, cream foundation drying in uneven patches, and she is talking to a beautiful bearded man with sad brown eyes seated next to her. He is wearing brown corduroy pants and a black-and-white checkered shirt. He has a black brief-case and a white lab coat. Their voices are raised loud enough to hear each other over the noise of cars honking through traffic, of bus tires grinding to abrupt stops on cold concrete and the voices of others conversing around them.

"Did I tell you my horse got stolen?" she asks.

"No."

"Yeah, it did. I still ride, though, whenever I visit the village."

"I have only ridden that one time." He laughs and shakes his head as though this is something no one else can believe.

"Remember that day my mother came to your house?" she says after a short pause.

This time his reply is hesitant, quiet. "Yeah," he says.

"When she came to drag me away? How she was saying, I have warned you about this boy, you can't be here, you have to leave."

She is laughing as she says it. And it's a laugh I know, one most women I know have. Mother has it, too. Laughter you use when nothing is funny, but you are lighthearted and resilient and eager to show it.

"Have you seen anyone else lately? Anita? Banke? Emmanuel?" she asks with leftover laughter in her mouth.

The conversation on his side is no longer loud or discernible. There is no way to be sure why he now mumbles. Maybe it's been a long day and he is tired and wants to ride the bus in peace. Maybe he has never liked her or maybe she just reminded him of the hurts he has also covered up with laughter, and muscles, and gorgeous facial hair.

"Banke is married, she has like six kids or something," she says.

"Really," he exclaims. "Banke. Married! I definitely did not see that coming."

There is more laughter, more exclaiming, more naming names, more asking what are they up to now.

"So, are you seeing anyone?" she asks, deliberate, flippant.

"No, I am just focusing on leaving this stupid country. Ties just make things difficult," he says.

If she says anything after this, I do not hear it. The bus conductor announces the next stop and several people shuffle and respond. When the doors open, she grabs the black briefcase and lab coat that I had assumed were his, he has a doctor's face. She gets out of the bus, shouting, Excuse me, excuse me, at all the people in her way. One of the public school kids now sits where she was sitting. There is quiet and there is noise.

She will walk to her apartment, where she lives with her older sister and her sister's husband, and wonder if the universe was helped by her vulnerability, if she will get any closer to living in her dreams because she laid bare her desires to a man like that. She will wish for a second encounter with him. One where the best decisions of her years are on display. Like he walks into the hospital where she is a pharmacist or the church where she sings solos on Sundays. Or they meet in the parking lot of a supermarket the weekend after salaries are paid so he can witness all the imported foreign things she can now afford to buy on her own.

I hope she finds someone new.

I wish her love without this shared lament of people who remain in a failing city when others who are not stupid have left. I wish her love that makes her less ashamed, love that is ignorant of the specifics of her failed dreams and unaware of the details of her lost youth. I hope she finds a loving gaze that will not see how her face has fallen and where her arms have swollen or how her family has lost all they took great pride in.

WE GOT HOME a little after five p.m. that day, bubbling with the ignorant excitement of young children who'd completed their first adult task. It did not occur to us to wonder why our schedules had changed or whether this was a permanent kind of change. We did not yet have the kind of familiarity with misfortune that cultivated a sense of foreboding. We could only assume that Father was too busy to come pick us up and Mother was beginning to understand that we were grown enough to navigate Lagos streets on our own.

WE ATE OUR dinner in a hurry and, while we ate, Andrew and Peter watched cartoons and argued with each other in the living room. As soon as we were done with dinner, Father and Mother called us into their room for a talk. I was absolute in my certainty that they were about to announce we were expecting a new sibling.

This was the first time we had been allowed in our parents' room. It was, until this day, an odd place, with regular fluorescent lamps for the daytime and a tiny blue bulb turned on at night. The lights were like secret codes for access—white light meant it was okay to knock, to ask to be let in; the night-light meant to keep away.

But on this day—the day things were beginning to fall apart, the day we were too stupid to notice—we swelled with the confident pride of new initiates. The room smelled like Cussons baby powder and Mother's favorite perfume, Elizabeth Arden's Red Door.

I sat on the rug in the center of the room. It was yellow, brown, blue, and black, stripe-patterned and soft. It made me think of Joseph and his coat of many colors. My sister lay on the brown leather armchair opposite their bed, folding herself in it like a bush baby, one foot swinging down the side of the chair.

Mother and Father sat next to each other on the king-size bed.

It was Mother who spoke first:

"You are big girls now, so behave yourselves. Something really bad has happened to this family and—"

"We will be all right, though. This is nothing for you both to worry about," Father interrupted.

"I am not telling them to worry," Mother said. "We agreed to tell them, so we can handle this as a family."

"A few weeks ago, your mother got into some trouble at work and she was let go," Father said. "None of it is her fault. We will get through this, I promise you girls."

Mother was with the Ministry of Petroleum for ten years. In the last two years, she worked as one of the three personal assistants to the minister of petroleum. Her boss, the Honorable Minister Dakuku, had been fired by the military president, and a new minister of petroleum was appointed in his place. It was this new minister who, rather unexpectedly, considering that civil servants existed, under the national laws and in the valid assumptions of many, in a labor-protected space where the worst thing that could happen was a transfer to a remote village, fired all those staff he considered close associates of the former minister.

The ex-minister's falling-out with the military president was over approval given to an American company for oil drilling in the Niger Delta. It was not until the agreements were signed and money was paid that the president became aware that the Americans were in fact an Israeli company incorporated in the United States. The military president was a great friend of Yasser Arafat, apparently, and an avid defender of his politics. He wanted nothing to do with the American company once these facts were revealed.

Father explained these facts to us in short, straight-to-the-point sentences.

"The ex-minister is in hiding. Some say he is in America."

"Many people were also let go. It was not only your mother."

As much as he tried, he did not help me understand how anything that happened was our mother's fault. Until that day I'd thought her job as an assistant was limited to serving the minister and his guests tea and smelling nice as she did this. Even though I was confused, I was not surprised. In Lagos bad things happened all the time.

My sister's dangling foot tapped the leg of the armchair over and over, a little loud, but no one told her to stop doing that. Father reached over and patted me on the center of my head, ta, ta, ta, harmonizing with the tidi, tidi, tidi my sister was making with her foot against the wooden chair leg. He patted me on the head several times, until it started to hurt. I started trying to think of something to say, something reassuring, sensing that Father had planned a more confident rendering of this tale, but he now sat quiet and absentminded, forgetting the words he planned to say or why he was convinced they would help.

I MAKE A pillow fort for Andrew and Peter under our dining table. I have modified a simple nighttime ritual. Every night, I sit on a stool in the boys' room. I tell my younger brothers stories before bed.

Today, Mother and Father are locked in their room yelling at each other again. So we sit in our dining room fort, talking and laughing. The dining room is right next to our parents' bedroom, there is only a thin wall between us, we are close enough to know when the first punch lands, close enough to scream if it continues. Peter sits next to me, his elbows are on the floor, his round face is nestled in the curve of both palms. His hair smells like Blue Band margarine. Sometimes after eating, he wipes his hands on the living room curtains, other times he wipes them on his hair when he thinks no one is looking. His face is oily, shining like a lamp in a dark room.

"Can you tell us a story?" he asks me. "You do not have to make it up. It can be one of Father's or Mother's stories, but nothing with a tortoise or a monkey in it."

"Should it have a song?" I ask.

"Yes," my brothers answer at the same time.

"But only if you really want to," Andrew adds quickly. He is the older brother, he does not want to appear too interested in childish stories.

"Way back before the rebellion, when animals and people could talk to and understand one another, a woman buys two hens on her way home from the market. They cost only half a penny each and so she buys them even though she really does not need any more hens. The woman soon gets tired of carrying her basket on her head and holding hens in both hands, so she throws one of them away, right into the forest, and thinks nothing of it. And a few months later when she is walking down the same road after a market day, she sees her hen walking along the path. Only this time, the hen has several chicks walking in a straight line behind her."

"How did she know it was hers?" Peter asks.

"Because, back then when you bought poultry, you cut a tiny piece off the edge of your wrapper and tied it around the legs of your hen. The rope was still there," I reply.

"People still do that today," Andrew says.

"The woman is excited," I say. "She chases after the hen, but the hen refuses to be caught. It scratches her a couple of times and then runs to the palace of the king.

"The hen gets to talk to the king, but decides to sing instead. She tells her story, the hen does, with singing. How the woman bought her for half a penny and threw her in the forest and how the lord of the forest fed her with corn husks and water from a well. The hen says she is now a mother of many children: her first son is called the Warrior Prevails, the second is called Finger of the Truth—"

"How many children did she have?" Andrew asks.

"What did the king decide?" Peter asks.

"The song says they were six or three," I reply. "I don't really know, *meta* and *mefa* sound the same, especially in a song."

We are singing the story's song, "Iya Elediye eyen ye kuye," whispering the words now because Mother is crying in the bedroom. Loud crying and hiccupping. And Father is shouting at her to stop.

"The king said the woman could take the first chick with her, and the hen was free to go back to the forest with the rest of her children."

"And that is how it ends?" says Andrew. "You should have just told us the one about the tortoise and the hyena."

Peter laughs because Andrew said *hyena*, he is laughing and laughing, and then Andrew and I also start laughing. Peter's giggle is laughter at its best, light and loud, floating around then resting on you, making you woozy and hopeful. Andrew already has a man's laugh.

Something breaks in our parents' room. We stop laughing to listen. Everything is quiet, Mother is no longer crying, and Father is saying nothing. Then Father comes out of the room. We watch his feet walk past the dining table, along the hallway, and down the stairs. We listen to the sounds he makes in the kitchen. A clank of metal, a swish, water splashing on a face. We watch him walk back to the room. There is a tumbler filled with cold water in his hand.

When he opens the door to their room, we hear Mother whisper, "Thank you, dear."

It is hot here in our fort. Peter is sitting close to me with his knees folded to his chin. He is sweating, his forehead covered in shiny droplets of sweat.

"Tell us about that time you saw them burn a robber in Fashoro," Andrew says to me. "Or about that time armed robbers came to the beer parlor and shot a man's ear off."

"I was going to buy pepper in Fashoro when I saw a boy running with a small generator on his head. Suddenly, one woman started running after him shouting, *Ole ole ole*, another woman came out of her shop and joined the other woman shouting. Then I saw the tailor who made your Easter suits come out of his shop. He started running after the boy. It was now that the stupid boy decided to drop the generator and run as fast as he could. The tailor was almost losing him, so he bent down and picked a giant stone and threw it at the boy. It landed right in the middle of his back. The boy fell down flat. Plenty of people now surrounded him. Iya Togo even came and said, Is this not Gbenga, the one who stole my pot of beans while it was still on the fire?"

"Was it Brother Gbenga?" Peter asks.

"No jare, did we not still see Brother Gbenga yesterday?" Andrew replies.

I am listening for sounds from our parents' room, but I hear nothing now.

"Then many other people came and started accusing the boy of stealing from them," I say. "He was crying, saying he was not the one, but your tailor kept slapping him. Then somebody brought a tire and put it on the boy's neck. He was screaming and begging. Someone else opened the tank of the generator and poured out the petrol. They poured it on his face and on the tire and then they set it on fire. He got up and started running but that just made the fire worse, then he fell on the floor and someone took a big brick and smashed it on his head."

"Did he die for real?" Peter asks me. He is yawning, so at first I think he asks did he die for *free*.

"Of course he did. He died, and several vultures came to eat his eyes," Andrew says.

"Don't listen to him, Peter. Nothing like that happened," I reply.

"What do you think happened to him?" Peter asks again.

"He went to heaven," I tell him. Someone must tell him about these things. "He went to a special heaven where only dead children go. And God gave him a room full of jean jackets that never get dirty and candy that gets sweeter while in your mouth—"

"And video games?"

"Yes, Peter, and video games, and TVs as wide as the walls of this house."

WHEN ANDREW AND Peter finally go to their room, I go to our room.

Ariyike is awake and listening to the sounds from our parents' room. I sit next to her on her bed and tell her this same story even though she has heard it all before. I tell her everything from the beginning—how the first time I saw the boy, I smiled at him. I told him I liked his FUBU shirt. He winked at me and walked away. And the end—that I saw the thief's mother run to where his dead body was still burning, take off her cloth wrapper, wrap it around his body to try to carry his body home, and fail. All she did was separate burnt clothing from skin, skin from bones. She stood there crying, "My daughter. My daughter. I warned you not to dress like a boy. Now see what you have done to yourself."

I told Ariyike that all the women who stood there earlier, accusing him of stealing food, laundry drying on the line, generators and coolers, came to the mother, pulling her away from the body, crying with her. That one of them gave her another wrapper to wear but she rejected it. Instead she stood there in her little green slip, crying and screaming, saying that they had stripped her naked in the streets and she would now be naked for the rest of her life.

I told Ariyike all the things I saw and heard, and she was as quiet as a mouse until I was done.

"He was just a stupid girl, Bibi, just a stupid girl," she said.

Then she put her arms around me and cried with me, and this was how I knew that she felt all the things that I felt, and we did not sleep at all that night because we were the same sad the same angry the same afraid.

NEW CHURCH

ARIYIKE
1998–1999

WE WERE SITTING at the back of the house, peeling the skin off black-eyed beans we had soaked in water for hours. The water was dark and particulate, black eyes and brown skins slid off the beans, away from our grasp, floating around the kitchen bowl. The skins reminded me of those newly hatched little tadpoles swimming in the drains out in the street. We could hear Jennifer Lopez playing from speakers in the neighbor's house. My sister was singing along, quietly because she did not want the neighbor to hear her enjoying it and turn it off.

"Jesus is coming soon, Bibike," I said.

"Okay," she said and continued singing.

"You can't be singing these types of songs. Do you want to be left behind?"

She was ignoring me. She continued singing along. She grabbed a handful of beans and swirled it quickly several times in the bowl, troubling the water until it moved around and around on its own, dark and misty, like a dirty whirlpool.

"I'm serious," I said. "Jesus is coming really soon. Like before the end of this year."

"Okay. You know this how?" she said.

"I saw it. No. Pastor David told us. But he prayed our eyes open and I saw, too."

My twin sister, Bibike, started laughing at me. She kissed her teeth, letting out a short but loud sound. She laughed hard, shaking her head, cackling. She is the one everyone calls quiet, so all the noise she was making was a surprise.

"Stop laughing at me. You are being annoying and rude," I said.

She did not stop. Her laughter made me think of water in the canal and how we loved to go there when we were younger. The canal water was usually calm and still. I hated it when it was like that. I used to throw rocks in the water just to disturb it. First, I'd cause a small ripple, which would create a larger one, and then another ripple, and then it was no longer calm undisturbed water but a series of unending circles. That's how laughter poured out of her, in waves and ripples. When I thought she was done, she only paused to laugh even harder.

"Are you done laughing?" I asked.

"Are you done saying stupid things?" she answered.

"Have you finished?" I asked again.

She did not answer. She just wiped her eyes with the back of her dress.

"These are the last days," I continued. "Everything the Bible talked about so far has happened. Wars, pestilences, rebellions. The only thing left is the Rapture. God told Pastor David that it's happening really soon."

"Ariyike, even if that is true, God won't tell anyone. Especially not Pastor David."

"Why won't he?" I said.

"Because it will be unfair." She got up as she said this, pouring the beans out from the bowl and into a large sieve, washing them under running water, splashing everywhere, on her dress, running down her legs, settling around her feet in a small puddle. "He will have to tell everyone or tell no one at all. God should be fair. Treat everyone the same. Like sunlight—"

"You're getting drenched," I said, interrupting her.

"I know. I will change before Mother gets back."

MOTHER HAD A new job. She was teaching business studies, shorthand writing, and typing at Oguntade Secondary. It was a private school, two streets away from us. She was offered a discount to enroll two children, but she didn't take it. We were enrolled in the neighborhood public school. She complained about her job every day.

"These children are so terrifyingly lazy."

"This proprietor is the most miserly man I have ever met. He is making us pay for tissue paper in the teachers' lounge, can you imagine it?"

"The parents want you to give their children marks they haven't earned; not me, let the other teachers cater to these nincompoops."

Mother was unsuited for this position. I felt sorry for her students. She was taking out her disappointments on them, I was sure. I hoped they knew that when she called them stupid or insolent, it was not because they were exceptionally incompetent. She just did not expect to be herding other people's children at this stage in her life.

Bibike and I were making moimoi. Mother sold moimoi wrapped in clear plastic bags to kids at her school during lunch. Lately we also had moimoi for lunch every day. We half joked to Mother as we cooked, "Can we eat something else? Peas will soon start growing from our ears o."

But her reply was: "You'd better be grateful you have any food to eat." She said this like it was the most normal thing to say to your own children.

Since she'd lost her job, Mother had been different, always angry, always tired, always looking for something to criticize us over. The boys, though, could do nothing wrong. One Friday, Andrew stayed out late. He was playing football at the stadium. Mother did not even notice he was not home. Or if she did, she said nothing. Bibike and I would never have tried something like that.

Father noticed everything but said nothing. It was harder for him, I assumed, because when Mother lost her job, he lost his inside connections and could no longer get printing contracts from the government. Father had never had a regular job. This was why he was our favorite parent; he had the time to do things with us. Before Mother lost her job and we all became poor, Father drove us to school every day. The first car I remember was a yellow '88 Mitsubishi Galant, but then he had it repainted to a brash red-wine color, because people in Lagos always thought it was a cab. They sold that car when Bibike and I were in primary 6, to buy a white Volkswagen Jetta. I loved that Jetta so much. Father washed it by himself every single day and it always had a fresh clean smell like a baby's bathwater.

Ever since selling the Jetta, Father had been home all the time. He had no connections, no car, and nothing to do. He spent most of his time indoors reading old newspapers, using a blue pen to mark them up. Other times, he was outside the house, "spending time with friends," "making money moves," "cultivating new business relationships."

"They are nothing but a bunch of time wasters," Mother said once, the day after Father's new group of friends visited him at home for the first time. "Time wasters. Roaming about looking for whom to devour."

We were all in the living room when she said it. She was standing by the dining table folding laundry. Father was sitting in his armchair, Andrew and Peter sat on the floor, Bibike and I lay on the purple couch. I could feel my face swelling with anger. Bibike was patting me on my back, calming me down without words. How could Mother think it was okay to talk about Father like that—and in front of him? All he was doing was trying. Trying to make something happen.

She would have continued like that, going on and on, if I

hadn't jumped off the couch and started singing, out of no-where, the reggae dancehall song "Murder She Wrote." Peter joined in singing, and soon we were dancing, swaying this way and that, flinging imaginary dreadlocks right, left, and right again. Andrew was providing the beat and shouting, in his imitation Jamaican accent, "Mderation Man," over and over, and Mother was saying, "Stop making noise," but no one was listening anymore to anything she had to say. She walked away, into our room, with a pile of folded clothes to put in our chest of drawers. Then Father said, "Stop making that racket. I want to watch the news.

Afterward, Mother spoke to Bibike and me yet again about the dangers of worldly music, that it was the devil's mascot, leading young girls to bad things, like boys and drugs, and how we had to be better examples for our broth-ers. And in this moment, I wanted worldly music more than I ever had. Nothing Mother was saying was new. I had heard it all in church already

I listened to Mother repentant now. I started crying not because of what she was saying but because I was afraid. I was afraid of failing God. My pastor, David Shamonka, the reason I knew Jesus was coming soon, had been in university studying medicine when God called him to win souls. He left medical school, he left his parents and siblings, he left everything to start his ministry. If God called me like he did him, what is worldly music that I couldn't give it up?

I hoped that God could tell that my heart wanted him more than it wanted worldly music, or anything else. I could sense that the world was changing, that big things were about to happen. Of course, I could not say for certain that it was the end of the world, the Rapture or the Second Coming or anything like Pastor David said—Bibike's mocking made it hard for me to believe everything he said—but I felt something.

On some days, right after I said my night prayer, when I focused hard enough, I could hear the voice of God in the evening breeze. It sounded like an old man speaking softly in the distance. I did not know, in the way Pastor David apparently did, how to decipher what the voice was saying. But I believed that someday I, too, would understand His voice. I think I love Pastor David.

Once, before Mother lost her job, a street magician visited Fadeyi. All of us children paid five naira per head to watch his act. I watched the magician swallow a whole python alive, only to vomit it up five minutes later. It was an unforgettable sight. Pastor David reminded me of that magician. The difference was that he was teaching me, teaching all of us his congregants, how to do all the same glorious things he did.

I had first met Pastor David six months after Father sold the car. It happened in my school principal's office. I was there that day because Mrs. Modele the math teacher had reported me for copying my test answers from Bibike. I was walking up the stairs past the courtyard when I saw him approaching. He was smiling directly at my face. I pretended not to notice him looking, but I walked even more slowly, waiting to see where he was headed.

When I got to the principal's office, after stopping to

drink water in the teachers' lounge, he was already there. Before the principal could say anything, he was sitting and saying, "Please attend to your student, sir. I can wait."

Then the principal, determined to embarrass me, started bringing up unrelated stuff, eye makeup, short skirts, and the pack of Benson & Hedges from months ago.

Pastor David seemed to fight back an amused, puzzled look, and when the principal was done, he said: "If you don't mind, can I pray for this little girl?"

Then the principal said, "Of course, she needs it. I don't think it will help. This one is already a lost cause."

Then Pastor David held my right hand gently and said, "Loving God Abba Father, reveal Your love to her," and then I felt like my brain was expanding and my heart heating up at the same time.

I later learned he had come to ask to use the assembly grounds for midweek church services, and so I started to attend his services. I was hoping to be friends, but joining the church made me see how big he was, and how small I am. Whenever he caught my eye from the pulpit during services each Sunday, I wondered if he could tell how much I loved him.

We exchanged gifts. Just before Christmas, it was the annual love feast, and Pastor David picked my name out of the Christmas partner names bucket, right in the middle of service, and everyone cheered. He gave me a bracelet and a note that was just a long list of Bible verses selected "For the Godly Woman You Are Becoming, My Darling."

We exchanged even more notes after that. Mine were

my meditations on the Bible verses I studied each day. I was trying to read the entire Bible in a year. His notes were more mercurial. Once, he wrote several lines describing the hills in Jos when he'd visited for an evangelical outreach. Other times, it was lyrics to worship songs, in full, name of songwriter included. At the bottom of one note he wrote:

Everything softens when I worship.

HE LOVES TO sing. He cannot sing. Singing, he sounds like a bush baby crying for his lamp and lantern. He says that people who are not broken by God will be broken by life. I do not know what that means but I think it means tears. Cry when you sing worship songs.

He loves Lagos. He once said that people who haven't visited Lagos have yet to meet their country. He said that Lagos is a mini–Nigeria, only much better. I thought then that maybe he was talking to me alone, trying to make me feel not so bad for knowing only Lagos. Someday soon, I will travel. I want to see the Mambila Plateau.

My sister, Bibike, is less yielded than I am. She comes with me to church sometimes, especially Thanksgiving Sunday, when rice is served. First time she came, Pastor David didn't know it wasn't me; I was folding prayer clothes behind the altar curtain, she was talking to someone from the choir. They were standing in front of the altar. He said, "Madam dancer, I saw you digging it during praise and worship, keep it up." She laughed her laugh and said thank you. I was angry at her for smiling at him, so I walked into their midst and said, "Pastor, hi, this is my twin, Bibike, the One Who Doesn't Believe in Jesus."

And so that day, the day Mother was speaking to us about comportment, abstaining from all that sex music, the importance of respect, self-respect, and respecting others—I was crying and pretending to listen. I was really wondering, wondering whether maybe this house, Lagos, maybe even the world, was melting away and I was the only one who could remember how things used to be.

I wanted to answer her with the thoughts I was thinking, but I could not form a complete sentence. My thoughts were choking me, draining me. I wanted to ask how she could have no faith in Father. But I could not say what I wanted to say. She was stern and angry, pitiful. She looked old to me, like one of those women who sold tomatoes at Sabo night market.

Yet, after that occasion, whenever Father's friends came by she was well dressed, commanding, funny. Mother was funny when she wanted to be, she would speak in the military president's voice, making solemn announcements: Fellow Nigerians, I Am Announcing the Suspension of Milk Subsidy with Immediate Effect.

I saw that Father enjoyed her new attitude. He stayed home longer, started going out only in the evenings. He was talking about starting a business of his own, being an entrepreneur. One of his friends had recently been deported from Germany. It was this friend, Mr. Gary, who had all these big ideas about what they could do for money. They were becoming motivational speakers for hire. Gary had the interesting accent, my father had the looks, together they booked deals in colleges and universities, speaking to graduating students about the job market. But their partnership lasted less than a year, ending things quickly. They argued about splitting profits and separated. Then Father became a recruitment consultant. After that failed to work out, he started a business magazine with some other friends.

"What's this?" Mother asked him when he brought home the galley copy.

"What does it look like?"

"Like another stupid way you're wasting my money."

"I am a businessman. This is what I do," he said.

"You are a lazy man," she replied. "Get a job."

When *Business Insights* magazine failed—they kept at it far longer than they should have—Father's group of friends disbanded. They had run out of courage and enthusiasm, each person moving on to independent pursuits. Father was keen to start something new. He wanted to convert the lower part of our home into a business-services support center. With a couple of computers and printers, some old photocopiers, the business would provide services to other businesses in the neighborhood, ones still dependent on traditional typewriters.

"I would rather convert it to a flat and rent it out," Mother replied when he told her his idea. "The Soweres next door paid two years' rent in advance; how much can a business center bring in?"

We were sitting at dinner while they argued. Peter was

making a mess: okra soup spilled from his plate, forming a tiny puddle on the table. He was putting his fingers in it, handwriting *shit fuck* on the walls. They did not notice.

Bibike and I had visited the Soweres the day before. Their daughter, Titi, was a year older than we were. Her parents were home early from work. I was impressed by how basic and transactional their conversation that afternoon was.

"Did you put on the water-pumping machine?" Titi's mother had asked.

"Do we still have yellow garri?" Titi's father asked.

"What time will you be back tomorrow?" Titi asked.

It was nothing like our house. In our home, everything was at stake. Nothing was inconsequential. Even the way you said good morning could set them off. The house we lived in was a wedding gift from Mother's father. Whenever they argued about Father's idea, Mother said, "I will do what I like with my father's house," and Father said, "Do what you like, endanger our children because of your being stubborn."

After a few months, the arguments were no longer as loud as they had been. Father was resigned, quiet. Mother was eating less and less, drinking schnapps and agbo, laughing even when nothing was funny. We entertained ourselves by dressing up with Mother's makeup and hanging out in filling station tuck shops. I am great at meeting new people; Bibike just went everywhere I did. We made plans to run away, to leave the country. Move to Ghana, make our own money, get our brothers, Andrew and Peter, into better schools. Bibike was to sing in a live band. I would work as a waitress in the bar.

We even met a man who promised to get us ECOWAS travel booklets. We wouldn't need visas to travel anywhere in West Africa. It was such a simple plan, really. He just wanted to take pictures of us in swimsuits, which was silly because we had already told him we did not know how to swim.

Mother announced one day at dinner that the school where she was teaching was closing in the middle of the school year. She said the owner had sold the property it was built on. The new owner was tearing down the school to build an apartment complex.

It was March of '98, and Mother was without a job again. We, *all* of us, went to visit Mother's boss, the proprietor of Oguntade school. He hadn't paid Mother any salary for the last three months before the school closed, and it was her idea to take the whole family to his house.

"I know that man made millions when he sold the school. Yet he refuses to pay me my arrears. If my pleas have not moved him, let him look into the eyes of the children he is starving," she said before we left our house. And so, the six of us got in a bus and went to his house.

It did not work.

"I will pay you as soon as I get the money, madam," the proprietor had said. "I cannot turn myself to money for you. My children are also hungry."

"So, will you now consider trying out my idea?" Father asked.

We were sitting in the back, the very last row of the danfo bus, when they were talking about this. Mother was whispering. The quietness made her voice sound like she was about to cry.

"It's not like I have a choice," Mother answered.

LATER THAT MONTH, our parents asked me what I thought of their business plans. I promised to work in the business center as often as possible. They had taken to including Bibike and me in every discussion about the family's finances. We did not give any opinions, we just listened and tried to look sad. Father's plan was all we had left. Money for the business center came from selling our parents' wedding bands and Nestlé PLC shares, the only other thing (apart from the house) Mother had inherited from her deceased parents. The money bought two used photocopiers, one desktop computer, one scanner, one laminator, and one printer. Father was excited to finally get his chance. He promised his business would bring in, every other day, what Mother had made in a month as a teacher.

The trouble with his new business started early. Our photocopy machines were temperamental and unreliable. They made faint and unreadable copies, they leaked ink all over the place, they consumed way too much electricity and even more petrol whenever there were power cuts. Our patrons were infrequent and often needed services rendered on credit.

It was during this season of hopelessness, when we were learning to wait for whatever money was to be made from the business center, to know whether there would be food to eat the next day, that an old work colleague, visiting the neighborhood and seeing Mother manning the typesetting business, had advised her, face contorting with the exaggerated sympathy usually reserved for victims of hit and run accidents, to attend Pastor David's church.

My sista! Please attend this meeting. You will receive a breakthrough. Your life will change.

I was so happy when Father and Mother told me they had heard wonderful things about my Pastor David and were going to see for themselves. They attended a Wednesday miracle night the week after. Bibike and I stayed home with our brothers. Later that night at dinner, they spoke of all they had seen and heard. Stories of people who had been worse off than they could ever dream of being who experienced great change through the church. There was the illiterate taxi driver who found favor with an expatriate and became his personal assistant, earning a salary in dollars. And the man who won the visa lottery after he was prayed for and who was leaving for America soon. And another, a man once so poor he sewed boxer shorts out of his wife's old wrappers, who, after prayers at church, won a government tender and made so much money, he bought three brand-new cars in one day.

It was the very best day of my life. Even though I wished they had joined because they loved Jesus, I was happy that the rest of my family had finally come to the New Church. We were desperate for better things, feverish with expectation that church was the missing link.

Andrew and Peter missed our old church, All Saints Anglican Cathedral. They were chubby, round-faced boys who had been doted on by most of the elderly congregants of the old church. Andrew had been nicknamed the King Himself, for his portrayal of King Herod at the Christmas play in '94, and Peter delighted everyone with his recital of the First Psalm in English and Yoruba. It was something they did every year after that, until we left: Andrew was always the lead in church plays; Peter always recited long Bible passages from memory.

My mother still struggled with being poor and needy. The women of the New Church discomfited her for this reason. They were, in many ways, unlike the women who attended the old church. Women from our old church, like my mother, had been raised as privileged Lagos girls, attended competitive all girls' schools like Anglican Girls or Queens College, lived in London for a year, perhaps taking Cambridge A levels, or perfecting their typing and shorthand skills, then returned to steady careers and marriages. Most of the New Church women usually had little or no education. They came to Lagos from their villages for the first time as adults, courtesy of born-in-the-village husbands who had found work here. They were very dependent on these husbands and other male relatives in a way that our mother found annoying in the beginning, but later began to envy.

Whenever they gathered together for prayer meetings in our business center, they generally had the same kind of conversations. Gossip, grievances, and barely concealed guile masking as prayer requests. "I asked my husband for money for food shopping and he did not give me." "My brother in Germany has forgotten the family." "My neighbor needs to come to the Lord. Her husband won't stop beating her till she becomes a praying wife." When they were around, Mother made a show of being a model Christian woman. Behind their backs, though, Mother mocked and mimicked these women. Bibike and I were glad to have Mother's attention again, and so we laughed aloud each time she did. We were fakers, but we were happy.

Pastor David's church was growing. The New Church moved out of the public school into a new, purpose-built church building. For the first time, there was a separate youth church, called the Burning Citadel, and it was one of the first youth churches in Lagos to attempt being simultaneously cool and godly. Sunday services were called "hangout sessions" and midweek services were called "meet-up gigs." There was an effusive worship band with electric guitars and large drums, which made Ron Kenoly and Don Moen songs sound super cool. The band took the music from "Malaika," made famous by Miriam Makeba, and turned it into a song of Christian dedication. We sang, "My lifetime, I give Jesus my lifetime," with contrite hearts. I no longer saw Pastor David and I did not care that much. I had Jesus, I had my family.

Father found himself a new group of henchmen, similarly smooth-talking, broke men with big dreams and loud voices. They congregated almost daily in our business center. The business was getting better at this time, and Mother had even expanded it to include wholesale office materials and beverages.

They were like Father's earlier group of men. Loud, noisy dreamers. These dreamers, though, said bless you instead of good morning, and "I am a winner" when you asked, "How is your day going, sir?"

One of Father's closest friends was a young man named Pastor Samuel. He was one of the assistant pastors and was always in a suit no matter how hot the weather. He came to the house, to our business center, almost every day. He always bought a bottle of Coke, first wiping the rim clean with a white handkerchief he kept in his shirt pocket. Then he told stories of all the business deals he was about to strike. The stories he told Father were rivaled only by the ones he told as testimonies in church. He spoke of connections with military administrators in various states of the republic. One Sunday, Pastor Samuel presented to the church a "sacrificial thanksgiving seed" of an imported fourteen-seater bus. He announced that he was thanking God for connecting him with the highest-ranking military men in the state. We were so happy for Pastor Sam's newest blessings. Especially because, like oil on Aaron's head, they were sure to trickle down to us.

Most days when Pastor Samuel visited Father at home, he paid special attention to us girls, dashing Bibike and me money. He was nice and friendly. He sat with us and talked with us, wanting to know what books we were reading, what music we liked, whether we had boyfriends. Mother hated the attention Pastor Samuel gave us and one day, after she walked in on him giving Bibike a foot massage, asked us to never speak to him again unless it was in church. Father agreed with her and began sending us upstairs whenever Pastor Samuel came to visit.

When the military president died in June of '98, things fell apart all over the nation. The chaos was particularly intense in Lagos. As commercial capital of the republic, the unexpected changes in political leadership led to pan-icked trading activity among the ruling class. People were hoarding food—rice, garri, yams. Gas stations shut down. Electronics stores moved their goods into more secure ware-houses, fearing a riot.

IT WAS DURING this time that Pastor Sam approached Fa-ther about a deal. He told Father that one of his connections, a top admiral in the navy, was in possession of a shipment containing foreign currency that the deceased military presi-dent had been taking out of the country. The admiral needed money to transfer ownership of the shipping containers to someone outside the military. The reasoning was a new gov-ernment in the impending democracy would most likely in-vestigate all past military personnel for corrupt practices.

The money, ten million naira, was the admiral's share of the container's worth, and he insisted on getting cash upfront. Pastor Samuel came to Father because he did not have that type of money. He offered to pay Father back the ten million plus 50 percent of the shipment. With such looming promise of profits, Father was convinced to secure a high-interest loan on our family home for the value of the proposed bribe. The home was conservatively valued at almost double that amount at this time; it was sitting on acreage that could support two other buildings. But being confident that once the shipment cleared and the money was shared, the mortgage would be paid in full, Father signed the loan papers. Mother noticed that the visits of Pastor Samuel were more frequent in this period, and the men's discussions intense. She asked Father several times what they were up to. "God has remembered us, dear. Something big is on the way," was all he said.

She responded by being even more protective of Bibike and me, keeping us indoors as much as she could. Father was a changed man this season. He woke up with songs of praise every day: "Isn't He good, isn't He good, hasn't He done all He said He would, faithful and true to me and you, isn't He good?"

His enthusiasm was easy to catch. Even Mother, who was usually cautious about his schemes, finally caught it, this exhilaration of faith. We the children were beyond excited. Every night, we sat in our fort and talked to one another about what would happen when the money Father was expecting arrived.

"Father will buy me a BMX bicycle," Andrew said.

"Me, I want a Game Boy," Peter replied.

Bibike and I dreamed of buying brand-new clothes from Collectibles, jeans from Wrangler, clogs, and Lycra skirts. We were going to be again what we used to be, and did not know until we no longer were, the prettiest, best-dressed girls in the neighborhood.

It would have been easier for Mother to handle if she had been aware of any of the particulars of the deal. Father said nothing to her about it until the day after he had handed over the money to Pastor Samuel. He waited all day for Pastor Samuel to bring over the bill of lading. Next, he went looking for Pastor Samuel in the New Church. Pastor David had no idea where Pastor Samuel was. In fact, no one could find him. It was almost as though he had never existed. The only proof was the Volkswagen bus the church had repainted blue and on which it had written EVANGE-LISM in block letters on both sides.

I supposed this was another way that the New Church differed from the old one. The older churches taught of a God who was responsible for everything, both good and bad. Believers were encouraged to accept their fate with good cheer, trusting the God who would deliver if He chose to. The God of the New Church was a good God, but he was only good, and He was good all the time. He took credit for everything pleasant and the blame for evil was shared between the devil and his cohort of doubting Christians. Evil of any kind, from an injured toe to lung cancer, happened only to the unbelieving or those with feeble faith.

This was the way the New Church handled our heart-break. First, they christened it the work of the devil, asking us to pray harder than ever—expecting the Holy Spirit to bring Pastor Samuel back. Later, we were denounced as agents of Satan, concocting a scandal to bring disgrace to the church.

In my heart, I knew it was just a temporary trial. Like Job, we were being tested of God. I gave myself to prayer and reading the Bible. I encouraged my brothers and sister as they wept themselves sore. God had not forgotten us. He would deliver us in His own time.

That Friday night, after we got the "last and final warning" from Fountain Mortgage Bank's lawyer posted on the front door, Mother woke me up in the middle of the night and asked me to help with tidying the boys' room. She gave me two hundred naira right then, so I asked her no questions, I put the money in my pillowcase and followed her to their room. We stood in front of the blue chest of drawers at the foot of the bed, saying nothing as we rolled up Andrew's socks one into the other and tied Peter's in knots. It was a little glimpse of the type of mother she once was, the type of mother who was careful to do the little things you asked from her. She folded Andrew's underwear into tiny squares, and Peter's she rolled into short scrolls.

We folded T-shirts, singlets, and trousers, and then we hung up all their church clothes in the wardrobe. My brothers slept soundly next to each other on a queen-size bed beneath a white mosquito net suspended with twine from nails in the ceiling. There was a ceiling fan that no longer worked. The windows of the room were wide open, letting in a misty draft. Peter coughed but didn't wake up, Mother looked like she wanted to go to him, but then she turned around and asked me to shut the windows.

I woke up late the next morning. It was nine thirty, and I was really angry with myself for accepting Mother's bribe and ruining my sleep. I had woken up late and missed the first part of Cadbury's breakfast television. It was a once-a-week, two-hour program on the Lagos state-owned television channel showing premium American television. They had, in the month before, begun showing *Family Matters* and *A Different World*. Cadbury's breakfast television was the only interesting thing available to watch on Saturday—the rest of the day's television stations devoted themselves to live soccer matches and replays.

I loved Carl Winslow. He was the perfect father. He even looked like a father was supposed to look: balding, round-faced, and old. For a few necessary minutes every Saturday, I would watch *Family Matters* and pretend he was mine. But on this Saturday, the television was turned off. Father sat quietly in his armchair, his *Dake Annotated Reference Bible* between his thighs. There was no one else in the sitting room. Bibike was still asleep and the boys were sitting on the kitchen floor, whispering. The note, a sheet torn off a reporter's notebook and placed slightly underneath the television, said:

My dear children,

I have gone to New York.
There is nothing left here for me anymore.
Peter, if God blesses me, I will send for you.

Love,
Your mother.

In the end, our mother was just the first to leave. My family unraveled rapidly, in messy loose knots, hastening away from one another, shamefaced and lonesome, injured solitary animals in a happy world.

HOW TO BUILD A CHICKEN COOP

ANDREW

2000

WE ARE BUILDING a chicken coop.

My brother, Peter, and I came up with this plan just last weekend. Already we have started working it out. We have no hens yet, but we know that Nonso's mother's hen always has eggs. When Nonso is over here trying his best to make our sister Ariyike smile, we will walk into their compound all majestic and what, go all the way to the poultry at the back, take as many eggs as we want, hope they hatch.

We have wood, gravel, and leftover roofing sheets from the time the local government built a shed with a roof for the transformers down the road because electricity shocks killed some boy's father during the last flood.

We have old wood, nails, and sawdust, and we will find old plastic bowls no one uses anymore.

All of Grandmother's things are old. She still has those green Pyrex dishes, teacups, saucers. They are older than all of us grandchildren. She still wears the aso oke wrappers she wore when Sister Kehinde and Sister Taiwo were baptized. We will not use any of Grandmother's things. She has given us the space at the back of the house for the chicken coop, and that's just enough.

We do not need a hammer. That's what stones are for.

We are digging the hole already. It's ankle deep and is wide enough for us to stand back-to-back in it. Already we have a heap of sand-dirt. Grandmother says that chicken coops do not need a foundation. We both insist that they do. So we promise that we will spread the sand-dirt all over the back of the yard instead of leaving an unsightly heap.

We do not have a phone. We are thinking of ways to get one.

We are alone at home. Grandmother is out shopping. Our sisters are at work. We are big boys, eleven and nine, old enough to be by ourselves staying out of trouble.

We have walked all over the carpenters' shed in the next street, picking as many old wood nails as we can find. We are sitting at the back of the house, straightening bent nails with a big stone. Sometimes we think we hear the gates opening, someone coming, but there is no one else here.

The boys next door are playing table soccer in their backyard. We cannot hear the sound of bottle caps falling off the table or large suit buttons pushed into a goalpost made of paper. It is their happiness we can hear, the sounds of boys our age cheering and screaming. It sounds like it is coming from a galaxy far away.

Last Saturday, we walked for fifty minutes till we got to Rita Lori Hotel in Ikeja. There was a wedding reception. We had two black shopping bags. We were going to pick up as many bottle caps as we could find, start our own league. I was going to take all the Coca-Cola covers; all the Fanta and Sprite covers were to be Peter's. If we got more than enough to split evenly this way, we were going to scratch the covers till the names disappeared and write our player numbers with red ink.

There was no guard at the gate, so we walked in. We searched for covers but there were none. We were too late; the hall had been cleaned up. We went outside to the dumpster behind the hotel. The guard was there smoking cigarettes. He offered them to us. I refused, and he chased us away.

When our hens are grown, they will lay eggs of their own. Then we will sell them for money. We will buy a crate of soda, and drink as often as we like. We will have our own teams and players.

Peter is unhappy with this work. He is focused on the nail in front of him, squinting like the sun is in his eyes even though we are in the shade of the cashew tree, straightening nails as he is supposed to, bottom first then the top, over and over. There is an interesting melody in this repeated banging, easy to get swept up in, gbam gbam gbam, shake your head, gbam gbam gbam, from side to side.

He is sitting with his legs crossed under him like he is in a mosque about to pray.

"Andrew? Are you hungry?" he asks. Looking up at me.

He is just like Mother, staring and squinting like that. I do not mention that. Instead I say, "Let us go and search for something to eat."

We leave our pile of nails there and go looking for our friend. His name is Solomon, but everyone calls him If You See My Mama. He is a good dancer. He dances all the time. Anytime there's loud music. Especially when there's a ready audience, like people gathered at the beer parlor or at Rosetta's snooker joint. People sometimes give him money. Most give him food.

I can do what he does, dance galala like Daddy Showkey, but I have no plans to dance for food. To dance for food, you have to be able both to dance and to eat anything. I don't like stew without pepper. I cannot stand vegetable soup with crayfish in it. Peter can't eat eggs or beans.

Solomon lives with his mother in the house where the TV repairman Uncle George lives. There is a pile of broken televisions on the veranda outside their house. There is a big one with a brown wood-paneled back, the TV like a long rectangle lying on its side. Sometimes, the littler kids sit in it and pretend to be newscasters reading the evening news.

I am Frank Olize
And I am Abike Dabiri
This is NTA Newsline

Today there is no one sitting inside the TV. We go into the house and find Solomon's mother's room. It is the third on the left. The one with a charismatic renewal sticker on the door.

It says HONORING MARY, NEVER WORSHIPPING. I have no idea what it means.

Solomon is inside. He opens the door only when he hears my voice.

"Andy dudu." He calls me by the nickname I hate. His room smells like freshly cooked egusi soup, so I let it go.

"If You See My Mama," I sing out loud.

"Tell am say I dey for Lagos," he replies.

"I no get trouble." Peter supplies this last part. Solomon and I laugh at him because he still makes *r* sound like *w*.

"Sit down," Solomon says as he laughs. "I wan turn garri. You go chop?"

"What type of soup do you have?" I ask.

"Egusi," he says.

"Nice," Peter says.

Peter and I sit on the floor. There is a curtain with little blue fish and yellow bubbles demarcating the bed from the rest of the room. Solomon kneels by the bed and pulls out a tiny stove and an old Mobil tin gallon out from under it. He opens the door and places the stove and keg outside. As he pours kerosene into the stove, I tell him what we are up to.

"We are building a chicken coop."

"Since when?" he asks.

"A few days now," I reply.

"For sell or for choppin?"

"Both," I say.

"For selling," Peter says.

Solomon comes back into the room, picking up a kettle and a box of matches. There is a covered plastic drum at the foot of the bed. He opens it, puts a cup in it, and fills the kettle with water.

"This is the perfect time for chicken business," he says to us. "It will be almost Christmas by the time the chickens are big, then you can sell them for even more money because of Christmas rush."

We did not think it would take that long to raise chickens.

"Let me tell you where you can get maize for free." Solomon puts the kettle to boil and comes to sit on a stool next to us.

"What for?" Peter asks.

"Where?" I ask at the same time.

"For feeding your chickens na." He looks at Peter like a fly is on his nose. He turns to me and asks, "You know where the bakery is?"

"Not really." This time I am not ashamed of not knowing. Solomon has lived here since he was five years old. Father brought us here this year to live with his mother, our grandmother. We do not know where our father lives now.

"It is bit far. I don't know how to describe it. There is the borehole with three huge water tanks right next to it," Solomon says.

"Our sisters will know," Peter says.

"Every morning when my mother goes to buy bread for sale from the bakery," Solomon continues, "there's always fresh maize in a calabash. She says people leave it there as offerings to spirits."

We will take maize offered to spirits for our hens.

When Solomon is done, he brings the food in two bowls, one for garri, the other for soup. He sets it right in the middle of the room. Peter and I sit next to each other, Solomon sits on the opposite side facing us. I have a feeling that I have been here before. That all this has happened already, and I am just now remembering it.

"You better don't touch my meat," Solomon says to Peter.

"Sorry. It was a mistake," Peter says, and the feeling is now stronger than it has ever been. I force myself to eat but I can no longer do it. I am searching inside my brain to know what I remember, what happens after this. There's nothing. My mouth is bitter, my stomach feels like I drank cement mix.

Solomon says something to me, but I don't hear it. Peter laughs and replies.

"—he say he wan free money."

They finish the food, but we do not get up. We are talking in this room, a multipurpose room where I can see everything Solomon's mother has got—plates, pots, and pans poking out of old moving boxes, a pile of old clothes in a brown leather box with a broken handle. There is a black-and-white TV with a wire antenna on top of it.

We are sitting on a scratchy faded green rug with spots of candle wax all over it.

We are talking about new music. We all agree not to like musicians who start their choruses with names of girls. ("Sade" by Remedies is a stupid song; "Omode Meta n Sere" is the greatest song of all time.) I am thinking about Mother and Father. Mother hates worldly music. Father hates it but smiles anytime our sister Bibike sings.

As we sit here talking, a short man I do not know walks in. He does not knock, he just pushes the door open like that.

"Welcome," Solomon says to him as he motions for us to get up, leave.

"Sit down and continue your enjoyment." The man speaks to us, smiling a wide white smile that brightens his face. His lips look too wide for such a small face. The man has dark blotched skin. His face is a perfect round shape. His eyes are swollen and red. He looks like Raphael the Teenage Mutant Ninja Turtle without the green. The man sits on the bed behind us and starts taking off his clothes. Solomon springs up.

"We are leaving. My friends have to be home before their grandma comes back."

"They don't have to leave. Okay. Take this money. Let the small one stay. The two of you go and buy something to eat—" The man is still talking. I get up. I pull Peter onto his feet. The man is still smiling, softer now, hopeful even. He is sweaty even though he has taken off everything but his undershorts. I do not know what he sees in my face but he stops smiling immediately. His transformation is instant, almost funny.

"Get out of here, foolish children. Shut the door," he screams. "And Solomon, you better not come back till your mother comes home this night."

We rush down the hallway, to the veranda of TVs and into the streets. Peter is humming. We are walking slower now, still saying nothing. Peter stops in front of a dusty Datsun that looks like it's been there for ten years and starts to write on the windscreen, "Wash me please."

We walk in silence until we get to our home. The boys next door are still playing a game. We can also hear some girls singing.

"Let's go see Stanley." Solomon does not wait for me to respond. He walks to their house, opening the gate.

Peter and I look at each other, then we go in with him. Their house looks just like ours—cracked plaster walls, a moldy well to the left at the entrance, a veranda made with red brick paving stones.

At the back of the house, the boys are playing table soccer in one corner. Stanley is winning. Their table is huge. They have taped a linoleum rug over the wooden top. The bottle covers just glide over it. Peter and I will never be able to make a table like that on our own. I must become friends with Stanley.

A group of girls are in dance formation. They have strips of aso oke tied across their chests. Longer ones cover their waists down to their knees. Girls are magic beings. They have to be not to die from itching, wearing scratchy aso oke next to their bare skin like that. They are singing in Yoruba:

> *We are here*
> *We are here again*

The eagle is the king of birds
The lion is the king of forest animals
We are greater than these by far
We are singers, dancers too

I am watching them but pretending not to do so. Soon they start to argue. One girl, the shortest, the one with blue stars drawn on her legs, wants the group to roar like a lion at the end of the first verse. Many disagree with her. As she talks, explaining her point, she keeps untying and retying her waist wrapper. It is a very womanly move and it makes me feel like my stomach is punching itself. It also makes me think of Mother. Mother once made us crowns out of her old gold aso oke. Peter and I hated it. We wanted store-bought crowns, like the other kids in the play.

As I watch the girls dance, I start to feel the feeling again. This time it is a different, more sure feeling. I am certain all of this has happened before. I have seen this before—little girls singing, dancing, smiling, one in the middle stopping occasionally to stare at me, saying nothing, just smiling. I feel like all I need to do is focus my brain and I will remember what I am remembering.

I notice a lizard running across the yard, it runs over my feet and then goes up the wall separating our house and Stanley's. Once it gets to the middle of the wall it stops, still except for bobbing its little red head every few seconds. I have seen this before. Even this red-orange lizard crawling over the wall, nodding.

The girl looks at me again. This time I smile back. I blow

a kiss. She spreads out five fingers, points them at me. "Your mother," she screams.

Girls are crazy.

There is a concrete slab in the center of this backyard. It is a long rectangle that extends almost to the end of the east wall. It's as if someone intended to cover the ground completely but ran out of concrete too early. The girls are dancing on one side of the slab. On the other, Stanley's mother has spread out yellow maize and red guinea corn to dry on a raffia mat.

Some white pigeons circle around above. The girls love birds, they wave at them singing the leke leke song, *Leke leke, give me white fingers, won't you?*

Sometimes the birds swoop down as fast as lightning. They pick bread crumbs or a smooth pebble or chicken feed. A couple of pigeons hover close to our heads then fly away. They want the maize, but they won't land because we are here. There are too many of us.

One of the boys notices the pigeons and says something. The rest of them stop playing to look at the birds. Then someone says, "I have an idea. Let's make a bird trap." Another says, "I know how to build one." They begin to argue about what is needed when Peter invites them to our house.

"We live next door. We have extra wood and nails. We are building a chicken coop," he says.

They want to see what we are up to. They want pieces of wood to make a trap. And so we walk away, a small crowd of boys in two lines. If the girls notice us leaving, they don't show it.

As we walk into our house, I see it the way they see it. Our moldy well has a pile of broken plastic buckets next to it. Our laundry is drying on the walls of the perimeter.

Solomon laughs when we get to the hole we have dug.

"Just look at this." He is laughing. It is the second time he has spoken since we left his house.

"You don't need this big hole, don't you know?" a skinny tall boy says to me. He is wearing a white shirt. His dreadlocks are long and dusty. "You just need four small holes for your four-by-twos, then you pour in a little concrete and it stays."

"We were going to fill the hole with stones," Peter says.

He sounds like he is annoyed and impatient. He must be unhappy with me. This is our house, I should not just stand there like a fool while these boys laugh at us.

"Which is easier? Stones or concrete? Where will we get concrete from?" Peter continues. It is hard for him to say concrete, so he is making everything worse.

"Okay. Do you want to help with the bird trap, then, or are you still digging your nonsense hole?"

"Just shut up. With your scanty hair like an abandoned mop."

Now everyone is laughing at tall-skinny-dreadlock guy. Peter just walks away, into the house. Not even glorying in delivering the perfect insult.

A gentle wind stirs in the cashew tree in the middle of our yard. It is becoming evening, the warm humidity is being replaced by the cool breeze. When the boys stop laughing to begin sorting through nails and wood pieces, I continue standing where I am, watching the wind make the leaves dance. I notice a lizard, I think it is the same one that was in Stanley's yard, dash up the tree.

The boys have gathered wood pieces of different sizes. Some the length of a walking stick, others short as a pencil. Skinny-dreadlock guy sits under the cashew tree and gathers all the materials to himself. He starts to arrange them in a pyramid-like pile. When he figures out the arrangement of sticks that makes up a perfect pile he splits them up in pairs, giving one pair to each boy.

"Take. Look for stone. Knack these two together," he says.

Peter comes out of the house but doesn't speak to me. He walks right to skinny-dreadlock guy and sits next to him. I do not know what he says to him, but he looks like he is apologizing.

When Peter was younger, he was so slim (even slimmer than dreadlock guy), his head was huge, his legs were super short. I called him Mr. Big Head Small Body because he looked like those cartoons in the Sunday paper. He hated it, but I couldn't stop. The more he protested, the more I enjoyed teasing him. One day, Father showed him a picture of a lion in a calendar and said: "That's who you are, son, a lion. A son of a lion is a lion."

A son of a foolish man who loses all his money to fraudsters is what? A son of a poor man whose wife leaves him is what? A son of a man who runs away, leaving his children with his mother, is what?

Father should see Peter now. He is no longer tiny. He is

tall, almost as tall as I am. His head is bigger and harder. No one can tell him nothing.

I watch the two of them talking. Then skinny-dreadlock guy picks up three sticks, he sets them in position, he makes a shape like a small letter *t*. He starts to nail them together. Peter reaches out to steady the longer piece underneath. The nail goes through both pieces of wood and into the thin skin between Peter's thumb and his forefinger.

"Oh my God."

"Sorry. Sorry. I'm so sorry."

We are all scrambling. The nail, the *t*-shaped sticks, are stuck in Peter's hand, like they are sprouting. We surround him. We hold him down and pull it out. There wasn't blood before. Now there is a lot of it. There is a lot of blood. Someone wipes it with his shirt. Another grabs a fistful of sand, pours it over the wound. The blood stops rushing out. Someone tells Peter to shake his hand. As he shakes it sand and blood fall to the ground at his feet.

I see the lizard fall off the tree, race over to be next to Peter, lap droplets of blood as they fall to the ground. I look in its eyes and see myself the way it sees me. I am dark and dusty like a school blackboard, my head is bigger than the rest of my body, my hands are tiny, plastered to my side. The lizard stops to look at me. He is nodding again and again. I think the lizard is laughing at me. I am sure of it.

I AM SOMETHING

PETER

2000

I LIKED TO think that no matter what happened, my older brother, Andrew, and I would always be close. This was exactly the kind of thing I worried about, growing older, being on my own, my sisters leading happy, glamorous lives, my brother busy and distant.

Many times, it felt like Andrew and I were only one argument away from being enemies. Other times, we were the best brothers in all of Lagos. I made it my business to try, to make sure we always were getting along, fun and happy. We were best friends only because I did everything he said to do, and I did not mind every time he ignored me to go play with Solomon, Babu, and Eric. Each time he said something mean, I tolerated it, pretending the pain was from something else, like a stomachache from food I did not enjoy, beans or something like that. I stored the hurt for a while in my belly, then I found a place to let it out. Other times, he was the nicest brother, taking care of me.

"I am something," Andrew said that day, to distract me from the pain he was inflicting as he was massaging mentholated balm all over my swollen palm. "I am tall in the morning, short in the evening, even shorter at night. What am I?"

"You are an old man," I said, after thinking about the riddle for a little while.

When he said that was the wrong answer, I did not argue. I watched him pour boiling hot water into the bowl we use for washing up before meals. He pulled out an old towel he had tucked in the back of his trousers and sat on the floor before me.

"The answer is a candle. I am a candle," Andrew said.

A CANDLE IS long, an old man was tall now shrunken, I wanted to say but did not. I grabbed the handle of the chair I sat on with my left hand, steadying myself as he pressed the heat of the rag against my wound. I did not cry out. I did not want Grandmother waking up and looking too closely at my hand. Better for her to sleep, I thought. Better for us that she sleeps as long as she wants to because then when she wakes, it will be easier to talk to her about money for Panadol painkillers.

Andrew leaned in with the full weight of his grip, applying pressure to my swollen palm. As he did, bloody pus oozed out in a slow and steady drip.

"Sorry," he said.

"I am something," I said, interrupting his pity. "I am light as a feather, yet the strongest man in the world can't hold on to me for more than ten minutes. What am I?"

"You are water," Andrew said. "Am I right?"

"No. Not really."

"What is the right answer?"

"It's air. Actually. Breathing air. No one can hold his breath for up to ten minutes."

The air around us was humid and difficult to endure without murmuring. My scalp was wet and sweat was going down my face, even into my ears. My shirt was soaked with sweat, but I could not take it off until Andrew was done cleaning my palm. It was early evening, and we were boiling a half yam for our night meal. I could hear the slices boiling in the pot a few feet away from us because Andrew used the wrong pot cover, so the heat was escaping, and floating bubbles were bursting and spilling all over the stove. That was just one more thing for Grandmother to be angry with us about when she woke up.

It was as if she considered us two children instead of four. Our sisters were one person, the girls, and Andrew and I were one person, the boys. Whatever he did, I was equally responsible for and there was nothing I could do to escape it.

Once, Andrew had dropped his undershorts in the hallway when he was taking his house clothes out back to wash. He did not notice them quickly enough. Grandmother found them and lifted them with a broken plastic hanger, waving them around like a flagpole.

"Do you see what I have to live with?" she asked, screaming

in Yoruba at no one in particular as she walked around the house. "Dirty smelling children. Underwear smelling like the penises of dead male goats, in the middle of the house where I get up each morning to pray to my creator."

"God, is this not too much for a little old woman? When did I become the palm nut in the middle of the street that even little boys are stepping on me so mercilessly?"

For days, she continued like that. She did not allow any of us to retrieve the underwear from the place she had mounted it, in the center of the living room right next to the pile of Father's university textbooks. Andrew waited until she left one evening to sing with a funeral procession for one of the commercial bus drivers in the neighborhood who had been killed in an accident with a delivery truck. He waited until the voices singing "Jesus, the Way, the Truth, and the Life, whosoever comes to Him shall never die" were a distant hollow, then he picked up his underwear and threw it in the trash along with the plastic hanger.

"This woman is pushing me to the wall. I am going to deal with her very soon," he said that day to me, his eyes cloudy with not-shed tears.

Andrew was not massaging my arm fast enough to stop the cramping in my back. My face felt hotter and hotter, so I asked him to stop.

"Do you feel better yet?" he asked.

"Yes," I answered. "I am just hungry."

Andrew stood up off the floor. He had the bowl and the towel with him. I let go of the chair and wiped my face with the back of my hand.

"The food should be ready now," he said. He was looking in the direction of the kitchen, nodding toward it. "Do you need my help to get up?"

I did not. I was dehydrated, hot, and my throat ached, but I did not need his help. But Andrew must have misheard me, I thought, for he reached out his hand and pulled me up out of the chair. I stood up, my legs burning and my steps shaky, taking off my shirt and walking into the house in nothing but my undershorts.

The palm oil came out in thick droplets as Andrew shook the bottle over the plated yams. The heat of the yams melted the droplets immediately on contact till there was a small puddle of oil around the yams. Andrew sprinkled a small pinch of salt over the plate.

"My neck does not feel so good," I said.

"Just eat this. Then I will go out to buy you Panadol Extra," Andrew said.

"Just Panadol. Panadol Extra is for adults only," I said.

"Panadol Extra is for stubborn pain. Children can have stubborn pain, too, you know," Andrew said.

He had made the yams soft, just how I liked to eat them. I squished them with my fingers into the body of oil, watching steaming white yam take on the red of palm oil. I took a little piece of yam then molded it into a tiny ball and put it in my mouth. This is how I knew how sick I had become, because Andrew did not complain about the mess I was making.

Back when I was younger, back when we had Father and Mother, Andrew twisted my shortest finger so hard it came close to snapping because I was playing with our food. Mother screamed at him for hours after that and she stopped serving us in the same bowls, even though Father told her that it was perfectly normal for brothers to fight over such things. *Rough play does not kill boys, it makes them stronger*, Father said to Mother. *You should have seen what my cousins and I got into growing up.*

That was before they were gone, before it became so hard to remember what they looked like. Sometimes when I watched Nigerian movies, I looked out for ones with actors and actresses that were around my parents' age. I did not remember them and so I imagined. It was easy to imagine Mother in a thick coat shivering in the London cold, her makeup bright and irreverent like Gloria Anozie in that movie. It was easier to imagine Father with a group of men arguing politics, his beard uncombed, short and thick like Sam Dede in any of his movies. I wondered about my ability to identify them in a crowd of people. I suspected that I would have been unable to pick them out, unable to remember any distinguishing fact about either of them.

"PETER?" ANDREW SAID my name. I opened my eyes.

"Yes? I am not sleeping," I said.

"I am going to get you medicine now," he said.

"Okay. Thank you," I said.

He went into Grandmother's room, where she was still asleep, and brought out one of her old duvets, covering my feet with them.

"I found some money," he said. "I will be back right away."

When he was gone, the house began making those empty-house sounds, the ones you hear only because everything else is quiet—water dropping from wet clothes recently hung on the line, a fly sizzling after contact with the metal body of the kerosene lantern, the curtains dancing in the breeze, the wooden doors shifting on loose metal hinges.

In the early evening quiet, our tiny house felt like a large expanse of forest with sounds from unseen sources I had to decipher to keep from being frightened and overwhelmed. In my little corner of the forest, I was like a squirrel in a hollow hole in a tall tree, all the outside sound first filtered, then condensed and magnified. I had to try to guess, to know and explain to myself what each sound was, to keep from being afraid of it.

When you're the youngest in the family, everyone tries to protect you. They lie to you, they cover for you. You learn to do your own investigating. You have to be both persistent and invisible. Sometimes it seemed like there was a duvet of silence over all the important stuff about our family. There was no one willing to lift it up for me, to let me see for myself what it was all about.

When we first moved to Grandmother's house, it took me three months to figure out that Father was not just job searching in Abuja.

When we walked around the streets, I liked to walk behind Andrew. He had no idea I was being slow on purpose. I hid it well. I stopped to pick up stones or write on dirty cars or hurl stuff at stray cats. But what I was really doing was waiting for Andrew to go ahead of me, so I could walk behind him, keeping him in my sights.

If he walked away from me, at least I would have seen him leaving. I wouldn't have been left to wonder if someone had snatched him and made him a houseboy. Or if he stepped on a charm and dissolved into liquid or picked up money off the floor and became a tuber of yam.

Andrew returned with the painkillers and a small bag of roasted groundnuts with the skins still on. He smashed the pills into a stony powder then stirred it into a thick mix, adding about two teaspoons of water. It tasted like drops from the stalk of the bitter leaf dipped into classroom chalk. When I was done swallowing the medicine, he sat next to me eating his groundnuts.

"Here," he said. "Take some." He was stretching out a fistful of nuts to me.

"Take that away from me. My mouth is too bitter." I said. "I may never eat again."

"Do you know what I was thinking when I was walking home just now?" Andrew asked.

"No, I do not," I said.

"I was thinking about porridge," he said.

"What type of porridge?" I asked.

"Any type," he said. "I think porridge is the worst food in the world."

"Because it looks like poop?" I asked.

"Nope," Andrew said. He did not laugh, so I wondered if he knew I was joking. "Only beans porridge looks like poop. Asaro does not."

"Tell me what you were thinking," I said.

"I was thinking about stories. The stories about porridge I know. In at least three of them, terrible things happen to people after eating porridge," Andrew said.

"Are they real life or just ordinary stories?" I said.

"It's in the Bible, okay?" he said. "That makes it real."

"Are all the stories in the Bible?" I asked.

"Just the one about a boy who had worked all day hunting for meat for his family and when he came home he was tired, but his brother was making porridge for lunch, so he was excited—"

"What type of porridge?" I asked.

"I have no idea, maybe the type you make with grains, milk, and cheese. What is terrible is how much the older brother lost because he agreed to pay what his younger brother asked for the porridge."

"What should he have done?" I asked.

"He should have just waited till his brother was done and served himself. Worst thing that will happen, they fight like men," Andrew said.

"Hmmm," I said.

"Do you remember that story of the tortoise dying because he ate the medicine the Babalowo made for his wife, Yarinbo?" he asked.

"I do," I said.

"Another tragic porridge story," Andrew said.

"That was medicine, not porridge," I said, laughing a little.

"It was porridge. Irresistible porridge. That is why it was so tempting to the tortoise," he said. "When I get married, I am never letting any woman send me on stupid errands. A person can meet their death just like that, no warning given."

Our front gate opened, then banged shut. From the antiseptic smell slowly filling the air, I could tell it was Sister Bibike coming home from the hospital where she worked as a cleaner.

"My favorite tortoise story is when Tortoise goes to heaven," I said to Andrew.

"Really?" he asked. "You know that it ends with him being thrown down back to earth, right?"

"Yes, I do," I said. "But before all that, there was a feast and he ate till he was full and bursting, and the angels waited on him."

Our sister hovered over me for a few seconds, her large work bag dangling from her shoulders like a third limb. She placed the back of her palm, clammy from the humid evening, on the right side of my neck.

"You have a serious fever," she said, her voice filled with the forced calm of a nurse.

"I just gave him Panadol. He is getting better," Andrew said.

"Look. Andrew, come over here. Look at this. Look at your brother's face," our sister said.

The two of them bent over me, the smell of chewed groundnuts mingling with the smell of medical disinfectant.

It was like being in the rain with an umbrella too feeble for the wind. It took too much effort to hold on, there was sense in letting go, giving in to the wind.

"My back. It hurts. Bad." I screamed as I gave in to the wind. It was liberating, comforting.

"Mama!" our sister shouted toward the direction of Grandmother's room, where she still was asleep. "Andrew, run down the street to Aminat's house, see if Alhaji Sule is home so he can drive us to the hospital."

My brother stood stunned for a second then moved away from his spot above me.

"Hurry," she said. "And if he isn't home, ask Aminat to lend us five hundred naira. We have to go to a hospital far away from here where no one knows us. So we can run away if the bills are too expensive."

I heard the gate shut with the loud precision of a gunshot. Andrew was out before the import of our sister's words hit him. Grandmother was helping to lift me up, and I felt like I was sinking into the floor no matter how hard they tried to lift me.

In the corner of my eye, I saw an old tortoise, his shell cracked in several places, smiling a tired smile.

"How are you feeling?" I asked in a voice I did not recognize for its cheer.

"Better now that you are here," the old tortoise said.

We studied each other in silence for several minutes.

"Was it worth it? Falling from the sky? The anger from your friends? Your imperfect shell?" I asked.

"Have you had food from heaven?" he asked. "Have you

had everything, every kind of food you ever imagined spread out before you, an expanse as wide as the sea?"

"There would have been enough for all of you to share, you should have just waited," I said.

"No, there wasn't. Don't you get it?" the old tortoise asked. "That was the moral of the story, that there was not enough for all of us."

"And you had it all. And you were punished for that," I said.

"But I survived," the old tortoise said. "I am still here. Where are all the others?"

The hospital was the teaching hospital affiliated with Lagos State University. The children's ward smelled like a buka—like fried meat, heat from woodstoves, and jollof rice. There were more guardians and parents than there were sick children. They hovered over them like musical mobiles attached to the cribs of babies, soothing their restlessness and cajoling food and drink into tight lips.

By my side, what was left of my family smoothed into something firm, thorough and lasting, like starched clothes dried in the open sun.

It began with my grandmother, who said to the doctors who were urging her to leave my side, "I am going nowhere, I have heard you people kill poor children, so you can give their organs to rich people."

My sister Ariyike, who read from the Bible over and over again till the rhythm of her recitals became the rhythm of my dreams:

"You will not allow your Holy One see corruption.

You will protect my soul from Hades.

Therefore, my heart is glad.

My glory rejoices."

My back settled into the stiff sweetness of the hospital mattress. Unlike on the woven mat Andrew and I slept on at home, I rested in the hospital. I felt my muscles relax, become compliant as I lay down.

It was my sister Bibike who explained to me:

"You are getting fluids as well as antibiotics. They expect to be able to save your entire arm."

It was my brother who said to me, "You are going to be a footballer anyway, you do not need two hands to score goals like Yekini."

When you are the youngest child in a Lagos family, you are the custodian of the most precious unacknowledged hopes. Every sentence to you is a prayer, every sentence about you is an expression of possibility, everything you hear is love. I did not know this at first. Around the time I was learning to use my left hand to draw superheroes, I learned to listen for those hopes like words from a new language.

The boy on the bed next to me had a clean-shaven head and a full body cast. His mother, a plump woman with two bluish green tribal marks underneath each eye, made a contraption from a metal hanger to scratch his body with. As she scratched underneath his feet, she reported all that was going on in their family.

"Fadeke lost her tooth yesterday. And she nearly swallowed it. Thank God your daddy was with her, he caught it right in time."

She passed along to us his uneaten meal, long-grain rice sitting on a bed of tomato and carrot stew, pieces of fried beef and cow skin in a second bowl.

"I am something," Andrew said. "If you do not have strong teeth, you cannot eat me. What am I?"

He dipped his hand into the bowl, picking up both pieces of cow skin at the same time. This was how I knew everything was going to be all right: my brother was eating food meant for me, and I was laughing with him.

2

HOW TO WEAR MOM'S JEANS

BIBIKE

2002

THERE WAS A black leather portmanteau filled with Mother's things sitting under the bed our grandmother slept in. The first time my twin sister, Ariyike, saw it, she pulled it out by its patchy leather handle and it snagged on a loose nail, making a small rip along its side. She was in the middle of cleaning up Grandmother's room and so she was sitting there in the center of the floor, her broom and dustpan at her side, staring at old photographs, when Grandmother and I came back from working at the hospital.

Ariyike had examined the portmanteau's contents, memorizing them without trying—one wedding dress, two ankle-length dinner dresses, two pairs of boot-cut jeans, one pair of black kitten heels, one shoebox filled with jewelry, forty-five photographs with Father in them.

"Did you know Mother and Father honeymooned in Spain?" she'd asked me that first time.

"They did not. They went to Tel Aviv," I said.

She did not argue with me, but she should have, because she was half right; they had gone to the Spanish border, had taken pictures standing at the foot of the Rock of Gibraltar.

"We should sell her jewelry," she said instead. "We should sell everything, even the portmanteau."

I laughed because surely she intended it as a joke. The portmanteau was old, torn and falling apart, no one wanted it. Besides, it once belonged to Justice Silver, Mother's granduncle. He gave it to her when she was about our age and traveling to Lancaster for A levels.

"You should not laugh," she'd said. "Let us take this stuff to Tejuosho market. We can sell it to those Mallams, get some money for new clothes."

She was sitting there, holding out the shoebox, a silver necklace tangled in the middle hanging from the end. I took the shoebox from her, pushed the tangled necklace inside a heart-shaped emerald pendant, and shoved the shoebox back in the portmanteau.

"It is not ours to sell," I had said.

My sister did not like that I said this. And she was right. She should have insisted. We needed money. We always needed money. Grandmother was still getting used to having four children depending on her. She still went on complaining about how much food we ate, how much soap was

left after we showered, how much noise we made. Sometimes she forgot how she spent her money, so she accused us
of stealing it, then made us empty our luggage and purses
searching for it. Once, a few months after we arrived to live
with her here, after she had searched us and found none
of her missing things, she made us walk with her around
the neighborhood, from the man who sold chewing gum
and candy in a tuck shop, to the woman hawking bread and
beans, to the old man mending plastic buckets with pieces
of scrap plastic. She made us stop at every shop, showing our
faces to them, telling all the owners to never sell us anything
because if we ever had any money, it was money we must
have stolen from her. We walked past Uche, the jollof rice
seller, and even though my belly was filled with water and
tumbling with anger, I wanted the jollof rice so much in
that moment that I would have stolen to buy it. By the time
we had walked to the houses nearest the canal, houses so
close together that you could stand at any point on the street
and tell which mothers had started dinner and which ones
hadn't, I realized that we were to blame for the shame we
had experienced. It was indeed my own legs walking behind
her, wasn't it? My own head, bowing shamefaced.

Ariyike and I decided that day to start earning our own
money. First, we started to sell sachet water we had kept in
plastic buckets filled with ice overnight, but too many kids
here already did that. We had to walk as far as the tollgate
and wait until there was serious traffic to make good sales.
We did this together, my sister and I, for a few months until
one of grandmother's co-workers at the hospital died and I

decided to take the job. Ariyike continued to sell water in traffic.

I worked mostly in the children's wing of the orthopedic department. Most of the time, all I did was empty trash bins and wastebaskets in doctors' offices. The favorite part of my day was running errands for doctors and nurses. Most of them were nice; they let me keep the change.

Sometimes the older cleaners did not show up and it fell on me to clean the toilets. It was on one of these days that I met and befriended Aminat. The supervisor had found me sitting beneath the stairs in radiology and said, "This girl again. Don't you have something to do?"

I had just come back from walking thirty minutes to and fro, buying lunch for some doctors. I could have told him that, but then he would have laughed, telling me that was "extracurricular." Instead I said nothing, pointing in the direction of the nearest toilets, and walked away.

The men's toilet smelled like boiling hot piss mixed with something superconcentrated, like hair dye or shoe polish. The cleaning bucket was in a corner by the washbasin but there was no mop or scrubbing brush. I made a makeshift bowl by breaking the top half off a plastic bottle I found in the trash. Afterward, I mixed some cleaning detergent with disinfectant and water then took to sprinkling it over and over around the bathroom. I sprinkled all around the steel pipes jutting out of the wall where the urinals were once erect. I sprinkled inside the doorless stalls, on the mirrorless walls. Unlike in the women's bathrooms, there was running water. I walked into every stall, flushing toilets repeatedly. I had spent what I considered enough time in there and was getting ready to leave when a woman walked in and shut the door behind her. I watched her lean against the door, sighing loudly as she pulled out a sanitary pad from a large red purse shaped like an envelope. It was the cheap kind of pad, not the flat type with wings, but one of the thicker ones, the ones that look like a long lump of cotton wool. She was a tiny woman. Her long box braids were waist length. They made slow, somber movements across her face as she pulled down her skirt to tuck the pad in. She was wearing one of those tight Lycra skirts with mid-thigh slits, so I had to wonder why a young lady would use such older-woman pads. She looked like the kind of person who would choose Always every day.

She did not care that I was watching her. I was not even pretending to be cleaning at this point. She stuck the pad onto her underwear then took out a Wet n Wild lipstick from her purse. She pressed it onto the pad, making a bold red stain. She drew a couple more poorly structured stains then pulled up her underwear. It was then she looked up at me and asked with that inventive mix of Yoruba and pidgin that took me months to get accustomed to, "Watch me like TV. You no get work to do?"

I realized then that there was no real way she was as old as I had assumed she was. She was only a little older than Ariyike and me, probably—eighteen, maybe twenty. It was the way she carried herself upright in the world that had thrown me off, like she knew things no one else did, like she had plans and she was thoroughly convinced of their brilliance. Her makeup of course contributed to it: she had shaved off her eyebrows and drawn thin straight lines with red pencil, and her lips shone with bright red lipstick. Her eyes were lined with the darkest shade of black possible and contrasted with her light brown skin; she looked like she had been punched several times.

The door opened and, once she was satisfied with who it was, Aminat moved out of the way to let him in. It was one of the technicians who handled X-rays. His colleagues called him Four Fiber because he held on to copies of X-rays until patients gave him at least four twenty-naira notes.

He motioned to leave as soon as he saw me, but Aminat caught him by the arm, pulling him to her. I was so happy to have spent enough time pretending to clean the toilets that I left immediately, kicking my cleaning bucket back into the corner. I walked into the nearest office and picked up their trash bin, waiting for a full minute before walking back to the toilet door, stopping to listen. I heard the sound of struggling, her braided twists smacking the small of her back as she tried to wriggle out of his grasp.

"I do not believe you," he was saying to her.

"Why will I lie about this. I have been looking forward to spending the weekend with you. Don't you believe me?" she asked.

"Show me, then, show me," he said.

"Someone might be coming. Calm down."

He pulled down her underwear, not listening to her protest. When he found the stained pad, he said he was sorry he did not believe her. He watched her as she pulled on her underwear and adjusted her skirt, then put his hand in the inner pockets of his coat, giving her all the money he could pull out.

He was sorry that he had given the girl a real reason to end the relationship with him. A relationship that had cost him a lot of money to begin and maintain. He was ashamed of how excited he became after those few moments of struggle, deflated by the possibility that all that potential had gone to waste.

He would be sad for a few weeks because Aminat will no longer have anything to do with him, then he would learn to accept it. One day, six months later, a tiny light-skinned girl who had been in the hospital for days taking care of a little brother in a hit-and-run would take the lab technician up on his offer for a hot lunch and a cold shower in his apartment. He would wait until she was fed and clean and initiate a struggle. It would be everything he imagined, then he would find another girl and do it again and again and again.

AFTER HE WALKED out of the toilets, Aminat waited a few seconds. Then she walked out after him. I was outside, right by the door, making a show of taking a broom to the cobwebs on the hallway ceilings when Aminat walked up to me.

"Here, take your share," she said, tapping me on my shoulder. She had two twenty-naira notes in her hand. She was trying to shove them down my bra.

"Stop it. I don't want that," I said.

"Why? Are you planning to broadcast on me?" she asked.

"Yes, I am. That is exactly my job here. Administrator of periods, chief commissioner of sanitary pads."

She laughed a loud hearty laugh and walked away from me, taking her money with her. I watched her go, wondering if she was walking home with the lipstick-stained pad still between her legs.

The next time I saw her, she was standing by herself in the sidelines watching our neighborhood boys play Saturday soccer. It was then I realized that I had probably seen her so many times before, but that there had been nothing about her that interested me back then. She was several inches shorter than we were. Ariyike and I tended to befriend tall girls because we do not enjoy towering over people, like their mothers. Aminat had her hair in two braided buns that Saturday. The buns were inelegantly knotted, as though she was trying really hard to look like a messy little girl.

She looked in my direction but made no attempt to acknowledge me. There were a couple of other girls with her. Maimuna, who was newly pretty, was getting a lot of attention because Agbani Darego had won Miss World. Thanks to Agbani, every tall skinny girl with skin like a dusty blackboard would forever think they were better than everybody else. Thank you, Agbani. Then Adanna, who always told the most ridiculous stories, like the time she claimed she knew someone who ate boiled yams and palm oil that she found at the T junction and now coughed up naira notes at night. Why aren't you rich, Adanna? Where the naira notes?

They all had on the same type of jeans, low waisted, light blue with horizontal white stripes around the hips.

They were talking, waving to the boys and calling the referee names. I was about to walk away when one of the boys kicked the ball in my direction. It was rolling out of the area, so I stopped it with my feet. Another boy ran up to me to get it, his feet dusty and bare. He said thank you with a shy smile, then walked away. A few minutes later, another boy threw the ball, and another came to get it. By the third time it happened, I started to suspect it was deliberate. Aminat and her friends were leaving. None of the players had paid much attention to them.

As she walked away, she came close to me and whispered in my ear:

"Next time put on some jeans," she said. "The boys have been making all kinds of excuses to look up your skirt."

I ran home like I was seven and a boy kissed me at playtime, my ears warm from embarrassment. Andrew was home by himself building giant kites from old calendars. I ran into Grandmother's room, pulling out the portmanteau.

My mother's jeans were too short for me and too tight around the hip. They made my legs look as long as the road to Oyo. I hated them. But we had only two thousand naira saved—actually, it was a thousand six fifty because Ariyike had taken three hundred and fifty to buy us Vanilla Ice deodorant spray.

When she returned from selling water, her bucket still half full, she found me sitting outside in Mother's jeans, watching the evening make way for nighttime.

"Why are you wearing that?" she asked.

And so I told her the whole story.

"You should keep away from those girls," she said. "I have heard many bad things."

"Do we have enough money for jeans?" I replied.

She sat on the floor next to me, taking off her top and then tucking it under both arms, covering her breasts.

"We can if we have to," she said.

"Look at this, what do you think?" I laid our mother's jeans on the floor between us. "I'm thinking of cutting it short right here, just under my knees."

She leaned back into the wall, wiping her face with her shirt. "You do not need my permission to do anything" she said. "I am not your mother."

A short distance away, Ibrahim the muezzin sang in his clear loud voice the call for evening prayers. There was no real mosque in the area, so the Muslims brought their mats from home and spread out in the corner of the football field that faced east.

Grandmother was making a soup dinner, but we called Andrew and Peter. Together we had bread and akara that Ariyike had bought on her way back from selling water. We sat there, the four of us, chewing and listening to the fading sounds of the neighborhood as it settled into nighttime.

In the morning, my sister woke me up before we headed out and gave me a list of all the things we needed money for, along with all the money we had saved. She did not have to. I knew what we needed and what we had. But I was thinking about more, I was thinking that most of the money was mine, anyway. Ariyike made barely sixty naira a day from water and always spent it before she got home.

We needed a new kerosene stove, lightbulbs for the living room lamp, sugar, rice, beans, smoked fish, dry okra, palm oil. Grandmother rarely did anything for us in those days, and we had learned to stop asking. She still accused us of stealing from her sometimes, and so we kept away, spending most of our time outdoors and in the bedroom that we all shared.

The next time I saw Aminat, she had a pimple the size of a bean on the side of her face. She spoke like her mouth was filled with warm water.

"Nice jeans, where you buy it?"

"A shop close by," I said.

"Your boyfriend won't like it?" She said it like a question. "You want many new toasters, showing off your hot legs—"

That was the way she acted. If the last time, she had made me feel like a toddler, now she was making me feel older, sophisticated, the kind of girl who had a jealous boyfriend.

"Who cares what anyone thinks." I laughed.

We had started off at the hospital and were walking toward her house. Her father was crippled in both legs and moved about on a wheelchair that had an exposed battery attached to it. She was telling me about her ex who was so jealous, and I could not tell if it was the technician or some other fellow, but I had never known another girl our age with an ex, so I listened to her stories about the time he ripped her blouse open in a restaurant because she was talking to some other man. By the time we got to her house, I felt like a stranger in my body. I spent a lot of time thinking about Aminat, how she was just a girl like me, we lived in the same neighborhood, but she was from another world. She made me think I could create a world for myself, but I was hesitant. I did not know how many worlds could fit into ours and not explode when they came in contact.

I had planned to stop at the entrance of her house, but by the time we arrived I just had to go inside. There are two types of ambitious families, I think. Some are so enamored with connections, they can live in the dingiest house in a nice neighborhood; others are more concerned with being considered wealthy, so they build the nicest house in a poor neighborhood.

Aminat's father was the second type. His house, a four-bedroom bungalow, had a white Mercedes 300 class in the driveway. There were numerous, similar-sized posters of Indian actresses on the walls of the hallway that ran from the front of the house to the back. Alongside them, in a strange kinship with them, was a wood-framed black-and-white photograph of a woman who had to be Aminat's mom. She was sitting, back straight, both hands clasped before her and resting on her thighs, looking into the camera with Aminat's same resolve. Her headscarf was loose around her neck, both ends falling forward in front of her chest, as though it had been a last-minute addition to her self-assured pose.

Their television stood over a sturdy bookcase overflowing with old books. From my position in the hallway, I could see those unmistakable James Hadley Chase covers.

"Those are all my father's," she said, "please don't touch anything."

In her room, she had several suitcases around her bed.

The wall was bare and without character, and her mattress was on the floor like she was resident in a dorm room, just moved in and already waiting for the end of the semester. She rummaged through a couple of suitcases and brought out baggy T-shirts with no sleeves, the kind all of us had been crazy about the year before, and long khakis with several pockets.

"You can have these if you want," she said.

I had laughed when she said that, thinking it was a joke, but she was serious. In a quick moment, I pretended my laughter was joy at the unexpected largesse of it. Andrew was already almost as tall as we were at this time, and because I knew he would be glad for those clothes, I laughed again and smiled with real gratitude for the unisex style of American rappers of the nineties.

It was harder to be her friend after that, for in that moment I had seen what she had, the bounty of it, all types of clothes slipping out of boxes, her bedroom untidy in the way only the rooms of girls with too many things could be. We had stood there laughing, sister-friends, with the same concerns and goals, and then she had looked at me and handed me clothes that she would never wear again. This was the summary of her estimation of me, I concluded, *Poor Bibike, she is desperate enough to be grateful for anything.* After, we remained friends for the sake of habit. There was no easy way to begin to avoid her in the neighborhood, no polite way to ignore the carefree persistence with which she ingratiated herself into my life.

My sister, Ariyike, hated that the "corrupting" influence

of this friendship. My brothers did not mind, all they cared was that Aminat's house had cable and someday they could visit with me—they really wanted to watch episodes of *Captain Planet*. I always said no to them tagging along.

They did not understand that being Aminat's friend was like taking a bus to a different part of town. She showed me a different Lagos, a happy Lagos. Aminat had grown up the richest girl in a poor neighborhood. She was used to a certain type of authority, her own brand of soft worship. I did not want to fawn over her, not over her beauty and not over the nice stuff she had access to. When she got CK One perfume as her birthday gift from her father a few weeks after we became friendly, even though I was impressed about the reach of her father's influence—a friend of the family had brought it all the way from New York just in time for her nineteenth—I still did not fawn. For her birthday party, I again reached inside Mother's portmanteau, modifying one of her old dinner dresses into a minidress, to my sister's chagrin. I told anyone who asked that it was vintage, and therefore priceless. They all laughed at my lack of shame. At the party, the red looked fluorescent on my skin in the dark lights of a nightclub. When two different boys tried to touch my thighs, I knew there was something about the dress. I was beautiful in my mother's dress, and sometimes beauty was just as powerful as wealth.

I met Alhaji Sule, Aminat's father, months after we became friends. It was after I had already gone to her house several times, attended her birthday party, taught her how to make moimoi to impress a new boyfriend. On this first day, her father rolled up in his wheelchair, sitting beside us as we watched dancehall music videos on Channel O. Aminat changed the channel to CNN immediately and motioned, her fingers slow, wary, pointing to her bedroom, asking me to leave the room with her.

"You girls should spend more time reading than watching all that junk," he said as he pulled himself out of the wheelchair to sit next to us on the sofa. He was a tall, broad-shouldered man; even beneath his jalabia, you could see the dips and curves of defined biceps.

He spoke with the cultured precision of the educated northerner, his vowel sounds not exaggerated, his *th*s smooth, his *r*s elucidated. As soon as began to explain the severity of America's actions in Afghanistan, Aminat walked away with the dismissive rudeness only children could exhibit to parents regardless of who was watching. I sat there polite and smiling, listening until the news report ended and he lifted himself back into his chair and rolled over to the bookshelf/TV stand, picking up three books.

After he had set himself as close as possible to me on the sofa, he handed me the three books, one Danielle Steele, one John Grisham, one James Hadley Chase.

"One for passion, one for wit, and one for cunning, I will leave you to figure out what is what," he said, and I laughed with him in spite of myself.

He was emboldened, it appeared, by my unforced laugh and the quiet of Aminat's room. He moved closer to me, cupping my chin and whispering, his breath warming my face. He smelled like dabino and sugarcane.

"You have a pure smile," he said. "It's golden."

I did not feel the disgust I would have expected to feel, but instead, a sense of relief, of superiority, that continued to accrete as he slid his hands down my dress, tugging on a nipple.

It was the way he spoke and looked at me, both shy and hopeful like a boy but also like a medicated puppy, the way he was polishing his words and making an effort to sustain a loud conversation when all I was saying was *yes sir* that stripped me of every kind of envy I had felt for Aminat. Instead, I realized how tenuous her position was, how vulnerable her life really was. Her Lagos was just as sad as mine.

"I have many Nigerian paperbacks as well," he was saying. "Do you know Anezi Okoro? He writes the best stories about what it means to be around your age."

I was wearing my mother's dress, the one I wore to Aminat's party, that neck-too-wide dress, that hand-stitched-hem dress. Aminat's father moved from one nipple to the next, watching my face for a reaction. His fingers were dry and cold, and if I had been as present in that afternoon as I should have been, his grip on my nipples would have hurt.

"I suppose you may not like Okoro as much as I do. He writes about teenage boys. But perhaps you will enjoy Nengi Koin's *Time Changes Yesterday?*"

He was slower and gentler and warming my belly, so I pulled his hand out in one deft move.

Aminat was on her bed, both ears covered with headphones, hands holding a bright yellow Discman. It was a recent purchase, and I performed, for the first time with delight, the friendly responsibility of admiring it and congratulating her.

My world had shifted and collided with Aminat's, and I could not tell my sister what had happened. I spent way too long thinking about how to frame it, so as to understand my reaction to it. Why did Alhaji Sule touch me like me that? He wanted to. Why did I sit there quiet like nothing was happening?

I was a parentless teenage girl living with my grandmother in the slums of Lagos. Beauty was a gift, but what was I to do with it? It was fortunate to be beautiful and desired. It made people smile at me. I was used to strangers wishing me well. But what is a girl's beauty, but a man's promise of reward? What was my beauty but a proclamation of potential, an illusion of choice?

All women are owned by someone, some are owned by many; a beautiful girl's only advantage is that she may get to choose her owner. If beauty was a gift, it was not a gift to me, I could not eat my own beauty, I could not improve my life by beauty alone. I was born beautiful, I was a beautiful baby. It did not change my life. I was a beautiful girl. Still, my life was ordinary. But a beautiful woman was another type of thing. I had waited too long to choose my owner, dillydallying in my ignorance, and so someone chose me. What was I to do about that?

THE LAST TIME I saw Alhaji Sule, Aminat's father, I was standing on a bed in a hotel in Sabo. He was sitting in his wheelchair, his head beneath my dress. The hotel building stood adjacent to the All Saints Girls Secondary School. Every time his beard tickled my outer lips, instead of laughing, I looked outside my upstairs window and watched girls in blue checkered dresses, worn with matching blue berets, playing, reading, and writing.

It was like any other ordinary day in Lagos. My sister, Ariyike, thinking I was on my way to work, had tucked in my purse a short list of things to buy. My brothers, also not caring where the money was coming from, asked me to buy the two Westlife audio CDs everyone had been talking about.

"I promise to take care of you, my little angel," Alhaji Sule had said that day, reaching up under my dress and pulling down my underwear. "You are too beautiful to be walking around in your mom's jeans."

Alhaji Sule kissed the back of my neck as he wrapped his arms around me, and his body was like mine, pudgy and soft, his skin unlike mine, wrinkly, tough and warm like a fake leather bag left in the sun too long.

I searched inside me for something to stop me, for a reason to say *no*. I found nothing. There was nothing to stop me.

HOW TO RECEIVE FROM GOD

ARIYIKE

2004

"WHEN YOU SELL cold water on the streets of Lagos, you meet different types of people. Mess with the wrong thirsty bastard, your day can be ruined just like that.

"You learn to separate them into people in cars and people in buses. If you sell water mostly to people in cars, you will have a good day. If you sell to people in buses, there are two things involved.

"You will sell water to women or to men. If the bus patrons are women, you are safe. But if they are men, there are two things involved. It is either that they are old men, or they are young men. If your male bus patrons are forty and older you are safe. If they are younger men, then there are two things involved. It is either that they are ass men or boobs men. If they are ass men, you are safe—"

"I don't think you can say *ass* on a live radio show," Bibike interrupted. "Or *boobs* for that matter."

We were practicing for my audition to be an on-air presenter for a radio comedy show. In the weeks before, I had been writing several original jokes for my audition. Unsure of which way to lean, I had run through many tactics, trying to find my own distinctive style. I had started with the obvious—things of concern to young girls my age, like makeup, lace shrugs, and long belts that hang loose around your hips.

My first jokes had been drawn from my life. They had included one about buying two used skirts for two hundred naira after waking up at five a.m. on a Friday to get to the Katangwa secondhand clothes market the day all the used clothes from America arrived. But then we got home and could not wash off the telltale smell of imported used clothes: cheap fabric softener and naphthalene mothballs.

The final version of the joke was not that funny, to be honest. Besides, like my sister Bibike said, it just made me seem poor and desperate. So I had decided to go for sexy jokes. To tell a joke with a punch line about jiggling breasts, bonus points being that I could perform the jiggling.

Then my sister again, wet blanket that she was, pointed out that there was a limit to all the things I could say on air. As if I did not know that. As if we did not know that the unacknowledged goal was to seduce the interview panel.

"If you sell water on the streets," I continued, ignoring her, "young men wait until the bus is driving off. They do this so you can run after them. They love to watch breasts bounce."

•

ON THE DAY of the scheduled interview, when I finally made it to the little flat at the back of the Karamorose restaurant on Victoria Island, I was aghast to find at least thirty other girls auditioning for the same role.

It was easy to feel immediately drained and defeated and, in that moment, I did, especially after I noticed that most of the girls auditioning spoke English with accents polished, it seemed to me, by international travel and private schools. Their sentences, as they spoke in loud whispers to one another, were cheery and bright, their diphthongs cleaner, glossier than mine.

I did not know anyone at the radio station, Chill FM. My referral had been DJ Angro, a friend of a friend, one of the few boys who in recent times had made it out of our neighborhood. He was trying to give a fellow ghetto girl a leg up in this world. I had met him only once at this time. He was short and stocky, loud and enthusiastic, with prominent round eyes always red with wine or something stronger. He wore his "hair" in a hairless shine, a clean skin cut that aged him and contrasted with the baggy jeans and baseball jerseys he always wore to affect a well-traveled-young-person aesthetic.

I liked the Chill FM offices. I liked the idea that I had made it to such an opportunity. DJ Angro had been calm and reassuring when he told me what to do at the audition.

"Dress sexy, be confident, smell nice, and if you are offered something to drink, ask for water first," he said. "If they insist, ask for something foreign and healthy, like green tea."

The job entailed everything I dreamed, a chance for the restoration of all we had lost. A sufficient salary working four shifts a week on air, four shifts off air. A furnished apartment in the gated Victoria Island neighborhood, for me to arrive early or sleep off late shifts. The job also included an allowance for clothes, for hair, for makeup. A glamour crew to help with celebrity interviews and public appearances, a driver to take me around the city.

DJ Angro had said his bosses were Lebanese and so they were more interested in natural talent, unlike other owners of FM stations around Lagos who had become somewhat notorious for being more impressed by pedigree. I laughed as he told me many stories about talentless kids from wealthy families—offspring of diplomats and politicians, who, eager for jobs on the radio, had been humiliated during Chill FM auditions. Many people wanted to be on radio: it required less skill than movies or music, with about the same access to celebrity.

I wanted the job so badly that it made me physically ill with longing. Not just because I wanted to make people laugh, but because radio stations were one of the few places in Lagos that did not care that I had dropped out of school at fourteen and barely made five credits in the GCE Bibike and I had written the year before. They were interested only in talent. The only other available profession with such lax entry-level requirements was stripping.

As I waited to be interviewed, I sat on a chaise in the

waiting area, watching a girl in a bright yellow midriff top sip water so delicately that it looked as if she was taking invisible sips, and I felt like I was about to scream. Whoever these women were, they were born to be stars. They were confident. They smelled like mothers who baked meat pies and made the sign of the cross over them when they sneezed, and fathers who had other kids' fathers drive them around.

A girl in a TM Lewin shirt with a boy's haircut, her hair wet and slick like she had just showered, sat next to me. She smelled like old cigarette smoke and hair gel. She reached into a side pocket of her jeans and pulled out a new pack of Orbit gum, offering me one. I smiled gratefully at the kindness of her gesture; I was beginning to worry about how my mouth smelled after sitting quietly for over an hour.

"The wrapping is still on," I said.

"I know. I was not really offering. You were just to say no thank you," she said, laughing. She unwrapped the pack, took two sticks of gum out of the first row, and tucked the pack back into her pocket.

As she chewed the gum with her mouth closed, her mouth twitching only a little at the corner, I wondered if the humming I could hear was coming from her or someone else. I was upset but smiling to keep from crying. For the purposes of this job, I was pretending to be twenty-one instead of my actual eighteen years, but next to this girl, I felt fourteen. I felt both alien and plain. It was as though I had accidentally sat at a T junction with my knees spread apart and everyone could see my lies and inexperience.

She was doing nothing but sit there, chewing gum soundlessly, and I was unraveling.

"You have the widest face I have ever seen on a not fat person," I said to her suddenly, without thinking. My voice carried above the whispers; three other girls turned in our direction then immediately looked away.

"Your cheeks are huge, you look like you have whole lemons stuck under there," I continued.

She stared at me, still calm, with only her widened eyes revealing that she had been surprised. But I was not even sure whether she was amused or annoyed.

"Well, not everyone needs to be pretty, being cultured is often enough," she replied.

There were other girls in that room, but it seemed in that moment that it was just the two of us. I knew then that I did not mind not getting the job, as long as she, this girl with the boy's haircut, was not the one to take it from me. I did not understand the rage I was feeling nor the discomfort I felt watching her get out of the chair to work the room, flamboyantly on display, a magician, mesmerizing anyone watching.

She introduced herself over and over as Erica. She gave everyone rich, wordy, flattering compliments.

"Your hair is so beautiful. It looks like it smells like fresh oranges," she said to one.

"Your eyebrows! Such a perfect arc. I am coming home with you for makeup classes," she said to another.

She acted like she was the hostess and all of us were guests at her home, like that wide waiting room with the

leather bar stools and earthen sculptures of Yoruba god-
desses and antique mirrors was hers, like she had seen the
world, made her money, and gathered us here together to
bask in her joy.

I immediately made it my business to be outside every
small group she was in, to work the room in the opposite direction to her, from the girls gathered closest to the elevator
to the girls gathered nearest the director's office.

What I'd really wanted was to run away, to go home,
to tell my sister that of course she was right, jobs like that
were reserved for a certain type of girl, to admit that the
false courage I had conjured to get me to the interview had
evaporated and I was without cover.

Instead, I steadied my heart, told myself that it was as
good a time as any to become someone else. No one knows
me here, I'd thought, no one knows I am a nobody.

The girl Erica was a somebody, she had lived in Senegal,
then France, then had gone to college in Florida. Her degree
was in art appreciation and history. The person I decided
to become temporarily, as a perfect counter to her cultured
charm, was Keke, former child model and aspiring actress.

It rained that day. I remember because some of the girls
who came in later had water in their weave and Keke was
there to console them with loud exaggerated sighs.

"Your hair, your makeup, you must have spent so much
time getting dressed," I said.

All my life until that day, I thought the effort it took
to be mean without reason could poison me, that I would
never be happy or comfortable with myself acting that

way. What I discovered instead was how empowered I felt, talking to the other girls like that. A well-calculated snide remark said with a smile, a small laugh that made another uncomfortable. I even tried something I had seen on a TV show, saying *darling* at the end of every sentence, rolling that middle *r*, caressing it like a long-lost friend. All I could think of, apart from the desire to not lose to Erica, was my sister, Bibike, waiting at home for me to come back with good news.

When it was my turn to interview, I went in as Keke. I walked into that interview room pulling my stomach in, all the way into my belly button, and pushing my chest out. I was smiling so wide I could taste the humid air.

In the middle of rendering a highly edited version of my education and work history, the lead interviewer, a large man sitting at the center of the group, interrupted me.

"Tell me something interesting. If you could change something about your life, what'd it be?" he asked.

His voice, one I had heard too many times over the airwaves, startled me. It was difficult to imagine that this large, dimpled man, beautiful in a way that was almost feminine, was the possessor of the sexy baritone of nighttime radio. I had expected that Dexter, the British Nigerian who had revolutionized Nigerian radio, would be on the interview panel, but I had not expected my physical reaction to his dimpled smile.

"To be clear," he continued, "I am not talking about physical attributes, especially because they are outside your control."

"Dexter, is it okay I call you Dexter?" I asked.

"Yes. Shoot," Dexter said.

"If I could change anything, I'd choose to not be a twin. Even though I love being a twin, and appreciate the intense connection I have with her, sometimes I wish I wasn't a twin. It's been difficult learning independence." I said of all these things without thinking, still smiling.

I had resisted by instinct the urge to talk about our parents leaving, about the unending challenges we had faced raising our brothers in a cesspit of a neighborhood, raising ourselves. I had been honest yet circumspect; if Bibike had known what I'd said, it's possible she might have laughed. She also would have insisted that it was a great way to be evasive, introducing new information.

But no, I had not been trying to evade. I was realizing for the first time my tendency to think always in terms of "us" instead of "me." The shoes I wore were ours, the clothes ours, the parents who left without saying goodbye, ours.

When we finally ended the interview and I freed my face from the burden of a smile, the sun was setting in the street below. To avoid the other girls milling around the elevators, exchanging numbers to keep up with who gets called back, I took the stairs to the floor below, then stopped to stare at a Ben Enwonwu painting in the hallway.

I FELT A man's shadow fall over the painting like the shade of a tree. He reached over and touched the painting's edges, wiping off a speck of dust I had not noticed until he touched it.

"We keep our replicas clean around here," he said.

The woman in the portrait was bare chested, her breasts, rendered without nipples, were lopsided and uneven, her eyebrows thin and shaped like a half moon, like Beyoncé in her "Check On It" video.

"In the original, the woman is wearing a long-sleeved cardigan or something," he said. "The original is called *Portrait of a Girl.*"

"Are the eyes in both pictures the same?"

I frowned as I listened to him. His deeper dimple broadened when he talked, making his face look lopsided, his smile artificial and forced. Perhaps it was just to me, I thought. Maybe to most other people, he was just a good-looking man with the face of a baby.

"I don't usually do this," he said, interrupting me. "I promise you. Do you mind coming with me? I'd very much like to show you something."

"I guess I can spare a few minutes," I said.

I walked behind him down the hall, toward a narrow stairwell. On this new floor, we walked past three locked doors, stopping at the fourth. He opened it with a key card. It was the first time I had seen one used, and I immediately felt smaller and more vulnerable. The room was a similar size to the type the interview had been held in; this one, however, had been furnished like a studio efficiency. Through a balcony overlooking the busy street below, I watched several of the girls just ending their interviews get into their cars and drive themselves away.

"What do you think about this?" Dexter said. He pointed

at a sculpted head in the corner of the room. "I had this made as soon as I could afford it."

"Oh, that's you," I said, laughing at the absurdity of it.

Dexter was no longer smiling. He was watching me, his eyes squinting with either concern for my sanity or anger at my effrontery.

"It is very accurate," I said.

DEXTER EXCUSED HIMSELF, disappearing behind a closed door. I had not realized until then that the room had a smaller connected room. Outside, I saw Erica wave to someone before taking a sip from a bottle of water in her hand. Another girl stopped beside her and they began to talk.

When Dexter reemerged, he saw what I was looking at. "One of those two girls is our new OAP," he said.

In the street below, a third girl walked up to them. I watched as Erica hugged each girl and then walked away.

"Which of them is it?" I asked.

"The one who walked away," Dexter said.

When I said nothing, he continued.

"It was an easy decision really, she was head and shoulders better, the most qualified."

In that moment, I remembered the chapter in the Bible, the one the night before Jesus was crucified, when Judas walked up to kiss him right at the time that the soldiers came to get him.

JESUS, WHO HAD always known who would betray him, seemed to me strangely hurt by the fact that Judas kissed him. I had always found that part of the story hard to believe. It seemed to me an exaggeration, included for dramatic effect, something to be easily memorized and repeated by children all over the world in Easter plays.

Judas, are you betraying the Son of Man with a kiss?

I stepped away from the window and sat on the armchair by the side of the bed. Dexter sat next to me and helped take my shoes off.

"Is there anything you can do about that?" I asked him, surprised by how shaky my voice sounded.

I HAD OVERESTIMATED this invitation to Dexter's privacy. Maybe it was an underestimation of how male desire worked, maybe none of it was true, maybe Dexter had choreographed several moments like this in the past. There had once been another girl, it seemed to me easily possible, and she had wanted a job almost as much as Dexter had wanted her.

"There is nothing I can do, Keke," he said. And as he spoke, my heartbeat sped up like a car losing control on a racetrack. "I do not want to lie to you. It is done."

Dexter reached down to my lap and stroked the top of my thigh, right above my knee. It was a slow, oddly calming motion, and we sat there in quiet for a few minutes.

"Are you really sure?" I asked. "Is this what you brought me down here to tell me?"

I WAS CRYING freely, crying ugly, the tears and snot and shoulders shuddering type of crying.

Dexter continued stroking my thigh, murmuring in what he assumed were calming whispers.

"Don't cry, baby girl. I promise you things will work out just fine," he said. "I'm here for you. Let me help you. Everyone starts from somewhere, this is just the intermission, not the end."

The room had gotten quiet and uncomfortable. The street sounds had lessened and the dark of night was beginning to cover us all.

"Do you know that all three Gospels report the kiss of Judas but give different versions of how Jesus dealt with it?" I asked him, even though I knew he did not understand the parallels my mind was drawing or my tendency to exaggerate my hurts.

"Well, I am not sure I ever paid attention to that," he said.

"Only Luke records, 'Are you betraying the Son of Man with a kiss,'" I said.

"What do the others write?" he asked.

"Matthew says something that can be read as completely opposite to Luke. According to Matthew's gospel, Jesus said to Judas, 'Friend, why have you come?' It may seem that in Luke's version Jesus was surprised about the kiss, but in Matthew, he was surprised that Judas actually went through with the betrayal," I continued.

Dexter was patient, if still a little stunned by the direction our conversation had taken.

"Maybe both recordings are accurate. Maybe each disciple just wrote what they were absolutely certain happened.

Maybe we are to read them all to get the full picture instead of looking for inconsistencies," he said.

"I guess so."

"Are you going to be all right?" he asked.

"I just don't understand all of this, why I am here, why you told me Erica got the job," I said.

"I was hoping to spend some more time with you," he said. "Getting to know you, figuring you out. Your interview was an act, it seemed. I was curious about the real you."

I do not remember exactly why, but I started laughing at this point. Maybe it was the audacity of it all. Maybe it was my inner mind confronting the utter folly of my permutations. Of course, Dexter wanted me, that part was obvious. I had imagined some negotiation, a quid pro quo, while he had planned to rely solely on seduction.

"Keke, are you okay?" he asked.

"I am fine. I promise you I am not losing my mind right now."

Dexter shuffled around the room. I wondered if it was strange that I was still sitting in the chair I had been in since I followed him up the stairwell into this room. I shut my eyes and listened to what he was up to. He seemed to be walking the length and breadth of the room without direction, like someone in one those Nollywood movies, demonstrating their mulling over an idea.

"Have you ever listened to my Sunday morning show?" he asked eventually.

"*How to Receive from God*? Yes, I have," I said.

"Do you know it has been sponsored by Pastor David of New Citizens' Church for the past year?" he asked.

There was no way for Dexter to know of my history with Pastor David or my family's experiences with his church.

"I did not know that," I said instead.

"Would you like to take over that show?" he asked.

"Really? How would that work?"

"Well, I will have to convince the station to hire you as off-air staff," he said. "You can help set up the studio, edit interviews, follow up with advertisers, but on Sundays, you would do the church show."

"Why? Why are you offering me this?" I asked.

He came over to where I was sitting and settled into the other chair, shifting his weight now and again to better fit the chair and extend his hand to clasp mine. I watched him do all of this but said nothing, waiting for his reply.

"You need this. And I like you. I want to help you," he said.

"I am not a fan of Pentecostalism. I am not sure I want to be a part of this," I said.

"Let me help you. This is the only way I can help you. And you will be good at it. Just now, you taught me Scripture without trying," he said.

If the church was coming again into my life as an answer, it was okay for me to be weary, but it was stupid for me to say no. Dexter was right. I needed a job. My whole family needed it.

"I will do it. Thank you so much, I am sorry for

overthinking it." I turned, facing him so that our faces were right in front of each other. He was smiling at me.

"You are most definitely welcome," he said.

Still smiling at me, he clasped both of his hands around my neck, pulling my face closer to him. He kissed me. At first, it was a gentle kiss. His lips against mine felt weak and beggarly. Just when I was about to pull away, irritated by his hesitation, he got out of the chair, pulling me up with him.

"Is this okay? Can I continue?" he asked.

I looked at his face, still smiling his dimpled smile, and down at his jeans, his unbuckled belt, and his bare feet. His hands followed my eyes, his face contorted in a small groan. The smile never left his eyes. He placed my hand on the bulge of him.

"I am ready for you, can't you see?" he said.

I was about to begin another bout of hysterical laughter when he lifted me and in three quick steps placed me on the single bed. As he stood at the foot, hurriedly stepping out of his jeans, I wondered about the bed, about how many other desperate dreaming girls like me had inevitably ended up on it, despite their initial hesitation.

Dexter got up on the bed, kneeling and crouching over me so that, in the moment, I was overwhelmed by his calm confidence, by the sheer size of him, the smell of him, the width of him. I surprised myself by thinking about our father in that moment. I was thinking that since the day my father left, I had yet to smell this stench of maleness up close, this sweat and lust and cologne.

"Hey, Keke. Stay with me. Why are you so quiet?" he asked.

"I don't know what to do," I said.

"Do you know what you want me to do?" he asked.

"Not really," I said.

A strange calm had fallen upon us. I told myself to stop wondering how much was planned, or whether or not I could trust him to keep his word to me. It was possible, after all, that even the Gospel show was a hoax, a part of this seduction plan.

"Do you like what I am doing?" He was kissing my breasts all over, rapid wet kisses that did nothing for me.

"You should maybe kiss my nipples," I said. "Slowly. Please."

Somehow in the middle of my clumsiness and his eagerness, we found a way to move right. We had not turned on any lamps in this room, so the dark of night had engulfed us. I could see nothing but the brightness of his eyes. It felt like I was remembering a past life, like I had stored up a peculiar specificity of desire for that moment with Dexter. I was filled to the full measure of it and in every place he kissed me slowly, more desire poured until I could not recognize the words pouring out of my own mouth, their need or their satiation.

WE HAVE TO TALK
ABOUT GIRLS

ANDREW

2005

I WAS A Ju-boy that year. My school father was Ricky, the sanitation prefect. Ricky had six other school sons from all three junior classes. Each of us had been assigned specific duties. I washed and ironed all Ricky's clothes. Every day after lunch, right before siesta, I went to his room to check in his laundry basket for whatever clothes were there. I returned them handwashed, ironed, and folded in twenty-four hours or less.

Ju-boys. This was what we called the younger boys in junior classes 1 to 3. Ju-boys were identifiable by their uniforms, white shirts worn over blue shorts instead of the full-length trousers all boys in the senior classes wore. The Ju-boys were the nobodies.

•

ORDINARY BOYS. THIS was what we called the older boys in senior classes 1 to 2. The ordinary boys were almost nobodies or nearly somebodies, it depended on how you considered their situation. Ordinary boys were greater than Ju-boys but less than the ordinary men. Ju-boys ran every conceivable errand for ordinary boys, but they were not assigned to serve them.

The ordinary men were the senior boys in class 3 who were not appointed prefects. The prefects were the senior boys in class 3 who ruled Odogolu secondary school.

All ordinary men and prefects had Ju-boys assigned to serve them each year. On the first day of the new term, the head prefect posted a list of Ju-boys and their school fathers on the dormitory's central notice board. It was normal to see boys, their faces fat, full, and fresh from the joys of vacation, burst out weeping after learning they had been assigned to serve someone with a reputation for cruelty.

We called them our school fathers. A school father was the ordinary man or prefect a ju-boy was assigned to. A school son was the Ju-boy assigned to a school father.

I WAS ONE of the luckier Ju-boys. It would have been beyond me to oversee Ricky's food, water, or bedding, because most of the time you had to spend your own money doing things for your school father. I would have been terrible at cuddling or singing him to sleep like my school brother Teddy, the round-faced boy with a girl's voice, who had all the nighttime duties. Fortunately, all I needed was soap, and I had lots of that. My sisters sent us to boarding school with more than a dozen bars of soap; they wanted Peter and me to have more than enough for ourselves and to give away.

Our school was a mixed boarding school. This meant we had girls all around us. There were so many girls, there were even more girls than boys. In our school, girls did everything differently. They served nobody. They had a different set of rules. Girls had their own prefects, called aunties. Our prefects could not punish them. When they got in trouble, they were made to write book reports or apology letters. They did not have to do chores around the school grounds like clearing the lawns or trimming shrubs. They had their own hostels with running water flowing inside their washrooms.

We had chapel with girls. We had classes with girls. We had meals with girls. All the places you would think we needed focus and concentration, girls waddled in, pretty in their purple-and-yellow checkered dresses and white socks with tiny bows.

We were obsessed with girls. All of us were. Ju-boys had games where we wrote down names of girls on pieces of paper, which we then all drew from and dared one another to go ask out. We never did. We were Ju-boys; we knew our place.

Senior boys were obsessed with sex. They all were.

As a matter of fact, I was not even supposed to be a junior boy. When Sister Ariyike got her job and decided we had to go back to school, on account of my age, I was going to be in senior class 1 and Peter in junior class 2. But we had been out of school so long, I had not taken the junior secondary certificate examination. The school principal was only following administrative policy by requiring me to enroll in junior class 3.

"It can't be helped," he said to our sister. "I have been a principal for almost eight years. If there was something I could do, surely, I will do it for you. Especially because it's you."

Sister Ariyike was some kind of celebrity in those days because of her radio job. Everyone, strangers included, was nice to her. Once in a supermarket, an older man recognized her voice and paid for all the stuff we had in our shopping basket. Our sister did not even have to pretend to be interested in dating him or take his business card. He just said, "I am so proud of the work you do, praising God every day with your pretty voice," and walked away.

A bagger is what you were called if you could not handle your school father's business as well as all your chores and schoolwork without falling apart. A bloody bagger is what you were called if your incompetence was so glaringly bad that your school father had to report you to other prefects for reprimand.

Community murder is what a bloody bagger got. A small crowd of ordinary men and prefects made a circle around the erring Ju-boy, shouting punishments.

"Bloody bagger. Roll in the dirt."

"Dirty stinky bloody bagger. Now let me see you do five hundred frog jumps."

Ordinary men and prefects were fully grown men,

unlike the rest of us. They shaved every day, they walked around smelling like cologne and Irish Spring bath soap. When they slapped your face or the center of your back, you wondered how it was possible that something that hurt so bad was not fatal.

There was a hard-won peace between ordinary men and ordinary boys. This was on account of soccer. Before Friday evening soccer became a regular thing at Odogolu Secondary, clashes between ordinary men and ordinary boys were said to have been so frequent, the school sick bay had to get a second full-time nurse in charge of deep wounds.

They brawled about everything; everything escalated easily into fracas. A tussle between a small-for-his-age ordinary man and a bigger-than-normal ordinary boy over seats on the school bus trip to the village market resulted in the Great Destruction of 2003. This was before we arrived, so everything we heard about it was hearsay. There are many versions of the story. The most consistent facts are that the ordinary man tried to take a seat in the bus the ordinary boy had reserved for his girlfriend. The ordinary boy refused to give up the seat. The smaller but older ordinary man, who had a reputation for wild anger—he was overcompensating for what he lacked in height—slashed the ordinary boy's cheek with a razor. The bleeding boy punched the man, knocking him out. Other ordinary men attacked the bleeding boy in a bid to subdue him. The bleeding boy's classmates and friends tried to help him. Soon no one cared how it had started, it was ordinary men vs. ordinary boys. According to the legend, the resulting free-for-all lasted hours.

It is, however, unquestioned that the police descended upon the school with antiriot gear, batons, and tear gas. They arrested at least twenty students that day. There was a noticeboard at the entrance of the teachers' lounge with the names as well as passport photographs of all thirteen boys expelled from school after the incident. We were in awe of all of them. We called them the League of Extraordinary Gentlemen.

Every Saturday, my school father, Ricky, assembled us all, the seven of us school sons, in a straight line at the foot of his single bed in the prefects' dorm.

They were only six boys in the room, which loomed large, imposing because I shared a room of the same size with about sixty other junior boys. Our walls did not have the same fresh coat of paint nor the full-length posters of Aaliyah and TLC, of Britney Spears. We did not have a wall dedicated to bras, thongs, and whatever else the prefects could produce as proof of conquest.

Every Saturday, Ricky assigned us tasks for the week.

"Andrew, make my whites sparkle, my trousers sharp."

"Temirin, I need warm water for my bath. Warm, not room temperature."

"Tarfa, I am the sanitation prefect, not the garbage truck handler. Polish my fucking shoes."

After the tasks were assigned, Ricky asked about our classes. We were required to show him results from any tests and any written reprimands from teachers or, worse, other prefects.

He certainly could have gotten away with not caring

about any aspect of our lives, but Ricky liked the idea that he was fathering us. He enjoyed the neatness of that description. A couple of prefects would walk over to his bed and say something like, "Ricky, your Ju-boys are having a blast. See how freely they are speaking with you."

When anyone said this, most of the time, right in the middle of him calling one of us a fucking bastard of a bagger for failing a mathematics test, Ricky looked up at his colleagues and smiled in his wide, clueless way.

"My guy, someone has to raise these bastards."

He called all of us bastards. It hurt me more than most on account of Father leaving me for God knows where, but I learned to hide it. Ricky could smell weakness and despair like a hungry leopard.

ON ONE OF those Saturday mornings when we were gathered together in the prefects' dorm room, I looked out the window behind Ricky's bed and noticed a senior girl walking up the courtyard. While Ricky berated someone for something that meant nothing, I nodded intermittently, faking attentiveness. I was watching the senior girl hide behind a tree; she seemed to be waiting for someone. She was crouching behind a stack of recently cut branches, her back to the dorm. From the distance, it appeared as if she had been trying to hold on to something for balance with one hand, and with the other was spreading a crumpled old newspaper so she could sit.

It took me too long to realize that she had actually been hiding behind the tree, unwrapping the newspaper as soundlessly as possible, so she could shit without anyone noticing. By the time I screamed, she had already begun flinging freshly released poop into the prefects' dorm through the open windows.

"Stupid muthafuckers, smelling bastards, mad men will fuck your mother's pussy raw," she was screaming, marching toward Ricky's window.

"I curse all of you demons," she said. "Every single one of you spreading lies about me. You will fail your final exams. No universities will accept you. You will die in roadside accidents. No one will claim your rotten bodies."

As though collectively released from a spell, most of the dorm emptied out, running toward the screaming female issuing death curses. We were terrified of the death curse. One of the prefects, the only one brave enough, grabbed her, attempting to restrain her by twisting her hands behind her in a lock. She fought him off successfully, slapping him all over his face with the leftover poop pebbles, wiping her hands on his shirt. A small crowd of laughing boys had gathered. No one tried to do anything, learning quickly the folly of interrupting this strange display of rage. It was easy to imagine what had happened. The senior girl had learned that one or more of the ordinary men and prefects had bragged about sleeping with her. It could have been even more vulgar; they might have included an aborted pregnancy or claimed she was a lesbian.

They were monsters, all of them, ordinary men and boys, iron sharpening iron to destruction. It would be a mistake to try to infer a logic or science to their taunts. They were just boys being teenage boys, drunk on power and lust, un-guided and free.

ON THE MORNING of the day the girl, Nadia, the girl whom we really have to talk about, first spoke to me, I had burned Father Ricky's school uniform trousers while iron-ing them. Instead of owning up to the accident, I had pulled someone else's trousers off the clothesline, ironed those ones, and given them to him. Just when I had begun think-ing I'd got away with the switch, Father Ricky found me on the class line in the assembly hall and began whipping me with his leather belt.

"You useless Ju-boy. What did you do with my trousers? Can you see what I look like in this trash? They don't fuckin fit right!" He was screaming and whipping and screaming and whipping.

The other boys in line made no attempts to hide their laughter. The boy nearest to me laughed so loudly, Ricky paused the whipping to shut him up.

"Shut up, you fuckin bastard. Am I now a fuckin clown to you fuckin Ju-boys?"

I could not bear to look at the girls. It would have been too much to turn around and see their disgust, or worse, their pity. When his rage was spent, he walked away. He wore those replacements till the end of the year. For the next week, welts the shape of his leather belt lined my face, neck, and arms like stripes on a flag. I considered it a fair trade.

We were in class, later that day. It was the end of English

period. We were waiting for the social studies teacher to arrive. Nadia walked to where I sat by myself at the back of the class and asked to see my stripes.

"No," I said. I folded my arms across my chest to create a distance between us, realizing too late that it only made my stripes evident to her.

"You think you always have to act so tough, don't you?" she said, as she tried to unfold my arms.

"I am tough. I do not have to pretend," I said.

She was standing before me, wearing ankle socks, so when I looked away from her face because it made me feel warm, I was staring instead at her legs, bare and long like prize yams.

"You should report him to the principal. He will get in trouble," she said.

"I hear you," I said.

I did not want to talk about it anymore. Nadia did not understand that things in our school worked differently for boys. She could not see the thing that was right under her nose; no girl would ever have been whipped like that. So could she be expected to understand how particularly different things were for me? I was not like the other Ju-boys. I was older, I was taller, I was meaner, and I was convinced that I could have beaten Ricky to a stupor if I had been allowed to fight back.

NADIA WAS THE most beautiful junior girl. It was not because her skin was brown and clear like still water, or because her eyes were huge and bright like a mirror, or that her hair was reddish brown without dyes. Nadia had breasts, full, round, grown woman breasts.

The story the junior boys told about Nadia was that she was full of herself. The story the junior girls told of Nadia was that she was the uglier sister. It was said that her older sister, who graduated the year before I enrolled, was even more beautiful, but I could not imagine a more beautiful girl.

I had seen Nadia's father walk around the school with her a couple of times. He was an older Anglican reverend, an albino who had married one of his parishioners later in life. This is one of the reasons Nadia had such pale beautiful skin; she was almost an albino, but she wasn't.

The walls of our classroom were without paint. Nadia reached over my head and sketched a sumo wrestler on the wall, writing below it this caption: ANDREW IS THE MI-CHELIN MAN.

"That is a terrible drawing. It looks like an amoeba," I said.

She laughed a loud, hearty laugh, and just like that, my arms stopped hurting.

We were both facing the wall, backs turned to the blackboard, when our social studies teacher walked into the class.

"The two of you standing at the back. Husband and wife," she screamed, startling us. "Come to the front. Now tell the whole class what is so funny."

We spent the rest of that class in a corner, standing next to each other, heads bowed in the perfunctory performance of shame. The teacher interrupted her class to mock us. Other times, she asked us pointed questions, trying to show us as ignorant.

"Which deposed king was allowed to return from exile when the British annexed Lagos?" she asked.

"King Kosoko," Nadia said.

"What year did this take place?" she asked me.

I did not know. I was bad with dates. I was terrible with all things involving the remembering and reorganizing of numbers.

"In 1840," I said.

"Wrong as expected. It was 1861. Keep playing with the beautiful girls instead of facing your studies. I am sure you can get a job as her driver when she marries a rich man," the teacher said.

Everyone in our class laughed out loud. My ears burned. I imagined running into the crowd of them with Ricky's two-pronged whip, slashing this way and that all over their smiling faces.

It was exactly the kind of day that made me wish I could go back home, but Nadia saved me. She was the kind of girl to make you smile on the worst day of your life. For a long time after that, we sat next to each other at the back of the class, never getting in trouble but barely participating. She was always smiling, always happy, shiny and bright in the way a few girls are, like a pink lollipop.

THERE IS A little Valentine's Day card with petals of a dried rose I still have somewhere in the house. It says:

To Andrew, who will grow up to be badder than
Tuface and Shaggy combined.
Never forget me.

The card does not tell the story of Nadia. Her face was round and pleasant from having a father who stopped by every other weekend to visit her, who loaded her with cookies, fruits, noodles in a care package. Her family had built her up with good fruitful words like:

"You are God's example to the world of godliness."

"You are the salt of the earth."

"You are the light of the world."

Her father visited her regularly without fail. Even in the bad weeks, those last two weeks when all the students had run out of provisions and no parents were visiting because it was almost time for the school term to end.

THE DAY NADIA asked me to meet her in the shade of the trees beside the girls' dorm to exchange Valentine's Day gifts, I showered twice. The first time, I thought I was ready to leave but then Father Ricky appeared in my dorm room, handing over to me his brown pair of boots to shine because he wanted to look good for his own Valentine's Day plans.

The second time, after I was done polishing and shining those shoes, I got dressed in the boys' bathroom and ran all the way to the girls' dorm, where Nadia waited. When I stepped outside, I could see several girls emerging from their dormitories with gift bags and identical white teddy bears with tiny red hearts. I held the single rose and the single bar of Kit Kat I had purchased with two weeks' allowance and ran to her.

My feet were fast and fluid and free. It felt like I was floating in the air. Nadia was there waiting. She was my dream, sitting on an abandoned granite heap, sipping from a can of Sprite and looking in the direction of the boys' dorm as though she wondered whether I was coming.

When I got to her side, I called Nadia the most beautiful girl in the world. Even though her hair was braided back in S-shaped cornrows and I could see the shine of her scalp, she was beautiful.

I TOLD NADIA that her mouth was the warmest mouth in the world, that inside it was soft and cozy like a nest, that I was settling in there. I said she smelled like lilies in the springtime field, and she laughed because she knew I had never smelled lilies or seen them spring. She made words fill my mouth and I poured them out and over her, without thinking.

We heard the last bell for the night ring, but we did not leave for our dorm room. Every time I tried to pull away, she asked for five more minutes.

"Kiss me again," she said.

I kissed her again.

"Consider the lilies of the field, how they grow," she said.

"What?" I asked.

"Consider the lilies of the field, how they grow; they toil not, neither do they spin. It's from the Bible, words of Jesus, one of my father's favorite scriptures," she said.

•

EVERY TIME SHE spoke of her father, I tried to change the subject. She did not like her father. He pressured her to be the perfect Christian girl. He was stern, demanding, and overprotective. He was brutal in his discipline. His regular visits were really inspections, as he looked over her class notes, her clothes, nails, hairdo. Her hatred of him was like black soot over her shiny soul, like a scar on her face, swallowing up her beauty.

"Do you know what my father will do if he finds out I have a boyfriend?" she asked me once.

I had almost smiled, because it appeared to me that she had formalized our relationship.

"What?" I asked instead. "Who is telling him anything, anyway?"

"He will beat me worse than Ricky beat you, a lot worse, then burn my feet with fire so I imagine the terrors of hell anytime I am tempted to fornicate," she said.

Even though I was thinking about the terrors of hell and her father's words, I let my hands travel down to her breasts and she did not stop me. Instead, she wrapped her hands around my neck and drew me closer to her. The school was as quiet as a cemetery when we finally decided to pull away and head back to our dorms.

Nadia stood at the top of the heap, buttoning her shirt, muttering the words to "Lucky" by Britney Spears. She was facing me and therefore did not see in good enough time to run away the bright flashlight and the two people who walked toward us.

"The two of you, stop right there," screamed one.

"Ju-boy and junior girl, I can see who you are. Run and get expelled," the other screamed.

They kept their flashlights in our faces, blinding us. I could hear Nadia's heart beating wildly. She tried to hold my hand, but I let the grip wane; I did not want to give the teachers who had just caught us together after our bedtime more to be angry about.

"We are really sorry," Nadia said. "We just slept off. We did not hear the lights-out bell ring."

One of the men laughed a loud laugh that reverberated in the emptiness around us.

"So what were you doing before you slept off?" the other man asked.

"We were just talking. About classwork. That is all. I swear to God," I said.

The man who asked me a question slapped me so hard I fell forward. That was how I was sure that he was not a student. It was one of the teachers; his palm was as large as my entire head.

Nadia began to cry. I sat back on the heap rubbing my face. The men stood at our sides, shouting at us, calling us disgusting perverts, telling us how we had to stand before the whole school and be punished for our crimes. It was hard to tell how long we stayed there, the night getting colder around us, when the man closest to Nadia, the man who had slapped me, pulled her to him, hugging her like a father would.

"It is okay. Stop crying. It will be okay, come with me," he said.

I tried to turn my neck to watch as they walked a little distance away from me, but the man standing before me screamed vile words at me.

"No looking. You will wish you were dead when we are done with you tonight, stupid boy," he screamed.

"Please, sir, I cannot do that, sir," I heard Nadia plead in the distance.

"Well, I am not going to force you. No one wants you to scream and bring the whole school here," the man replied.

"Please stop this. I beg you in the name of God," I heard Nadia say.

She soon began gagging and choking. Every time it sounded like she was about to stop, it started over again. I turned to look in spite of myself. Nadia was on her knees before the man, and he was leaning over her and moving his hips back and forth. Nadia was pulling her head away and he was pushing her head back onto him.

The contents of my stomach rushed out of my mouth with the speed of running water. It was a lumpy mess of chocolate and bread and sardines. In that instant, the man by my side forgot to shine his torch in my face. Instead, he pointed it downward, checking to see if any of my vomit had spilled on his shoes. As my eyes traveled to those shoes, I realized that they were the same ones I had cleaned and shined earlier. I stilled my stomach, but another rush of vomit exploded all over the place.

It was past midnight. The clouds over us had merged into one big lump of gray, covering the moon. The air was dry and there was nothing to be heard but Nadia's gagging and my retching. The smell traveled far. The smell of that night, vomit and shoe polish and fear, surrounded the school.

Ricky, my school father, hunched over. I flinched because I had assumed he was about to hit me again.

"Run and don't look back," he said instead. I ran. My legs ran before my head could convince them to stay. The smell of sorrow stayed with me. I took my shirt off and wiped my mouth as I ran. I was crying like a little boy. I turned around as soon as I could hide in the cover of the night. The shape of two bodies huddled over one lying-down girl swelled over the granite heap like the orange of a large traffic cone. Then their hold broke. I watched her try and fail to pull herself up. Her legs were kicking up granite dust, writhing weakly like an injured snake.

"Andrew, please, please, help me."

I turned toward the path. I continued running. The door to my dorm seemed like a faraway mirage, like a gateway to another world.

Everyone was asleep like it was any other night. I ran on. I found my brother half asleep in his own bed. He made space for me and asked no questions, even though we were both in trouble if we got caught sharing a bed. I could not sleep. Around me, several cone shadows danced. My ears were ringing from being slapped so hard. My mouth tasted of blood and granite. Then my heart began to rise to meet the shadows, to demand they cease their dancing and move away from my brother's bed. But it was a shadow of fathers. My father and Nadia's father and Ricky were all dancing in the room. I opened my mouth, but no sound poured out. I had forgotten how to talk to fathers. The dancing fathers stared me down, and the angrier I was, the better they danced. I shooed them away with my hands, but they did not leave. They danced and laughed and danced some more, and no matter what I did, no matter how angry I got, the fathers did not stop dancing and I could not bring my mouth to say the words, "Go away, fathers."

HOW TO BE THE
TEACHER'S PET

PETER
2006

SHE WAS HIRED to teach you English and elocution because your last teacher, Mr. Atogun, had died after being attacked by a horde of bees in the yam farm he kept behind the school fence. You all attended his burial service. Seventeen government buses had taken all students living in the boarding house to Atanda cemetery that Saturday in November. You treated that bus ride to the cemetery like any other school trip to the city, singing Tuface songs out loud in the bus, shouting hoarse cusswords at people driving past in fancy cars, the better the cars, the nastier your insults. When a taxicab driver drove close enough to the bus, you yelled with all the other boys, "Oko ashawo"—husband to prostitutes—"watch where you are going."

The Monday morning after the burial, Miss Abigail was there in your junior secondary class, teaching English language and literature. She was dressed like those women in old English textbooks, her natural hair pulled up high over her head, her blouse wide with big, fluffy sleeves, her skirt—well, she always wore skirts.

You were not happy at the quickness with which there was a replacement teacher. You imagined that for a couple of weeks at the minimum, you would spend your English and literature class periods sleeping, eating, and talking with friends.

There was nothing lazy about wanting free, unregulated time in a Lagos boarding school. Every single moment of your waking life was regulated by the bell—which was technically just a rusty wheel from an abandoned lorry—hanging in the center of your school. At six a.m. and every thirty minutes after until your nine p.m. bedtime, some person unlucky enough to be appointed timekeeping prefect rang the bell, telling you all it was time to do something else.

Catching all the junior boys, and some of the junior girls, giving her tired, annoyed looks that first day in your class, Miss Abigail assumed you all were upset to see her because you all missed your old teacher. She decided to begin your class that morning by saying prayers for the safe repose of Mr. Atogun's departed soul. Unfortunately for her, she called on—with no clue of how bad an idea it was—Adebayo, the tallest boy in your class and the most incorrigible class clown, to say this prayer.

Adebayo began in his best attempt at invoking reverence,

his voice hoarse from early puberty, projecting as far as he could:

"Dear Lord, we are nothing but stories written in pencil by your hand. When you bring your giant eraser in the sky, you wipe us away, no one will remember us.

Do not wipe us away, Lord.

Do not erase us, Daddy Jesus.

Do not remove us, Jehovah.

Do not delete us, Almighty God—"

The class erupted first in giggles and then, as he continued praying in that manner, outright laughter. You all laughed with glee at his audacity. You, Peter, laughed especially because Miss Abigail stood there before the blackboard, her eyes wide with shock, her lips thin from restrained anger.

The new teacher allowed him to go on like that for at least five minutes, then interrupted him with her calm, "In Jesus's name we pray. Amen."

Later, Miss Abigail, after you had become the teacher's pet, would tell you she knew that Adebayo was making a mockery of prayer. "I have been a teacher for a long time," she said to you. "I can tell who the mischievous children are just by watching how the class reacts to them."

The rumors began spreading a few weeks after Miss Abigail joined the school. First, it was said that by being a stickler for rules, promoting to higher classes only those students who had a 60 percent average, she had made enemies in her former school, the all-girls school in the city. They said this was her last chance to teach in a government school.

Later, it was modified to include a story where she had quit because the teacher she loved had jilted her without warning, marrying some other lady. She discovered his deceit by stumbling upon his village wedding photos while cleaning up after him in his off-campus apartment.

You did not often believe things just because of the number of times you heard them repeated. You needed to see with your own eyes, this cruelty, this naivete. This was why you watched her closely, any chance you got. You sometimes saw Miss Abigail talking to herself as she walked the path to her apartment in staff housing. Sometimes she held in her hands a pile of books. Other times it was a grocery bag filled with fresh fruits. Once you watched her eat a bunch of tangerines. She peeled the skin off each one and then, instead of littering the path like anyone else would have, she wrapped the skins in a white handkerchief, tucking them back into her grocery bag.

Miss Abigail had a way of talking about the world that made her different from all your other teachers. Before she became your teacher, English literature class was the one place where you struggled to stay awake. You had no interest in dead or almost dead white men writing about springtime and snow. You definitely had no interest in memorizing lines from Shakespearean plays so that, like Mr. Atogun, you could say things like "Yet, to say the truth, reason and love keep little company together nowadays," laughing at your own little joke.

She was hired to teach English literature from books

written by the English, but she taught you about the fall of Rhodesia, the fight for black freedom in South Africa, and black dignity in America.

She was asked to teach poetry, but all she did was ask her students questions like, "If you are in prison or separated from your family because you have to flee an oppressive government, will you write poetry? Is writing or reading poetry an appropriate response to pain?"

You all laughed. You all said you would not have time for poetry, but for forgetting your sorrow or remembering the good in the past or imagining a better future. But you were beginning to understand what she meant. Poems are tears of the soul. You had never imagined that poems could help a person survive. Then you read "Nightfall in Soweto" by Oswald Mtshali, then you read "Letter to Martha" by Dennis Brutus. Then you read.

After you first arrived at your grandmother's house, after Father left you one evening with nothing but clothes in your backpack, telling you he was going after a job lead in Abuja, you spent the first few weeks waiting with patience for his return. You sat on the veranda looking out into the street from the moment you woke up. You were there early enough that it was before the women hawking bread and beans began their rounds and before tricycles overcrowded with schoolchildren hobbled down the street. You were still there when nighttime arrived, when the entire neighborhood began to shut down in a dependable rhythm. First, the giant lights of the gas station went out, then the generators of the beer parlor got turned off, and finally the small kiosk owners turned off their candle and kerosene lamps and locked up their stalls.

MOST OF THE time your grandmother left you alone with your watching. Sometimes she even let you sleep out there on the veranda without waking you. She never said anything about it to you. You were not even sure she noticed or even cared. Then one day, when she thought you were sleeping, you heard her crying. She was standing over you, covering your feet with a blanket, mumbling to herself, *Ibanuje ka ori agba ko odo ki la fe se ti omode.*

"Sadness inverts the old person's head, what won't it do to a little boy?"

It was the first time you heard anyone use the Yoruba noun for "sadness"—*ibanuje.* You had no idea what the word meant; your literal interpretation made you think of a disease, of a rotting of the insides. That frightened you, because you wondered whether maybe you were sick and dying, which was why your grandmother had left you alone to sit and mope.

THEN YOU ASKED your sister what the meaning of *ibanuje* was and she said "sadness," adding, when she saw your confusion at her interpretation, "It's just classic Yoruba overstatement."

The first time Miss Abigail had your class read "Nightfall in Soweto," you thought immediately about those nights.

You knew nothing of the world outside Lagos. You did not know that the world outside Lagos was just as hard for many people. You would never have imagined that it was sometimes even harder.

Surely, there were kids like you all over the world with missing parents who also could not go to the police station and say, "Excuse me, sir, policeman. Can you please find my mother or my father? I am not greedy; either of them will be enough."

The television shows you watched at home with your brother and sisters only showed loud and happy families, kids with parents who drove them to school and read bedtime stories. Where were all the shows for children like you? The ones who went to bed screaming, or the ones without beds.

You realized then from reading those poems that every language in the world must have a word like *ibanuje*, a word for "afraid" and a word for "sad" and a word for "tears." You did not tell Miss Abigail, but the more you read the *sufferhead* poetry she gave your class, the less alone you began to feel.

Miss Abigail said, one day in the middle of class, that she was up at night reading your original poem, turned in as part of your midterms. She said that her heart broke and fixed itself, that you are pure of heart and full of empathy.

"We want to hear this pure poem," some junior boy said.

What choice did she have? She made you read it out loud to them all. She must have imagined that you liked that type of attention. Or that you were glowing with pride at her praise.

> *Rain*
> *There is such a thing as too much rain.*
> *It is too much rain if we grow nothing.*
> *It is too much rain if it hides our pain.*
>
> *What does one do with heads that turn to mash?*
> *And hearts that flee in fright?*
> *It is too much rain because we grow nothing.*
> *We grow nothing because there is too much rain.*

When she asked you to read it again, slower this time, for the benefit of the members of your class, those ones you called backbenchers, the boys and girls who sat all the way at the back committed to nothing but disorderliness, you acted like you did not hear her. You sat back in your seat, putting your head on the desk. You thought about your disobedience later and decided it was a pretty harmless way to make the point that you were not soft. You were under no compulsion to keep standing there reading, looking like the teacher's pet, but then, after class was over, you began thinking about the look of pain or confusion she had on her face as you ignored her. You decided to be better to her.

Miss Abigail arrived for her next class with copies of the class list and announced a surprise quiz, a thing she had never done, not even in the week the state inspector visited your school and all the other teachers had chosen to have surprise quizzes so that they were not nervous and shaken when the inspector stopped by to listen to their classes.

On her way out after the test, she called on you and another student to carry the test papers behind her. You did it in a hurry. You picked up all the papers so there were none for the other student to carry, so that he went back to his seat. You were the picture of efficiency. You wanted her to think of you with kindness when she read the incorrect answers you had written out.

When Adebayo shouted as you walked out of the class, "Peter, the teacher's pet," you laughed and said to Miss Abigail, "I am sorry about that, Ma. I think he is just jealous."

Later, after you have become the teacher's pet, Miss Abigail will tell you that you broke her heart that day you refused to read your poem the second time. That you embarrassed her.

You talked about Miss Abigail to anyone who would listen. All your brother, Andrew, who did not have any classes with Miss Abigail because he was two classes ahead of you, said was, "Peter, just begin falling asleep in her class and she will leave you the fuck alone."

You talked to Fat Fred, the boy who sat next to you in class who just laughed and said, *Miss Abigail doesn't want you, I heard she had to leave her old school because she was teaching the junior girls lesbianism*. Your friend Irene just said you had a crush on her and it was beyond disgusting.

Miss Abigail never acted like there was something special between you when other teachers where around. When her best friend, Miss Ufot, the math teacher who was also the soccer coach, was around, Miss Abigail acted like you did not exist. Sometimes, Miss Ufot stopped by as your teacher began her lessons, her smile wide as she listened in to Miss Abigail's teaching.When Miss Abigail stopped you one evening as you walked out of the dining hall to ask if you had eaten dinner and if you liked what was served, you said, "I'm sure you have seen the trash we are served. I would have to be a goat to enjoy that."

Miss Abigail shook her head, laughing. She reached into her purse and held out a fifty-naira note.

"Okay. Go buy bread with this. Things will get better. Cheer up," she said. She did not ever get angry with you.

Later, after you have become the teacher's pet, Miss Abigail will tell you that your anger frightens her. When she tells you this, you just shrug and say nothing. In your heart, you say to yourself, that is just what boys without mothers do.

Almost every night, you dreamed about your mother, only it was not your mother but your older sister Ariyike, only she was not loving you, she was asking if you remembered to hang your towel out to dry. Sometimes she was sitting at the edge of your bed, shouting at you to put some lotion on.

"Peter, look how scaly and ashy your elbows are," she said in those dreams.

You answered, "Auntie mi, I cannot see my own elbows."

The day you became the teacher's pet, Mr. Ahmed, the Islamic teacher, who was the new head guardian of the junior boys' dormitory, led all the boys in your class to clear out weeds from the soccer field. It was a Saturday morning, and all students had to do weekend chores. You walked at the very end of that procession, rehearsing over and over how you could explain to Mr. Ahmed that weeding was one of the few chores you could no longer do because your right hand had no grip. In the past, Mr. Atogun had let you be in charge of taking attendance and giving boys water to drink.

All your rehearsing did not matter because Mr. Ahmed insisted that you grab a hoe like the other boys. When you did not do that, he asked one of the boys to get two branches from the guava tree. The boy bought three. When Mr. Ahmed began to whip you, some of the boys began to scream.

"Please, sir, don't beat him. He has sickle cell disease," one said, lying.

"Sir, he is suffering from beriberi, he is not strong," Adebayo, the class clown, said jesting.

"Sir, he has fainted three times this term already, please leave him alone," a different boy said.

Mr. Ahmed didn't listen, even though your face had swollen from crying and the fresh bark of the tree branch had left numerous green stains all over your limbs and on your clothes.

It was Miss Abigail who ran all the way from the other side of the school, who lifted you up in her arms as though you were a feather pillow, who walked away without saying anything.

When she put you down with the same gentleness with which she had lifted you, it was on the front lawn of her staff quarters, and you had stopped crying. You sat in the armchair closest to the door. She went into her kitchen, making a large mug of warm cocoa. She brought it to where you were sitting, with a red straw inside it so you did not have to lift it up.

There was no TV in her living room, but her battery-operated radio was tuned to a station playing country songs.

"Do you want to talk to the principal about what happened?" she asked right after an advert for insecticide ended and Kelly Clarkson's soft voice began singing "Because of You."

"It is fine. I'm okay," you said.

She walked back into the kitchen and even though you wanted to tell her to turn off the radio because you were about to begin crying again, you said nothing. Miss Abigail was doing dishes and humming along with the radio and you did not want to ruin it for her.

"Teachers like Mr. Ahmed do not belong in government schools, I can tell you that right now." She walked into the living room, her hands dripping with water.

"That man did not even study a proper subject in the university, that is, if where he went can even be called a university. He studied Arabic and Islamic studies."

You had no idea why she said it like it was a bad thing. To you, Arabic seemed like the right subject for an Islamic studies teacher.

"Can you imagine that, Arabic studies? Yet he is probably going to become principal ten years before someone like me can even be considered. Do you know why?" She stood in the center of her living room, towering over you like a statue.

You did not know anything about how teachers in government schools were promoted. What you knew was that her question did not need an answer as much as she needed reassurance that it was okay for her to continue. You nodded, giving her permission to continue unburdening.

"Federal character is destroying civil service. Let me tell you right now. Federal character is destroying us all. Every time promotion comes, the government must make sure an equal number of people are promoted from all the states. Can you imagine anything more bonkers? People like Ahmed, who come from states with few teachers, always get promoted. Do you know I have a master's degree? I have a master's degree from OAU, and Ahmed, with his National Diploma, is two levels above me."

She walked away from you as she spoke, back to her kitchen, stopping at the doorway to pat her hands against the lace curtain. She did this several times absentmindedly.

"That is why he is impudent. He is so arrogant. He doesn't care what anyone does. Even our principal is afraid of him. Ahmed could become principal within the next two years—even state inspector."

The radio stops playing music. The announcer reads out the next program; *Storytime* for early readers. The story is titled "Pot of Gold." Miss Abigail walks away from the curtain with dry hands, she sits next to you, her cold hand rests on your knees.

You have heard many versions of this story, it is the story

of a rude little girl who demands a pot of gold from the ancient forest spirit.

"Once upon a time, there lived a poor orphan girl in
the village of Iperu." The radio announcer reads quickly in
a deep voice, it sounds like a waterfall. This story, in the
version your sister Bibike told you, begins when the poor
orphan girl helps an old stranger do some chores in the
stranger's home. In that house, a wood shack up a hill, the
orphan girl is asked to pick a fair price for her labor from a
hidden room filled with great treasure of all types—gold
necklaces, diamond rings, colorful waist beads. The orphan
girl picks the thing she needs the most, a clay pot. However,
when she gets home, the clay pot cracks, hatches, and becomes an unending stream of gold.

The rude little girl, from the richest family in Iperu,
hears the story and runs up the hill to the old stranger's
home, demanding her own pot of gold. The strangers leads
her to the hidden room. She is also asked to pick whatever
she wants. She picks a gold necklace. When she gets home it
becomes a hive of bees and the bees sting her to death.

As the radio announcer reads his version of this story,
you think about the orphan girl, about what she wanted and
what she got instead.

Miss Abigail sat in the chair next to you, and you could
smell the citrus scent of her dish soap.

"Huhh! I know this story," she said.

"I don't like this story." You did not even know you had
said it out loud.

"Yeah! It's a problematic tale, like most of our traditional stories," she said.

You could smell something else, something dry and dusty like old shoes.

"Give me my own pot of gold, I want the biggest pot you have," the radio announcer continued in his loud voice. The two of you sat in silence, listening as the rude girl met an unfortunate end.

"Do you want something to eat?" she asked.

"I really hate this story," you said.

A smile spread across Miss Abigail's face. "Oh, Peter. You're so smart. You are thinking that there is nothing wrong with wanting good things, right? A little greed is in fact a good thing." She laughed. "Don't worry, you can ignore it, it's folklore, not doctrine."

"What about what she wanted?" you asked.

"Who?"

"The orphan girl, what about what she really wanted?"

Miss Abigail looked at you from the corners of her eyes like she had words to say but did not want them to leave her mouth. She pursed her lips together and nodded slowly but said nothing.

You were thinking about the orphan girl who got a pot of gold from an ancient spirit. "I bet she would have asked for something else, if the spirit had asked her what she wanted. I bet she would have asked for her parents back, or a new family, not money, not gold. Why will a spirit give an orphan girl money?" you said.

Miss Abigail turned her face to you with sad eyes.

"I think the spirit just gave her what he had," she said.

"Yeah. That's it. When you are like me, people give you what they have, and you are supposed to be grateful, say thank you, sir, thank you, madam. This is going to be my whole life, isn't it, being thankful for things other children don't have to be? The spirit should have asked what she wanted and she would have said, Can I have my parents back, even for one day, and then even if that did not happen, if that was beyond the spirit's ability, at least the story would be about family, not gold. What type of orphan cares about gold?"

Miss Abigail placed one slim finger on your face and wiped underneath your eye. She did it quickly and quietly like she needed to make sure the tears did not fall all the way down. This made you cry harder, fuller, and freer. Soon you were wailing and hiccupping, she was cradling your head in her breasts and rocking you back and forth, back and forth.

This was how you became the teacher's pet, by talking about what you wanted. By reading poems, by writing your own poetry. It was not the life you would have had if your mother had not left you, but it was a soft and quiet life. As much as you hated school, with the hundreds of boys living in small rooms, the loud bells, numerous activities, unending chores, Miss Abigail made it bearable, even pleasurable for you to be there. She was constant and available, always there when you needed her to be.

Even those times when you did not know you needed her, she showed up swiftly for you, like that Saturday when all the junior boys stood in line for the visiting barber, who charged twenty naira a cut to make you all look like wrinkly grandfathers. Just when it was almost your turn, she appeared before you in line, interrupting the order of things, asking the barber what sterilization process he used for his clippers. She did not leave him alone until he poured some methylated spirit on the clippers' teeth and lit it on fire for five seconds with a cigarette lighter.

"See, now it is safe," the barber said to your teacher. "Nothing survives fire."

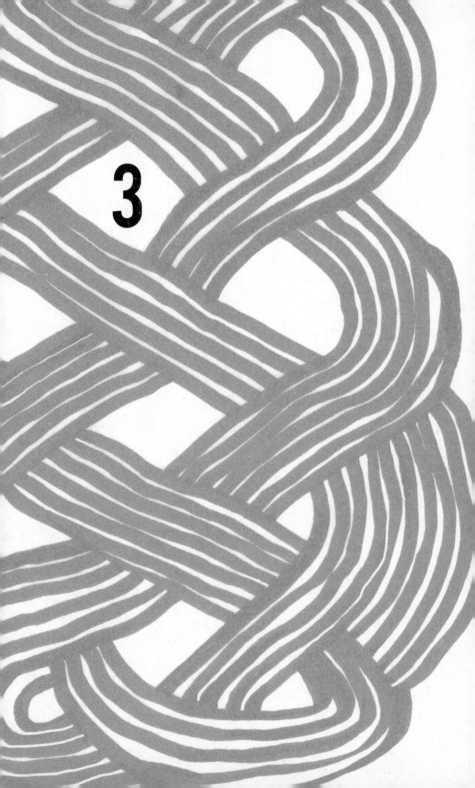

3

HOW TO LOSE YOUR LAGOS LOVER

BIBIKE

2006

WE MET BEFORE I was ready. It was the year I turned twenty. All the signs were already there. The earth was instructing me to prepare my heart for a solitary life. But I am not a good listener. I was not watching for signs. My mouth was instead wide open like a crocodile's, begging for more.

His face was like the Benin moat; firm, brown, and wide like it was built to keep strangers out. He had a big mouth filled with crowded teeth struggling for space, like a deep ditch overflowing with water. There may be other ways to describe the fullness of his lips, the hollow of his cheeks, the four equal parts his bulging forehead split into when he frowned, but even now I can only think of the cultivated inaccessibility of it all.

His face really was unapproachable, believe me. It was like the run-down house in our neighborhood where the boys who worked in long-distance transit buses gathered to smoke weed at the end of the day. His eyes were small and always red. When he looked at me, he made me want to apologize for all the wrong I ever did.

But the first time I saw him, I was not looking at his face. I saw only his legs. It was a Saturday at the start of the rainy season. I had hurried out of the house without my umbrella. The winds were bellowing before I arrived at the bus shelter, but I could not go home and come back in time for the bus. He saw me before I saw him. I felt the warmth of a gaze at the back of my neck, but when I turned in his direction all I could see were those legs. I was wearing a happy dress and the wind was battling with it, I was gathering the tulle with my hands, tucking the skirts between my legs. His legs were thick and long, majestic, like the trunk of a leadwood tree. He must have noticed me staring at them, for he moved them with swiftness to my side, covering me beneath the shade of his umbrella. It was already raining. It really was only a light drizzle, but the drains around us were blocked with refuse, so soon my feet were soaked with murky water. He was looking at me, saying nothing, as I watched the water ruin my work shoes and caress his ankles.

All those people waiting for the Rapid Transit Bus, sheltered under raincoats, umbrellas, polyethenebags, all their noise, all their muttering—about the morning crowd, about the clogged drain, at the lateness of the bus, about the unnecessary earliness of the Lagos rains—was nothing but the incidental music to my destiny.

I waited until the fifth time I saw him to speak with him. When I did, it was to ask him if he lived alone.

His name was Constantine, like the emperor, but I called him Aba for the city where he was born. He did not speak often of Aba, except to say, "A man must go where the money is. Aba will be there when I get back."

His mother was a fisherperson. She was getting older so no longer went out to sea, but her boats did, and once a month she sent him a basket of fish smoked in her coal oven.

I never saw him shave, but he was always groomed in that way few Nigerian men are, clean and only a little prickly with stubble. He would kiss me all over and my toes would twist with need. When he slid into me, my mouth erupted in a tangy sweetness. He was from the river and so everything about him was full and wide, his nose wide like the ocean, his navel full as the deep blue sea.

HE WORKED AT the wharf. He took the Rapid Transit Bus to Apapa every day, like I did. He did not believe in destiny, God, or the internet, but when I bent my elbows and knees, when I lengthened my torso and stretched like a yogi in compass mode, he believed in me.

I was becoming a grown-up madam of a woman. It was happening like my grandmother once said, "A girl becomes a woman when she finds a man she would do anything for."

I had found a man. I had taken a loverman for myself. My loverman did not laugh when I tickled. He did not cry when he was spent. He shuddered, like a possessed man at the command of the exorcist, like he was expelling whatsoever joy was trying to lay a hold on him.

My Aba was exacting and exhausting, like all my favorite sad songs, so I rolled around when he asked and played him over and over. I played him like I was a little girl again, sitting at home singing myself sore.

Back then, before our mother disappeared like smoke, before I had any real reason to weep, I would sing sad songs and cry so hard until I was sick with a high fever. My mother never could figure out how I got so sick sitting at home all by myself. But I knew what I was doing. I was sick with longing. I was sick with the curse of sensation, with all the world's sadness seeking and finding a resting place in my bones and in my marrow. One day, I was just a little girl who sometimes got out her seat in the neighborhood bar to dance, even if no one else was dancing. Then the next day, I was in love, I was a woman.

Did the world end when I lay on top of him? I think it did. The first time my hands traveled down his hips and I found the place where he had taken two bullets to protect his post from smugglers at the border, I placed my fingers on scars the size of a coin and asked Eledua to make the world kinder to men.

Did the world become nothing but a treasure trove when he kissed the back of my thighs? I expect that it did. I had formed a habit; a time-tasking habit of listing all the kinds of happinesses a grown-up in-love woman could feel. Every time I found a type I did not know by taste or a level I had not yet ascended, I shared it with my Aba and he showed me how to get there by myself.

WHAT IS THE morning? How did Oluwa mi make my morning like ten thousand mornings and my nighttime like one unending night? One day, as I was walking to my business place, my bunch of keys in one hand, my letter opener in the other, I watched a woman who had my Aba's face printed on the white T-shirt that she wore cross over to my side of the street. I stopped to let her walk ahead of me. The back of her T-shirt said

GONE BUT NOT FORGOTTEN
FEBRUARY 27, 1972–May 22, 2005.

She was one of those bony, shrunken women, and as she said her good-mornings and how have you been to other pedestrians, her thin voice scratched my ears. I walked discreetly behind her for a couple of miles, wondering about the least intrusive way to ask about the shirt she wore. When she arrived at her destination, a store where she sold all types of phones, cell phones and landlines, I waited a few minutes then walked in, acting like a customer in search of a new phone.

She smelled like her store, like sawdust, mothballs, and sunlight. When she replied to my greetings, her smile was weak and brief, her lower lip quivering after it ended. I complained about her prices, but she did not argue. One section of her store was dedicated to phone covers. I walked to that section, picking a case that was both phone case and wallet, neon pink and blue, altogether garish.

I turned to her. "How much will you accept for this case?"

We were no longer alone. A man had walked in, wearing the bright yellow branded T-shirt of the telecommunications company most people in Lagos used. He had placed at the top of one of her display cases a large expanding file folder, and they were looking through a small pile of forms, receipts, and price lists.

"Excuse me?" I said to her again.

"What do you want?" she asked me.

"I want to know how much this is," I said, holding out the ugly phone cover.

"Do you want to buy that?" she asked.

"Why will you not just tell me how much it is?" I asked.

"Please can you help me drive this woman away," she said, turning to the man with her. "I do not know what she wants, she has been here almost an hour, she has nothing to buy."

Time had run away from me like butter running from a hot spoon.

"I'm sorry for wasting your time, I just wanted to ask you a question. Please, who is that man on your shirt? He looks like my boyfriend," I said very quickly, not giving the man in yellow a chance to throw me out.

The storekeeper laughed for a long time. It was a sad laugh. When she spoke again, it was still to the man in yellow.

"You remember my brother Constantine, the one we hired your company bus for, to take his body to bury in Aba last October?" she asked.

"Yes. The customs officer. The one who died in Yobe," the man answered.

"Please, he did not die. What is die? My brother was killed. He was shot right here by smugglers." She slapped the right side of her pelvic bone hard, pointing out where our Constantine was shot.

Ta ta ta.

The fat around her hip sounded soft, tender, firm like the sound a cut of meat makes when a meat seller slaps it on his table in the market to convince you of its freshness. She did not hit me, but I felt on my own hips the intense force of her raging.

"This useless government killed him with that stupid job and their useless hospitals with no doctors. Is that how a grown man dies, just like that?" she asked.

It was like I was standing outside my own body, watching it fall from the world's tallest building.

The man in the yellow shirt walked to the other side of the display case. He placed one arm around the angry shopkeeper.

"Sister, please leave this place. You have upset her so much," he said to me.

I walked away, even though I had several questions with no one to answer them. I wanted to show her the pictures on my phone. The one with us in the mall, taken by a stranger, the one where we are holding hands going down the escalator. The one with us in his bedroom, the one where he had my blue bra around his head like oversize headphones. The one I took myself, where he was shirtless in his kitchen, frying plantains.

I wanted to show her his teeth marks on my thigh, fresh from that morning. I wanted to show her his seed still caught in the spaces between my own teeth. I could imagine her surprise, or anger, her mouth stretching taut then erupting, flowing with cursewords. I wanted her to feel this same disorientation I was feeling, like my face was filled with air and I was floating about without arms.

I wanted to tell her about all the names my Aba called me—Nkem, Ifunaya, Obidia. I wanted to talk about all the stuff my Aba taught me. Sometimes, when he sat next to me on the bus to Apapa, he would point out all the cars he would have detained for further checking at his duty post at the border.

"Kehinde, look, that red '88 Honda Accord, why is it getting stopped?" he would ask.

"Too old to be legally imported," I would say quickly, without even looking at the car. "Personal cars have to be fifteen years old or less."

Other times, it wasn't so easy. I did not have the discernment to notice unevenly balanced vehicles suggesting contraband hidden in their undercarriages or number plates much older than the car, suggesting stolen plates. Constantine was a patient teacher, saying everything with a smile.

My sister got her period first, weeks before I did. Our

grandmother called her into her room the day she got her first period, and they had a long talk. When I asked Ariyike what they talked about she refused to tell me.

"Don't worry, it was just her normal Yoruba spiritual nonsense, she will tell you herself when your time comes."

Six weeks later it was my turn to get the talk from Grandmother. She told us we were twins, therefore the elect of gods. We were to be careful not to get pregnant as teenagers; there is nothing sadder than a young mother of twins, she said. More important, she warned me to be careful when I chose my sexual partners.

"Before you have sex, remember you are Ibeji, you are a disruption that is tolerated only because you are good. We are Ibeji, the benevolent spirits, we bring fortune and good luck. But we are spirits, never forget that. So be careful of malevolent spirits. Do not befriend Anjonu. Abiku and Ibeji will wage war on their family, Ibeji and Emere will pollute the earth, Ibeji and Atunwaye will destroy each other."

If Constantine had indeed died a full year before I met him in Lagos, did that not make him Atunwaye, one who returns to the earth? Was he now Akuudaaya, one who creates for himself a second life after an abrupt end? I had many questions without answers, big questions pregnant with smaller questions. There was no one I could trust to give me the answers I needed, especially not my grandmother.

What do men want? What do they want from the earth? What do they want from love? I think all men want to live like trees. I think they want to be rooted in the earth, growing indeterminately, first as tall as they want and after that, as wide as their frames can carry. I think men want to die with their leaves green but their trunks hollow. They all want a slow, painless, gentle, suffocating death—not this sorrow, this terror, this fear.

I wandered around the city until it was dark. I had planned to say to my Aba when I saw him again, "You know how they say everyone has a second somewhere in the world? I think I met your second today. Although, I did not technically meet him, I saw a picture of him."

This is what I was going to say. When I arrived at his apartment, he was standing at his front door, a large suitcase packed, like he was ready for a trip and was just waiting to say goodbye.

"My mother has sent for me," he said. He did not give me a chance to ask questions.

I looked at his face, his hooded eyes swollen and dry, and I was surprised to find them completely without sadness. He looked resigned, even bored. Instead of all I planned to say, this is what I said:

"Constantine, who is your mother but me? Where are you thinking of going without me?"

I took the suitcase from him, walking into the kitchen. Everything in the kitchen was gone. From the gas stove and the oven mittens hanging above them, to the stack of washed dinner plates drying on the stainless-steel dish rack we had purchased together at the Lagos city mall.

I kicked off my shoes, running into the bedroom. The first time I visited him in this apartment, he asked me to be quiet because his neighbors in the next apartment just had a baby. I had tiptoed theatrically around the house and when that did not make him laugh, I coated my face with corn-starch baby powder and began to mime.

We were in the bedroom. He was sitting on the bed, both feet to the ground. My mime began with this—I believe I began with the basics—getting out of a box, eating invisible food, winning a tug-of-war. He sat there still staring, still saying nothing. Next, I stood with all the weight of my body on my right leg. With my left hand, I mimed knocking on and leaning against a door, waiting for whoever was home to come open up.

"Why don't you just come sit next to me?" my Aba said eventually.

I sat next to him and let him ease me out of my clothes. I was nervous and shaking that first time. This was the time before I knew I loved him and before the time I learned that the taste of him was smooth and filling, like coconut wa-ter. To distract myself, that first time, I thought about Saint Genesius of Rome, the mime who converted to the Chris-tian faith as he mimed what he had planned as a mockery of the ritual of baptism.

I thought about the way his mind must have had to re-arrange itself to accept a new reality. How was it so easy for him to believe that a voice from heaven had spoken to him, reporting his record of sins, washing them with water, de-claring him forgiven?

Often, as Constantine wrapped himself around my na-ked back, I wondered if records were being kept about my sins, and if there were records, how detailed were they? I wondered if there was, somewhere, a long list of all the times I licked his legs, or all the times after the first time and before the next, when I was by myself at home yet feeling aftershocks of how he made my body move.

ON THE DAY I lost him, the room had been emptied before I arrived. The bed was gone, the covers, the sheets, the area rug, all gone. His wardrobe stood emptied of everything but a pair of black shoes, four shirts, and two full sets of his customs officer's uniforms.

I walked out of the bedroom. He was standing at the door where I had left him, a suitcase in his hands as though I had not just taken it out of them.

"I am going to Aba" was all he said. "I have just spoken to my mother, she needs to see me now."

The part of me that loved him beyond words, that is my mouth, fell before him, kissing his feet. He did not move, even as I reached up to his knees, kissing and pleading with him to stay. The part of me that would miss him for all time, that is, my hands, rose up to his waist, pulling down his belted jeans. What I found was the quiet of the ocean in the morning, slithering and slim like a baby fish. He did not move away, so I filled myself with him in every way that I could. I filled my heart, I filled my tongue, I filled my womb. I took my calabash to the ocean, but the longing had arrived by boat.

··

SOMETHING HAPPENED ON THE WAY TO LOVE

ARIYIKE

2010

A YEAR AFTER I began co-hosting the Christian-themed radio show at Chill FM 97.5 Lagos, we included a segment where we had famous Christians—pastors and their wives, mostly—telling our listeners their love stories. We called this segment "Letting God Write Your Love Story." Most of the time, it was the same regurgitated boringness: the couple always met in church or in a university campus fellowship. The Lord Jesus told the man that the woman, usually a one-of-a-kind beauty and from a wealthier family, was to be his wife. The woman, usually much younger, and lacking in any personal, distinctive ambition, prayed to God and received her own sign that the rising gospel star was her husband.

I hated doing those interviews. I wanted more than

anything to ask those pastors about their ex-girlfriends, about how many women had refused their advances, about their failures at love. I would have given anything to ask these stunning wives if they truly were attracted to these plain men, if they loved having husbands who were never at home. Ask them what it's like to fuck a man who believes he hears the voice of God.

I am not a fan of love stories in general. I find the entire subject absurd and contradictory. By the time you decide to make a relationship into a story, the love part is already ending. My favorite books and movies have always been those dealing with anything but love. I remember seeing the movie *Dogville* with my twin sister and our brothers. I LOVED IT. They slept through it. My sister, Bibike, hated the blunt bleakness of it.

"If I want to think about misery and injustice, I just look outside my window," she said right after the movie ended. "You know I like my movies entertaining; next time, rent a happy movie like *Drumline* or *Love Don't Cost a Thing.*"

I loved *Dogville.* Even now, I consider it one of the best movies of all time. I loved the sense of compounding evil evoked throughout the movie and the fact that the towns-people got worse, instead of better. They were exactly like I have come to realize most people truly are, completely evil and irredeemable.

I THINK PEOPLE who, like my sister, say they can only be entertained by happy love stories are selfish and hypocrit-ical. They want to pretend that only happy stories are real stories. They want to hear a great big love story. It is not, I think, that they care that Mr. So So and Miss Do Do have arrived at happiness and are on the way to love. No, they are taking notes for their own journey. They are inspecting their own lives, comparing it with the stories they hear. They are wondering, when they meet an old couple married forty years, whether their own loves or lives will last that long. It is also that they are unwilling to confront the reality of the world we are all creating together. We all are both heroes and villains, both lovelorn and callous.

"These people are our bread and butter," my boss, Dexter, always said to me. "Do not antagonize them."

And he was right, as usual. Our loyal listeners, the ones who had made us so popular, were church people and, like people who only watched romantic comedies and read romance novels, they had come to expect a specific brand of sanguinity from our show.

The month before Dexter announced plans to leave Chill FM to start the first-of-its-kind sports radio station in Lagos, he had introduced his fiancée—a tall, mixed-race European named Cindy—to all of us at the office. Cindy and Erica, the other on-air personality hired the same day I was, became fast friends. Sometimes they stood right outside the sound booth whilst Dexter and I recorded our show, *How to Receive from God*, sipping from tall foam cups and smiling wide smiles at each other.

It was also the month Dexter and I resumed fucking everywhere we could—in the staff bathroom, in the service elevator, in the rarely used staff director's personal kitchen. It was a mix of the knowledge that he was on the brink of becoming truly phenomenal in the industry and the idea that I had the ability to hurt someone as beautiful and carefree as Cindy that I found so addictive and intoxicating.

It was also the month when I learned in a staff meeting, instead of from Dexter, that our show was ending because the New Church had decided to invest in a church satellite TV station instead. The station was cutting the whole religious programming schedule, and I was to be without a job. Stunned, I looked around the meeting room, from Dexter, whose face was without fear or remorse, to Erica, who made no attempt to hide her grin. No one was looking at me.

It was, therefore, the month I decided to go see Pastor David Shamonka again for myself, even though it had been almost ten years since we had last spoken.

BANKOLE, MY FATHER, had left us suddenly that October, ten years before. He had called my twin sister and me into the bedroom, after the boys were worn out and asleep, asking us to take care of our brothers.

I called a taxi at the crack of dawn, took it all the way to the New Church to see Pastor David. Pastor David was not as easy to see as he had been ten years before. It took me seven tries calling his office to be passed on to the assistant who wasn't too frightened to ask him if he wanted to see me. A few hours later, I received a call back from another assistant, telling me that Pastor would see me if I could make it to the Nigerian capital, Abuja, for the Full Gospel Business Crusade.

It was the month before Cindy found out Dexter and I had been fucking. She had found a voice note he had sent to me, a voice note that was nothing but sounds of us climaxing that he had recorded surreptitiously. Dexter, of course, insisted that the voice note was recent, but the recording old, and that it was born from nostalgia and nothing else. Even though his Cindy believed him totally, with the typical gullibility of a woman in love, she still was heartbroken that Dexter could be engaged to her and still miss me.

It was the month I surprised Dexter by continuing our situation even after he told me he had asked Cindy to be his wife. I did not care about her feelings, and I told him so easily because it was absolutely normal for us to talk about stuff like that. Back then, I had yet to grasp how little men, no matter how old, know about women. Most men have no idea how female resentment works. I was not sorry she found out the way she did. I enjoyed it. I wanted his Cindy to hate me. I was not even trying to hide it. Dexter, bright as the morning sun, never understood that.

More and more after that, I let Dexter kiss between my legs even though I did not enjoy it. He would lick and spit and nibble until I was irritated enough to smack him in the face. I never told him to stop. Instead, I would close my eyes and imagine those same lips that were licking me instead kissing Cindy's pale face, and my heart would quicken with joy. I did not realize then why I did what I did.

If a person has never had agbalumo, no matter how hard you try to explain the unique balance of sweet and sour to them, they cannot comprehend the reality of the "African star apple." Even for those familiar with agbalumo, very few are skillful enough to determine just by looking at the outside flesh which ones will taste good. The key, I think, is to focus on knowing several irrebuttable distinguishing features of great agbalumo.

I wish I could tell what makes good girls go bad. I wish I could identify, before becoming entangled, which people are traps and which are true friends. Maybe I am the kind of woman who will never have any real friends because I am always aiming for more, always seeking increase.

I cannot give anyone the experience of living my life, of knowing how I felt. I am still trying to understand these things myself. It is obvious to me now that back then, when I was desperate and needy, even though I was many years and several income streams removed from that girl who hawked water in traffic, running after cars while young men made fun of my bouncing breasts, I was nothing in my own eyes.

Yes, I was so small in my own eyes that the idea that the same penis I buried deep inside me could be in the pert mouth of part-Italian, part-German, part-Nigerian Cindy made me feel bigger, brighter, and better than anything else I had ever done at that point. Even earning my first one million naira did not compare. I told myself that Dexter, by sleeping with Cindy and me at the same time, made us equal. I told myself that Dexter, by risking hurting Cindy to continue fucking me, made me better than her.

As teenagers, my twin sister and I dressed the same way every day, continuing the tradition our mother had started when we were little girls. We wore the same jeans, same tops, and dragged around the same little purses popular with the girls in our neighborhood. We had to be matching, always. The first morning after we bought our first pair of jeans, we put them on and took a walk around the neighborhood. I was so uncomfortable at first. I felt vulnerable and on display immediately. The tightness of those jeans, combined with the shortness of the tops we wore over them, made me feel like everyone around us was watching our booties jiggle. My sister, who always thought everyone was trying to sleep with us, enjoyed the attention, as though she was glad, finally, to be proved right.

I kept the jeans, even though I hated them. It was easier, more comfortable, to sell water in traffic wearing jeans. I ran faster in them, and when men in cars stretched out their hands to smack my butt, I was comforted by the barrier of jeans between us, that they did not feel the texture or soft of me.

Before the radio station, I got a full-time clerk job at a beauty supply store. I spent the day giving women suggestions on the right hair extensions and makeup for their skin tone. Sometimes, my sister visited me at work. She made the day brighter; the customers stayed longer, bought more weaves, left bigger tips after listening to our team efforts at marketing.

One evening while Bibike visited, a tall, middle-aged man came to the shop. Having a man dressed so formally, as though he were on his way back from his job as a bank manager, was such a surprise. We sometimes had a few men come in to buy stuff as gifts for lovers and wives, but this man was different. He wore the darkest black shoes I had ever seen. He smelled like old wood and rich-man tobacco. He had a BMW saloon car parked right in front of the entrance. He picked up several Kanekalon hair extension bundles in black and came up to the counter to pay. He left a significant tip, then asked me to walk with him to his car. Even though it was stupid to be interested in a customer who was obviously committed to someone else, I still allowed myself to dream. I made several excuses for him. It was possible he was single, I reasoned. Maybe he was shopping for a family member or an acquaintance, I let myself think.

"That's a lot of hair, who is it for?" I asked as he got into his car, sitting behind the wheel.

"My wife and my two daughters," he said. "They are getting braids done. They are traveling abroad for holiday and want something that will not need to be redone until they get back to Lagos."

"Okay. I hope they like it," I said, turning around to leave.

This man, Lucky—I remember his name like it was yesterday—smiled and called me back.

"Wait, please, I want to talk to you," he said.

I turned back to him, standing as close as possible to the driver's window.

"You and your sister are such beautiful girls, can the both of you come visit me at home next week?" he asked.

"Why? Where do you live?" I asked.

"I live in Fola Agoro, it's close to Shomolu," he said. With one finger, he rubbed his left eye as though something had gotten inside it. "I will pay you thirty thousand naira each."

"Thirty thousand naira for what?" I asked.

"See, my wife is traveling. I don't want to be alone. I have never been with twins at the same time. The house will be empty, we can have so much fun together." He was frowning as he said this, angry, it seemed, at my bewildered questioning.

I AUDITIONED FOR and got the presenting job at Chill FM a few months after this, and quitting that sales clerk job was one of the best days of my life. It was even more satisfying than getting the new job. But that day, and all the days of my life, are colored by incidents such as the day with Mr. Lucky. I do not expect that I will ever be able to forget that feeling, like an old rag, dirty and dispensable. I did not tell my sister what the man had said, but after that day I stopped dressing up identical to her. If she got braids, I was sure to wear a weave. When she wore bright colors, I wore dark.

And so, that Saturday morning, the day I saw Pastor David again, I walked into the conference hall of the Ibeto Hotel in Abuja dressed in my best corporate skirt suit and black peep-toe high heels. I walked out of the elevator into the nearest women's bathroom. Standing in front of the mirror, I willed myself to speak with Pastor David again. Several groups of women walked in and out of that bathroom and I stood there, saying nothing to anyone. The floor was white and shiny, as were the tiled walls. Everywhere I turned, my

reflection—a put-together businesswoman in a gray suit—
stared at me. She made me want to run away.

I was unprepared for the nervous energy stirring inside me. Within the conference room, a crowd of mostly
younger men in dark-colored suits stood with arms raised
or outstretched, singing worship songs The only women I
could see were ushers and greeters scattered across the room.
I grew even more nervous. My scalp was sweaty. The air-
conditioning was failing to contain the dampness and heat.
I walked around for a little while until I found a place to sit,
an empty seat a few rows away from the makeshift podium
set up in the conference hall. Just as I was relaxing into the
chair, a fat man in a bright orange suit, his high compact
belly straining the buttons of his jacket, walked up from behind me, asking me to get out of his reserved spot.

Pastor David walked in right as I was standing up out of
the chair. Before I turned to look at the stage, I could feel
him. It was as though a gust of wind blew into the room,
over all of our heads. People screamed. Some cried. Everyone was clapping, even me. It took him several minutes to
hush us up, and then he began to sing. His voice threw me.
It was still as hoarse as I remembered but it was skillful now,
tempered by better musical equipment. He sounded more
than tolerable. His voice was pleasant. Arresting.

He moved from worship song to worship song with such
passion and ease that when he was done, almost no one was
left standing. We all were on our knees singing, praising
God. "There is no one like you God, our Father."

Finally, Pastor Shamonka began his message on the

Cave of Adullam. He read from the Amplified version the story of future King David seeking refuge from King Saul.

"In the first book of Samuel, chapter twenty-two, we are told David escaped to Adullam. Just like some of you. You have escaped your town and village. You are in Abuja hiding. Trying to make money so you can go home with pride. Or maybe, like David, you are hiding from the enemy of your destiny. Like David, some of you have left your father and mother. Like David, you have the promise of God in your life, but life has forced you into hiding.

"Book of Samuel, chapter twenty-two, verse two, says, 'Everyone who was suffering hardship, and everyone who was in debt, and everyone who was discontented gathered to him; and he became captain over them. There were about four hundred men with him.'

"Can you see what happened here? That is the difference between you and David. That is why David won and you are losing. David did not stop winning souls. David did not stop building his army. He did not stop leading.

"But I have come in the glory of God Most High to raise up the new mighty men of David!" he screamed into the crowd.

"I am here to raise up glorious men. Men who will not give up or turn backwards. Men who have been brought up to fight.

"You will fight for your money. You will fight for your job. Fight for your business. And when the enemy comes against you like a flood, you will raise up a standard against them. Somebody scream, 'I am a standard!'"

As the audience screamed, Pastor David took two steps off the podium. For a moment my heart stopped beating. I thought he was walking my way. He began to touch the foreheads of all the people in the front row, and as he did, he screamed into the microphone.

"You are the standard. You are the best man for the job. You are anointed for victory. Success is your birthright."

One woman in a yellow blazer over a black skirt began to scream. She was loud and unrestrained, as though she were in pain. Another man shook like a vibrating phone. People were falling on their faces, this way and that. My hands began shaking on their own accord. Waves after waves of something like electricity ran from my wrists to my fingers. Before long, I was praying like everyone else at that meeting. I was crying and weeping, I was praying with all my heart. I was pleading with God in Yoruba and English and asking him to help my family. I was not asking to be rich, a standard, a mighty man, or whatever. No, none of that was for me. I just wanted to have enough.

That service ended about three hours after I arrived, and it was not enough time to calm my nerves. When Pastor got off the stage, I realized to my dismay that I was on a long queue of people waiting to speak with him. Up close and away from the bright yellow lights of the stage, I noticed that his hair had begun to gray at the edges. His cheeks were full, round and wrinkly, and his eyes had a yellow tint to them, a yellow that contrasted with the deep dark circles around his eyes. He yawned at least three times in the minutes I waited in line.

During my wait, I chatted with a man next to me about the Word we had heard and the blessing we had received. The man had a large shipping envelope of papers with him, related to his manufacturing business.

"I just need Pastor to bless this," the man said, showing me the contents of his envelope. "I don't even need prayer. If he can just touch this. I know my business will revive."

The man was going on and on, and because I was being polite, standing there and listening to him, I realized too late that Pastor had decided to stop his one-on-one meetings. He was headed out of the venue. Without thinking, I ran after him and his entourage, screaming, "Daddy, Pastor, Daddy Pastor, I am here to see you, sir."

Immediately, the men around him linked arms, making a human fence around him.

I persisted with my screaming. I screamed even louder.

"Daddy, its Keke from Chill FM, we have a meeting for today. Daddy Pastor, sir, I just need five minutes."

Pastor David turned to his right when I said this. He did not turn around to look at me, he spoke inaudibly with the man closest to his right. Then he walked away. The man Pastor David had spoken to walked up to me with a wide smile.

"Good evening, Sister Keke. It is okay, Pastor says to bring you with us to the hotel."

"YOU HAVE GROWN into the most beautiful woman in the world. And I am not even the man I was ten years ago," Pastor David Shamonka was saying to me later that night in a voice hoarse from all that preaching. We were sitting next to each other in the L-shaped sitting area of his penthouse suite. "I think I am better in many ways. I am richer, of course. But I know I am no longer young and hip."

I told him he had never really been young or hip. He laughed gently at this.

"You are loved by many people," I added quickly, keeping the mood light.

"People will love anything under a spotlight," he said. "Especially troubled people."

I did not agree with him. "Well, they must like what they see."

"I am just God's conduit. If I die today, someone else will take my place. Blessed be the name of the Lord," he said.

"Blessed be the name of the Lord."

"You are the reason I never married," he said then, with a small sigh.

I laughed without thinking. The large power inverter next to the mini fridge hummed loudly. It was an awkward and foolish laugh, and immediately I tried to remedy it.

"I'm sorry. I didn't mean to laugh," I said.

"Are you courting anyone right now?" he asked a few quiet moments after.

"Courting? I think so. I don't know," I said.

"I thought about you every day back then. You were so young, and the ministry was so young, and I did not handle many things very well," he said.

He had gotten out of his chair as he spoke. He picked out a candy bar and two bottles of water from the mini fridge, handing the candy and one bottle of water to me before sitting back down.

"When did you realize I was the one working at Chill FM?" I asked after taking a bite of the candy.

"I knew right from the start. Who do you think told Dexter to hire you? You do not know this, but I saw you arriving for the interview. I had planned to sit on the panel, but I left when I saw you in the lobby," he said.

I laughed again, this bout longer than the last.

"Please do not cancel the show," I said finally. "Andrew, my younger brother, I'm not sure if you remember him. He is about to start university, and I am his sponsor. I need this job."

"We are starting our own satellite station, my dear. The radio programming was canceled months ago, did you just now hear of it?" It was the impatience in his words that wounded me.

"Have you heard about our new station?" he continued. "It will be called New Hearts TV. We will be broadcasting from South Africa and Lagos. We have spent millions of dollars on it. We will change this world. I promise you."

"Amen," I said.

I felt a gust of wind blow through the room and all over me. I realized that I was sitting on the floor, with no recollection of when I got out of the chair. I wondered if I had fainted from shock but did not realize it. How and why can it be so easy to fall again into poverty, after having come so close? I had paid my dues. I was always on time, working as hard as a donkey. I built a solid reputation as a Christian radio presenter, supported controversial public topics like anti-gay legislation and the criminalization of adultery. No reputable radio station was willing to hire me. It was hard to believe I was being cast away so easily.

"What is your boyfriend like?" Pastor David asked. He was a little bent over, looking down at me and smiling, the kind of bright smile a father might force to comfort his daughter.

"Which boyfriend? I never said I had a boyfriend."

"There's someone in your life, you said. You don't have to tell me who he is." He was frowning as he said this. "He should be taking care of you. You shouldn't be here begging for your job if he is doing his job well." He took a long gulp from my half-filled bottle of water, then set it down before me.

"Well, I have nobody to help me. I'm all my brothers have right now," I said.

"You are so wrong. You have God and you have me," he said. Water dripped down the side of his mouth and, without thinking, I reached out to wipe his face.

"Amen. Daddy, I believe. Blessed be the name of the Lord."

His phone rang at that moment and he reached to the top of the coffee table to pick it up. He did not leave the sitting area. Instinctively, realizing it was what he expected, I got up off the floor next to him and walked toward the door, giving him space for his call. I considered leaving at that point; it was obvious already that my job was gone and Pastor had other plans. I imagined the look on my brothers' faces when

I told them. Andrew had been so excited to begin studying at the University of Lagos, he had taken entrance exams and practice O levels before getting to his final year of secondary school. We were beyond surprised when he was admitted to study public administration. Finally, it seemed, good things were happening to us. We were lifting off, ascending, and we were doing it together as a team.

PASTOR DAVID'S CALL lasted longer than I expected. I stood quiet as a statue for at least thirty minutes, then I walked briskly past him and into the bathroom. I was just seeking a place to be quiet for myself. Every time Pastor David laughed during that call, it felt like he was laughing at me. I sat fully dressed inside the bathtub and began to think up a plan.

In the bathroom was a second door connected to the suite's bedroom. Opening the door as quietly as I could, I went into Pastor David's bedroom. I spent time looking at his briefcase, his computer, his international passport. I picked up the phone and, in my most businesslike voice, ordered room service.

When the meal arrived, he was still on the phone. As the bellboy opened the door, I realized that two assistants stood outside. They were the ones I had seen at the start of the service, but not the two who had driven the pastor back here. His life was organized and opulent in ways beyond my imagining.

I ate most of the dinner and was beginning to contemplate taking a shower and changing into a bathrobe just to scandalize him into ending the call when he in fact ended the call and came into the bedroom.

"Did you order the catfish pepper soup? It is usually really good," he said, opening up the covered plates on the cart.

"I haven't had any food all day," I replied, embarrassed that every plate was empty.

He laughed. "That is okay," he said.

Pastor David turned on the TV in the bedroom as he sat on the bed. If he thought the moment with both of us in this hotel bedroom was awkward, weird, or un-Christian, he did not show it.

"You can come work for me," he said suddenly. The TV was on some news station, but he was not looking at it. He was taking off his shoes, then his socks. He rolled both socks into one ball then picked up both shoes and socks, placing them in a shoebox in the corner of the room.

"What kind of job do you have in mind?" I asked.

"Our director of programs will be able to find something for you at New Hearts TV."

"That would be wonderful, Pastor," I said.

"Don't thank me yet," he said. "It probably will pay a lot less than you are used to. But the reward is the Kingdom."

"Hallelujah," I said.

"Can you call the desk and ask why we do not have TBN or CBN? Also, ask the assistants at the door to go get me my dinner," he said.

As I made the phone call in the living room, I heard the shower turn on in the bathroom. I was surprised to hear him call me some minutes later.

"Can I come in?" I asked.

"Yes," he said.

He was inside the wide tub with the curtain drawn all the way around, but I still could see the clear, full outline of him.

"Taiwo, did you call reception?" he asked.

"Yes, Pastor," I answered.

"What did they say?" he asked.

"They described how to set up TBN or Daystar here on this TV. They have a second network that is programmable," I said.

"Great," he said. "Let me know when the food comes."

"I have to leave now," I said. "It's getting too late."

"What? Don't leave." He flung the shower curtain to the side, water droplets splashing around. Pastor David stood in the shower, naked and wet, his penis erect and as long as a schoolboy's wood ruler. "Please don't leave yet."

I stayed until morning that day, like he asked. I stayed because I was hoping to negotiate a better life for myself. I stayed not because I was still the girl who had had fan girl crushes on this man as a teenager but because something had happened to me in all these years. I did not believe in love, in marital love, in righteous men or justice.

I did want to plant myself like a parasite at the side of Pastor David for as long as I could. I wanted the penthouse, the designer suits, the poorly paid people making my life easier, I admit it. I knew what he was doing by asking the girl he used to know to stay over. I knew he was trusting her—me—to be quiet and discreet.

I was falling asleep on the living room sofa when the assistants returned with Pastor David's dinner. They did not acknowledge my presence. The food tray was rolled in on the branded hotel cart even though it was obvious the meal had come from outside. There were gold-rimmed tureens of fish, gizdodo, and brown rice. A small serving of coleslaw and eggs.

One after the other, both assistants served portions onto gorgeous china, then took full spoons out of the tureens' remnants, making a show of chewing and swallowing and drinking the water.

I walked into the bathroom. It was misty from Pastor David's bath. I looked at my reflection again, wondering if it was not too late to leave. Surely there was something else I could do. I had some money saved, I could start a business. I got in the shower instead and washed all of my crevices with hotel soap.

When I was done, the food-serving assistants were gone and Pastor was on another conference call. I went into the bedroom, still naked under the bathrobe, and willed myself to sleep. It must have been almost morning when Pastor David made it to bed. I looked up and he was kneeling between my legs. My legs were spread apart and raised, my heels balanced on both of his shoulders.

"It is okay, you can go back to sleep," he said in a hoarse whisper. "I'm wearing a condom."

I did not go back to sleep, even though I pretended to be asleep. Instinctively, I realized that my nonparticipation was important to him. I realized he had come prepared and had waited it out. It hurt more than I expected. Everything hurt. He dug his fingernails in my ankle flesh, digging and pinching, harder and harder with each thrust. The first time I thought he was done, he had only paused to reach for the television remote, making TBN louder in the background. The second time he paused, he pulled out a soft penis, smacking hard at my vagina and inner thighs over and over until he was hard again. He was, all this time, singing along to the worship music filling the room.

It was a small surprise to me that I could make my body so still that nothing moved as he shook me—not my hips, not my breasts, not my hair.

"I'm sorry for shushing you," he said after he was done. He was lying next to me and whispering again in my ear. "I did not want to make any sounds my assistants could hear."

"I understand," I said.

"I am going to find your mother and father," he said, still whispering. "I am going to ask their permission to make you my wife."

Good luck to you and good luck to me, I thought to myself.

STACY'S BOYS

ANDREW

2011

On the day she came back for us, I ran away. I ran as fast as I could down the street, away from their scent. I noticed him first, he had a sweet, sharp scent cutting through the stale air of Grandmother's house. It was his hair I smelled, some loud citrus-based baby shampoo, announcing their arrival, announcing their strangeness, overpowering the smell of Grandmother's garden egg soup boiling on the stove.

Not even the stench of my brother Peter's soccer cleats, fresh from the field and sitting at the entrance to our room, or the rotting garlic cloves Sister Bibike had hung over all the house, on the doorposts and pinned to pillars to drive away bad spirits, could muddy his scent.

I saw him first, the back of him. His hair was brown, thick and curly. An alphabet onesie with a hood attached covered half his face. He looked less like a baby, more like a short, fat wrestler eager to jump into the ring. He was making those loud baby noises, saying gu gu gu ga ga over and over. As soon as he saw me, he turned so fast he slid halfway down to the floor of our grandmother's living room before his mother, my mother, caught him in her arms.

My mother saw me in the same moment I saw her. She said nothing at first. She just looked at me, from the top of my head to the shoes on my feet, and smiled a small smile.

It was Grandmother who spoke to me, disintegrating the peace.

"Andrew, leave your shoes outside," she said in Yoruba. I looked at her, surprised to find that her eyes were teary, even though she sounded joyful, even energized.

My mother cradled her baby in one hand. With the other, she searched around in a large handbag shaped like a boat. She found it, a little yellow pacifier. She unscrewed the cover and put it in his mouth. The baby went gu gu gu ga ga ga again then slumped in the nook of her arm like a half-filled bag of rice.

"His name is Zion," she said to me. "His father is an American soldier." She was still smiling that smile, wiping drool off her new baby's face.

"Where are your sisters?" she asked. Talking to me like it was nothing, like she had a right to be here, like everything was normal and fine.

"Did they go out? Grandma said they don't work on Saturdays," she asked.

Before I found the words to answer, Grandmother rescued me again.

"Andrew, there is rice in the pot. Go have some, take some garden egg soup with it," she said.

It was a short distance to the kitchen. Twelve steps end to end. I made it to the pot in six.

"THE RICE MUST be cold. Let me turn on the stove to heat it up," I said.

I took the pot from its position on the wooden kitchen shelf and was about to place it on the stove. Instead, I put it down, back onto the kitchen shelf, and I just ran. I ran out of the kitchen, through the back door, into the street.

Grandmother did not try to call me back. If she had, it is unlikely that I would have listened. My feet were swift and sweaty. The insides of my shoes felt like I had been wading around in a flood. As I ran, I caught glimpses of my reflection in car windows and the glass doors of storefronts. I was running like a thief being chased by an angry mob.

When I turned into the street with the many potholes, I realized where I was running to. I could see various men, some with faces stained with engine oil and car grime, washing their shirtless bodies at the sides of the street. A couple of men were washing their motorcycles with water collected from puddles. I walked the row of small houses, shacks really, on the corner, houses built with reclaimed wood from the old civil defense corps training ground. The house I was looking for was painted blue. The paint was the wrong kind for wood, so the color was faded, cracked, and peeling. There was mildew growing in the spaces between the boards. I stopped a few feet away from her door, trying to convince myself to turn back home. She came out of her house right at that moment, startling me. She was wearing a short white dress, and in her right hand was a small transparent bucket filled with black-eyed beans and sliced pepper, tomatoes, and onions.

Just as I was getting ready to leave, she saw me.

"Andy dudu. Were you about to pass through my street without visiting me? What is this type of life you're living?" Her voice was louder than necessary. Some of the car mechanics turned to look at us, then, immediately dismissing us, they continued washing their bodies and motorcycles.

"Good evening, Stacy. I don't want to disturb you. I can see you are busy." I was walking toward her as I spoke.

"Come over here. I have been looking for you," she said.

When I got to where she stood, she hugged me. Her body was both soft and firm, like a good-quality mattress. She handed over her bucket and continued walking. I walked beside her. Her pace was slow and leisurely. It was hard at first for me not to run ahead.

"Where were you going?" she asked.

"Nowhere. I was just taking a walk. What are you making, moimoi or akara?" I replied.

"Moimoi," she said.

Stacy and her mother had come to the neighborhood around the same time we moved in with Grandmother. She was only a little older than me but she was never really a girl, even back then. My friends and I used to play soccer on this street. We dug large stones from the ground, marking out our goalposts. Stacy was always quiet, not trying to join in like the other girls. She just stood there, watching us. I always played midfield. Peter was always goalkeeper, even after he nearly died from tetanus infection. Stacy watched us every day, saying nothing until the day her mother left and didn't return and she walked to Tamuno, the oldest of us, and asked him to give her fifty naira for a chance to look at her breasts.

For most of us boys in the area, Stacy's was the first adult female body we saw naked. We did not think much of it. We played football and went to Stacy's house and took turns watching her bathe.

When any boy tried to touch her, and there always was one foolish enough, the rest of us beat him up and dared him to tell his parents what happened. I think we liked to believe we were taking care of Stacy. We helped her eat, go to school, buy clothes. In return, she taught us what no one else would teach us about girls.

"If I go with you all the way to grind these beans, does that mean I get to eat some?" I asked.

"Of course, even if you didn't help, you are always welcome," she said.

"Are you going to work later tonight?" I asked.

"No, I am not, my boyfriend is coming to visit tonight," she said.

Stacy worked as a dancer/bartender in one of the adult clubs on Victoria Island. Her boyfriend, an older man in his thirties, was someone she'd met at her workplace. Whenever he visited, driving his white Toyota Camry through the puddles and mud, Stacy always paid boys in the neighborhood money for the "protection" of her boyfriend and his car. Of course, if any damage happened to the car, it wouldn't have been by any outsider. Stacy was just cunning in that way.

As we got closer to the mill, Stacy sang gently under her breath. It was one of those Igbo hymns, but she made it sound like something Mariah Carey would sing. I wondered then if anything ever stunned or disappointed her. She still had the same peace from when we were kids, when she'd run up all the way to the goalposts just to stand in silence for two hours.

"Do you think he loves you?" I asked.

"Who?" she answered.

"Your boyfriend," I said.

"I think so, but I do not really think about things like that," she said.

"What do you think about?" I asked.

"The important stuff. How to get money, how to be happy," she said.

It was Stacy who explained to me what a period was. Once, while I was watching her get dressed, she pulled out a face towel, folding it into four parts and tucking it into her underwear. After she explained everything about periods, I began stealing Always pads from my sisters and bringing them to her.

"So? Does Andy dudu have a girlfriend?" Stacy asked just as we arrived at the mill.

"Why do you keep calling me Andy dudu? I am not even that dark skinned," I said.

Stacy took the bucket from me, handing it over to the

girl manning the mill. The mill girl had one of those faces whose age you could not really guess. She was either a young-looking sixteen-year-old or an older-looking twelve-year-old. The mill was old and loud, but we stood right next to it. Stacy watched the girl's every movement even as she talked to me.

"Andy, are you angry with me? Don't be angry with me. We just call you Andy dudu because everyone else in your house, your sisters, Peter, even your grandma, is yellow like pawpaw," Stacy said. "But truth be told, eh, you are the most good-looking one. Auntie, isn't he good-looking?" She nudged the milling girl as she spoke, screaming all the sentences without pausing.

"Yes, he is. Tall, dark, handsome, like Desmond Elliot," the milling lady replied.

The first time I saw Stacy naked, I remember thinking she looked quite ordinary, like a little baby, spotless skin all fresh and shiny. I did not understand the excitement all the other boys had from the experience. It was a strangely painful feeling, like scoring a goal and having it unfairly disqualified by the referee. Then, one day, I saw her walking home and she was wearing a pair of those low-ride jeans and pulling them up every time they rode down to her hips and revealed her butt crack. When she turned around once and saw that I was watching her, she smiled a wide, bright white smile that was almost a laugh. And just like that, I understood what it was all about. After that, whenever it was my turn to watch her, I always tried to make her laugh or at least smile.

"I look like my mother. She has the dark skin. It's my

father who is, how did you say it again? Yellow like pawpaw, even though everyone knows pawpaws are orange, not yellow," I said.

"Hold still." Stacy placed the bowl of pureed beans in my hand and shut the lid. "I'm sorry if I offended you," she said. "It is just a funny nickname. You're funny, you always make me laugh. I thought you liked it."

I stopped for a moment, allowing her to walk ahead of me. A car was passing by and there was no room for us to walk side by side anymore.

"It's okay. Not such a big deal," I said.

I did not think she understood, but she was trying to. She laughed out loud for no reason. She walked ahead of me until we got to her house. I walked in right behind her. It was dark inside. Standing in the darkness while she fumbled around for matches and a candle, I imagined what would happen if her boyfriend arrived and I was still here. I daydreamed that he would go crazy with jealousy and start a fight. Then all of us, the boys in the neighborhood, would gather together to beat him senseless, then send him away.

There was one full-size mattress on the floor and one bean bag in the corner. I sat on the mattress. Stacy brought out some blankets and covered my legs with them. It was always too cold in her house. Once, I asked her if she cared that people knew what she did for money. "The people who love me are more than those who hate me," she said. "But I try to be the kind of person who is hard to hate."

As she poured the pureed beans into small tins and set them in a pot filled with boiling water, I lay on my back and looked up at the ceiling and thought about Stacy living here alone for so long. Maybe that was why she had us come here. Maybe that was why she did not pick just one for so long. Did she need all of us to feel less lonely? Was a prostitute just another type of lonely girl?

When she was done, she came to lie right next to me. Her breath was warm. She smelled like smoke and kerosene.

"I heard your Mother is back," she said. "Is it really her?"

"Yes, it is. She came this morning," I said.

"If you are worried about what happens next, you should not be. If her absence could not kill you, then her presence cannot kill you. Look here, you and me, we are like the barracks. Like Fela sang, 'Soldier go, soldier come, barracks remains,'" she said.

I put my left hand in her right, then I squeezed gently. We locked hands for a few minutes and then we let each other go. Just like we did when we were younger, our hands went beneath the blankets. I shuffled my way out of my boxers and jeans; her waistband made a *smack* sound as she pulled it down. I waited until the air smelled different and the force with which she moved rocked the little mattress and then I began rubbing myself. Remembering that she always finished first, I rubbed valiantly, trying to get to the end before her. I worked in vain. She went to the kitchen to tend to her moimoi and I remained on that bed. The room was cold and I was going so fast that my heart was racing, beating so loudly that I could hear it in my own ears. The blanket alone was failing to keep me warm; my legs were tingly and it felt as if I were about to lose feeling in them.

Stacy was moving about in her tiny kitchen. This made it so much harder to keep my focus. Just when I was about to give up, she started singing again. Her voice lifted, pulled, reinvigorated me. I worked faster, thinking that if she realized what her singing *Follow the ladder the heaven* did to me, she'd laugh and I would never stop feeling ashamed.

I pulled the first thing I could grab from a pile of clothes in the corner. It was a black-and-yellow headscarf. I wiped my hands all over it and sat up, my back to the wall.

"I will wash this and bring it back," I said when she came into the room.

"I know," she said. "You always do what you say."

When I left Stacy's house in the morning, I saw that there was a basket of fruit sitting on her doorstep.

I considered going back in to wake Stacy to tell her what I had seen. It was six a.m. on a Monday and people were opening their stores or homes, sweeping out dirt and debris, all evidence of a weekend of carelessness. I picked up the basket and walked away with it. I imagined that someone was watching me walk away. I imagined that the someone watching was cheering me on.

It took me almost thirty minutes to walk back home. I was slow, absentminded, hesitant to see my mother again. When I got home, there was nothing but three soft limes in the basket. I threw them in our trash can.

The next morning, two days after Mother arrived, I woke to the sound of loud arguing. My sisters were in the living room, and our mother was there with her baby, and they were talking all at once, over one another. I borrowed one of Peter's jalabias, got dressed, and walked into the living room. I was startled immediately by how ordinary it all seemed. As though we had been this family forever.

Sometimes, Mother would pause right in the middle of what she was saying to take a sip of water. As she did, I just stared at her. Her fingers seemed crooked, the skin on them wrinkly and hyperpigmented. My sister Ariyike, the one who was marrying Pastor David Shamonka, the one all the commotion was about, had a giant number 2 pencil in her hand that she waved this way and that as she spoke. The pencil was bright yellow and thick, making a wisp through the air as she waved it. Their voices over one another sounded both pleasant and weary, traveling through the air and landing in my ears. It seemed to me that whatever they were arguing about, the point had been made long ago and they were persisting just for the privilege of hearing one another, over and over, like the pleasant hook of a catchy song.

IT WAS FOR this reason that I sat down but said nothing.

"We all know that man is too old for you," our mother said.

"Age is just a number, madam," Ariyike replied.

"You are too young to be married, you have done nothing, gone nowhere," my sister Bibike said.

"I have done enough and I will do more," my sister Ariyike replied.

"We all know you do not love that man," our mother said.

"He loves me. That is enough for both of us," my sister Ariyike said.

"You are too pretty to end up with someone like that," my sister Bibike said.

They went on and on like that for a while. Sometimes, for a couple of minutes, Sister Ariyike pretended to be engrossed in the list she was making. She smiled as she scribbled in her notepad, looking up only when asked a direct question. She did not appear to be offended by their questions. It made me think of the types of argument strangers had in public places about soccer, how passionate people got and yet how no one fretted because it was all jocular, harmless fun. Soon enough, they were talking about dresses, decoration, colors, about the numbers of guests coming to the wedding. Did our mother have anyone from her extended family she wanted to invite? Would there be a camera crew? Had Ariyike met any of Pastor David's exes?

When our mother first came back, it was hard for me to believe our family could fit together again like an old jacket after a little mending. I would have been quite sure, once, that this jovial teasing was fraudulent—there was a suspicious ease in it, a hollow sweetness in their kindness to one another. However, as I watched them that morning planning for a wedding, I thought about Stacy and my heart ached because I realized how lucky she would have felt to have her mother back to argue with, to laugh with, to lie to.

THE BEAUTIFUL PEOPLE
AND THE BELOVED COUNTRY

PETER

2011

MY MOTHER, WHO had appeared again in our lives easily and without warning, like a pimple on my forehead, asked me that Saturday morning to go to Tejuosho market with her. My grandmother, placated by gifts she had received—packed foods from Walmart and shiny fabric from Mother's stopover in Dubai—assured me that it was okay to go.

When her encouragement was not enough to make me decide, our grandmother tried tears. She made a production of weeping and wailing, accusing me of ingratitude.

"Peter, you have only one mother, for God's sake. You are too young to be this unforgiving. Can't you just be grateful she's here with us now and be thankful to God she is alive and well?"

I was nineteen. Old enough to keep a grudge until I decided for myself it was time to let go. Tall enough to look down into the center of Mother's head where the repeated doses of blond dye had thinned her hair into near baldness.

My mother, who stood there staring with hope-filled eyes, looked up at me and patted my right shoulder.

"My dear, please come with me. I will leave Zion with your grandmother. It will be just the two of us," she said. "I just need to buy some sandals and ankara fabric to take back home with me. You can get whatever you want."

My mother picked up her handbag, flinging it over her shoulder as she pleaded, wrapping her blond hair in a thick green scarf and exchanging her fluffy pink slippers for flat sandals.

"Have you decided? Are you coming along? Are you gonna wear those?" she asked.

She motioned with a flick of her wrist in the direction of the half-a-size-too-big shoes she had bought me, black-and-white sneakers I would not have dreamed of wearing around our neighborhood. It would have been nothing more than an advertisement to thieves or an invitation for a violent beating from jealous boys.

"I am not wearing those," I said. I slipped into the tried and trusted rubber slide sandals I wore everywhere those days. My toenails were dirty and chipped, but I pretended not to care about what I looked like. Our mother looked at me, her eyes narrowing with hurt by what appeared to her to be my rejection of her gift.

"I will wear them. I promise," I said without thinking.

"I will wear them when I have someplace nice to go, not to the market."

She said nothing. I was not sure if my reply satisfied her. She walked out of the living room, through the veranda, out to the gate. She said nothing as we walked down the street to the closest junction hoping to find a vacant taxicab.

When we arrived at the end of our street, Mother stopped by the last of the small goods kiosks. There was a bench in the street next to the kiosk, and Mother sat on this bench. I stood next to her. We waited.

It was Emmanuel's mother's kiosk. She was the young widow who took over her late husband's business selling fried yams and potatoes in the night market. After her husband died, her friends had encouraged her to start taking new lovers in the city to help pay her bills. It was said around the neighborhood that she went out with one man her friend introduced her to and the very next day, her mouth began to swell up like a balloon. Within a week, her gums had turned black and all of her teeth had fallen out. Grandmother was the only person I knew who acted like any of it was normal and expected.

"Mama Emmanuel knows that her late husband was a very jealous man. What did she expect?" she said.

Mother ordered some fried yams and peppered snails. She waited for Emmanuel's mother to finish wrapping them up then she handed the pack over to me. "There's something I want to tell you, son," she said. "Something I've not yet told your sisters or your brother. Can I tell you? Then you can let me know what you think. Is that okay?"

"I think so," I said.

"Peter? Think so?" she asked.

"I don't know what else to say," I said.

"You can try to say something definite," she said.

As she talked, she flagged down a private car. The driver stopped, and Mother got closer to the car, leaning over the front passenger's seat with the exaggerated giddiness of a teenager as she asked for a ride to the nearest bus stop. Her voice was bright and calming, with just a hint of her American-influenced accent. I did not hear what the driver said but I watched her move away to let the car drive off.

"That man wasn't nice. What happened to all the okadas around here?" she asked.

"The government banned all commercial motorcycles," I said.

"How do you all get around, then?" she said.

"We walk everywhere," I said.

"Of course. No wonder you are all so skinny," she said.

I almost said something about hunger, but I did not. I unwrapped the fried yams and began to eat.

"What do we do now?" I asked.

"We walk. We walk to the bus stop," she said.

We walked for several minutes, saying nothing to each other. I focused on eating the yams as quickly as I could, hoping none of the neighborhood girls I liked passed by. We walked past many people. None of them paid too much attention to us. We walked past Maisuya, who appeared to be on his way to the bus stop as well, but he was slower, a thick roll of newspapers tucked under one arm, a working transistor radio hanging from a rope on his shoulder.

"Peter," he called out in jovial tone. "Peter the goal-keeper, the magnet, Sanu," he said.

"My customer, good evening. How's the Amariya? How's work?" I replied.

There was no need to introduce Mother to him. I did not want to have to explain her absence or be asked to relay greetings when she left again.

"Fine, everyone is fine," he said as he stopped to fiddle with his batteries. It seemed to me as though he was just giving us time to create distance. I did not like that even this neighbor, who knew me only through my fame as the one-handed goalkeeper, could sense how uncomfortable walking down the street with Mother was making me.

"So, I can talk to you about it?" she asked. Again.

"Yes. Go ahead," I said.

She reached into her handbag and pulled out a smaller clutch made of some type of velvety red material. She handed me a folded photo.

"I was in a detention center for eighteen months," she said. "Those are the friends I made there."

In the picture were four women, all dark and slim like my mother. They wore oversize men's clothes and brown boots.

"I was arrested for being an illegal alien. They got me six months after my visa expired. It took eighteen months for my asylum application to be granted."

Ori-ona, the mentally ill woman who claimed to talk to God, was screaming close to a bus parked in front of the beauty-supply store. She was dressed in her usual attire, two woven poly sacks formerly used by farmers to pack red beans, repurposed into a knee-length dress. Her head was clean shaven, her face glowing with a bright shiny oil. Apart from the odd choice of attire, she looked quite clean, almost ordinary, like any other woman in the neighborhood.

"I am the voice of one crying in the wilderness," she shouted as we walked past. "Prepare the way of the Lord."

"Who is that?" Mother asked.

"No one really knows. We call her Ori-ona," I answered.

"Ori-ona? Because she always knows where to go?" Mother asked.

"Well, it has been said that she hears directly from God," I said.

"Who said?" she asked.

"Everyone around here. People take her warnings seriously."

"Well," Mother said, "I guess that makes sense. God can use anyone, even babies."

A few months before Mother returned, the government had hired a construction crew to strengthen the pedestrian footbridge above the highway. Ori-ona made her camp inches away from the construction workers' tent. No one paid her any mind. Every morning she was awake before the sun was up, screaming till she was sore, "Repent, the kingdom of God is at hand. Repent, the kingdom of God is here."

She went on like this until one day a part of the footbridge being repaired collapsed. Just like that, without warning, one of the pillars cracked, killing more than fifty people. All of the construction workers died in the rubble. The government arrested the head of the foreign-owned construction firm

who had won the contract. Nurses from the Lagos psychi-
atric hospital removed Ori-ona from her spot in the street.

We did not see Ori-ona in the neighborhood for months
after that. Then, one day, she was back. Just like that. No
one could tell why she was released from the hospital or how
she found her way back to her old spot on our street.

I did not tell Mother about any of this. There was no need
to. I did not care if she believed it or not. It did not matter.
There are stories you can appreciate or understand only by
living in a particular place at a particular time. Ori-ona is
necessary for us here. In the middle of the worst type of tragedy, we got strange comfort from the idea that it was possible
someone somewhere had been trying to warn us, to prevent
it. This is how we know that we are not completely forgotten.

Mother and I walked for a few more minutes until we
arrived at the bus stop. We got on a danfo bus going to Yaba,
sitting next to each other in one of the two rows of passenger seats in the middle.

The moment we got into the bus, I noticed a middle-aged
woman outside in iro and buba running and heaving toward
our vehicle. She held two large covered plastic bowls, one in
each hand. They seemed full and bubbling with liquid. As
she ran, she stopped several times to catch her breath.

"Look at that yeye woman," the bus driver said to a male
passenger in the front. "When I married her, she was slim,
fine lepa shandy, now just look at her, like Agege bread
someone threw in the river."

The passenger laughed. We watched the woman hurry to
the bus. She was the driver's wife, bringing him his lunch.

Several passengers grumbled as the driver got out of his seat to meet with her.

"Sorry, just give me five minutes to quickly eat this food," he said to the grumbling passengers.

They sat in the waiting area attached to the bus shelter. We sat in the bus and counted the minutes until it was time to leave. He was softer, kinder, in front of her. I watched as she tended to him, how he spoke with her; he was so different talking to her. I could see that she excited him and I wondered why he had sounded so ashamed of her a few moments earlier. Why, in spite of how obviously fond of her he was, did he disparage her to a bus filled with strangers? Maybe this is what love is for some people. It requires them to do nothing, only receive.

My mother was also watching them, saying nothing to me. I appreciated the silence, the way she permitted me the illusion of thinking. Many people feel pressured to fill silences with words, to give more information, or to ask you to convince them that what they have spoken to you is still on your mind. I do not like forced discussions.

I was not thinking about her time in the detention center, not at first. I was thinking about Father, wondering how much he knew, wondering if learning what had happened to her was what broke him. Why did he leave like that? Why did she, who went to prison in another continent, come back first?

The bus driver returned to us. He had a cassette player. He made a show of turning off the radio station, slotting in his own tape. The first song began with the distinct mumbling we all associated back then with Craig David.

When the chorus began, half the bus, as if on cue, sang along to lyrics about taking a girl for a drink on Tuesday.

The bus driver screamed at the entire bus like a principal to a restive group of schoolchildren.

"All of you settle down! Don't make so much noise before the police stop us for no gotdamn reason."

My mother was laughing gently. She paused as I turned to look at her.

"This song is at least ten years old, isn't it?" she asked.

"I guess so," I said.

"How is it still so popular here?" Mother asked.

"Because it is not America, we don't get the songs as soon as they are released," I replied.

"I know what you mean," Mother said in a low voice. "Prison is a terrible place, you miss so much of the outside world, music, news, fashion."

After Craig David, we heard Shaggy and Sisqó and Des'ree. People all around us were smiling and humming along. There was a kind of peaceful silence happening inside me because the bus was noisy and hot. It was almost as if I could no longer sense what was going on amid the music, the arguing, people chewing food, the lady in the seat in front of me loosening her shoulder-length box braids with the cap of a Bic pen.

I was thinking about this woman, my mother, disappearing one day like smoke, gone for almost ten years, and then reappearing just like that, expecting everything to be okay.

There was nothing for me to do but watch her. What were her expectations? Love? Respect? Compassion? What did she suppose would happen after all this time? Whatever she expected, I was glad to disappoint her. As I listened to her talk, I was even more determined to make the fantasy she had built crumble before her.

She was so happy and satisfied with her life's choices. That was what I found most surprising about it all. In my mind, I had imagined her always sad, tired, frail, barely alive without us. I imagined her showing up, falling at our knees, crying like actresses in Nollywood movies, begging to be reinstated in our lives, promising to never leave us again. Instead, Grandmother was treating her like a tourist, making the best meals, asking us to show her around the city as though it were no longer the same Lagos she had been born in.

I was thinking of the story Sister Bibike often told my brother and me when we were younger. The story of the woman who threw her hens away because it was too hard to take care of them. When she found that one of the hens had produced seven healthy chicks by itself in the forest, she wanted it back. She demanded the return of the hen and its chicks even after throwing it away without remorse. I remember that story because of the song we sang. I remember that story because I always thought the king who asked the hen to go free but to give the woman one of its chicks was a wicked king. Now I realize that the king, kinder, fairer than I could ever be, was also very wise. No matter what your mother does, this is Lagos. Society will never let you cast her away. Especially when she wants you back.

"Peter, look, when did they build that there?" my mother

asked, pointing out the window at a new estate the state government had set up for civil servants.

"Who knows?" I answered. "We all just woke up one day and it was there."

If Mother had a problem with my tone, she did not show it.

The bus stopped, and two people got out. One person, a tall man carrying a small loaf of bread, got on.

"We should come here tomorrow and go in, see what it looks like," Mother said.

"If you want to, I am sure they will let us in. It's definitely open for everyone, not just people who live there," I said.

Mother said nothing to me after that. I was beginning to feel bad. It is difficult to fight with someone who will not fight you back. The bus arrived at the final stop, the railway tracks adjacent to Yaba market. At the entrance of the market, a group of teenagers, boys and girls around my age and younger, called out to my mother.

"Auntie, we do fine braids."

"Auntie, come and make your nails."

"Auntie, I will fix for you fine eyelashes."

"Things are so different around here," Mother exclaimed. "I cannot believe that in this same Lagos, boys are making hair in the market."

We turned away from the group, walking through the wide gates to the first row of shops. There were two sets of traders in the market. The first were those with shops and goods inside them. These were the minority. Most of the traders were those with mobile stores. Some had their wares in large steel bowls balanced on their heads, others had wheelbarrows filled with stuff for sale. Traders selling the same type of stuff were grouped together in the market. In a Lagos market, there is no reason or means for individual distinction.

The first group of traders were mostly women selling stuff for newborns and babies. Mother stopped in front of a shop. She grabbed at a large yellow bath towel hanging on a nook above the store's entrance. She shook it off the nook, then, squeezing and gripping, asked if it was made in Nigeria.

"And how much is this?" she asked, after the trader told her it was imported from Turkey.

"Three hundred naira," the woman said.

"Three hundred naira? How much is that in dollars?" Mother asked. She had turned to me as she said this, but she was not really talking to me. She was talking to the trader. I said nothing. She continued making a show of inspecting the towel closely. When she found what she was searching for, a loose thread, she picked at it.

"Look at this. This looks like it is made in Nigeria, such poor quality," she said.

"It is a great towel. How much do you want to pay, my sweet auntie?" the woman asked. The trader's voice had a very determined joviality to it. I immediately envied it. I wanted to also be able to talk to the most infuriating people like I couldn't see through their nonsense, and didn't care.

"One hundred naira," Mother said.

She paid two hundred and ninety naira for that bath towel. She seemed pleased with it even though we had just spent a fraction of an hour haggling for a mere ten naira in savings. I said nothing about that. I figured it was best to save my irritation with her for the big stuff. I think families who spend a lot of time arguing about the small stuff do it because they do not have the courage to talk about the big things.

I had learned from my sister Bibike to ask myself: Peter, what is the true source of your anger? Peter, what are you really afraid of? I am angry because I know she will never truly be sorry. I am afraid I will forgive her, trust her, and give her the opportunity to hurt me again. No, I am afraid that I would be unable to forgive her even if I wanted to. I am afraid I am the kind of boy who hates his mother.

After buying the yellow towel, we walked casually around the market, stopping in shops for Mother to try on several sandals and buy none. "I am sorry this is taking so long, Peter. I need to buy a few pairs of sandals to give the neighbors as gifts when I go back home," she explained to me. "But these are not comfortable, no one will wear this."

In a tiny shop at the end of the shoe section, we found a man sitting on a little stool. He rose up when he saw us come in. We could immediately tell that the man had only one good leg; the other one was limp from the knee down. It dragged behind him as he walked.

"In America," Mother said to me, but loudly enough for the man to hear as well, "he would not have to work, the government would pay him over a thousand dollars a month just because of his condition."

The man said nothing.

I said nothing.

"Do you not believe me?" Mother asked. "I know another African who got one hand cut off during the war in Liberia. He has his own house and car, everything from government money."

"Which shoes will you like to take a look at?" the man asked instead.

Mother pointed to a pink pair on the topmost part of the display shelves. The man picked up a long stick I hadn't previously noticed. It had several bent nails attached to its head. With the stick, he hooked the ankle portion of the sandals, pulling them down in one deft move.

The sandals were replicas, one of the many made in Aba as designer dupes. Mother bought several of them from the store owner. She haggled a little more and paid much less than he had asked for. As we walked out, several owners of neighboring stores called out, telling us they had real African leather sandals, handmade. Mother ignored them all as she walked away. I followed. We went back the way we came.

Once we were outside the market gates, Mother asked where we could go get something to eat.

"There is a Mr. Biggs in a plaza close to this place," I answered.

"Really? Do they have meat pies?" she asked.

"They better," I said.

This time, she realized it was a joke and laughed with me. There was something sad and vulnerable in that brief laughter.

"We should go to Chinatown before you leave," I said, feeling the need to say something.

"There's a Chinatown? Here in Lagos?" she asked.

"Yes, there is," I answered. "They have loads of great stuff for sale. Cheap, too."

"I'd love to get some orange chicken and Szechuan dumplings," she said.

"You will have to wait till you get back to America to eat that. There's no restaurant there. Just shopping," I said.

Mother looked down at her watch, then into the wide windows of a perfume shop. There was a sign announcing 50 percent discount on Perry Ellis perfumes.

"Do you think all those perfumes are real?" she asked me.

"Not sure. Probably not. At least expired and repackaged. You know how things are in Lagos," I said.

We arrived at the Mr. Biggs. A security officer wearing a black-and-white shirt and black pants greeted us with exaggerated warmth.

"Madam the madam. Beautiful madam. Is this your brother or your son? You are too young to have such a big man o," he said.

"You should see his older sisters then," Mother said, laughing. This time, her laugh was relaxed, genuine. She reached out to him and dropped in his hand all the change she had received from the shoe seller.

"He must make a ton of money every day, lucky guy," I said.

After we ordered our food, we sat in a booth and watched soccer replays on the big screen.

"Do you get to watch soccer in America?' I asked.

"No. Not really," she said. "American football is way

more interesting," she added quickly. "Basketball is really big there as well."

What was this place, this America she now called home? Who were these people? I wanted there and then, in the market, to scream at her, to ask how she could go to prison just for the chance to live in another country? What kind of country demanded that people make such sacrifices?

I took a loud gulp of my Coca-Cola. Two girls in the booth next to us turned around and laughed loudly at me.

"Mom, I do not want to go to America with you," I said.

"Why?" she asked.

"No reason. I just want to get into Unilag. Like Andrew. Maybe study medicine," I said.

"Andrew is coming along. He is coming with us," she said.

"Has he told you that?" I asked.

One of the girls in the close-by booth turned around and caught my eye. She shook her head slowly. This I interpreted to mean, *You, crazy ungrateful boy.* I said nothing more after that. Mother said nothing as well. We continued to chew and sip in quiet.

The television in the corner began playing church music. My mother pushed her uneaten coleslaw and chicken toward me. All the booths in the restaurant were filled. Another girl joined the girls at the table nearest to us. They were singing along with the songs on the television.

"Is there sugar in this?" Mother asked, pointing to her coleslaw. "I don't like how it tastes."

I shrugged and said nothing. I was looking at the girl

who had just joined the next booth. She had brought a book with her and was trying to read while her friends talked to and over her. The book was open on the table, next to a glass of orange juice. She had placed her dark brown wallet on the thicker side of the book, to hold the pages in place. There was something so calming about watching her read peacefully in all that chaos, and for a moment I wished I was like one of those guys in American sitcoms who could walk up to a strange girl.

"I had no idea," Mother said, her voice startling in its loudness now. "I had no idea your father would leave. I would have stayed if I knew he would do that. Do you believe me?"

I looked around. No one was watching or listening to our conversation. Outwardly, we were just like everyone else here, eating, enjoying our air-conditioned respite from the Lagos heat.

THE BOYS IN the neighborhood who called us abandoned bastards when we argued had been around when Mother arrived a few nights ago. They had helped with getting her boxes out of the taxi. They did not leave until she had handed out several packs of sneakers and Kit Kat bars as thank-you gifts.

"Are you listening to me?" Mother continued, her voice quieter this time. "Peter, I did not know I'd spend all that time in jail either. No one makes plans for suffering."

Above the headboard in the room Grandmother slept in hung a framed picture of Mother and Father at their wedding. Once, when someone shut the front door so hard the walls shook, the frame fell to the floor. Grandmother picked up every shred of glass, patching it all together with clear tape. Two weeks later, I picked up that frame, ran all the way to two streets away, and threw it in a dumpster. For weeks after that, Grandmother shouted and ranted about that picture, but I said nothing. I still haven't told anyone it was me.

"I was set up," Mother said. "I worked as a nanny for a Nigerian doctor and his wife. They were to pay me after six months. I planned to come back within a year. But they called immigration on me instead of paying. You have no idea what I have been through." She was whispering now. "Please just forgive me."

The girl at the next table was still reading. Her neck had been bent, so I had not seen her face. One of her friends raised a piece of sausage on a fork to her lips, forcing her to eat it. As she did, I caught a small glimpse of her. She had been crying, her eyes a dull red, the skin around her nose as brown as a bad tomato. Was she crying about characters in a book?

"But you got your papers years ago. You only came back because Pastor David sent you money. You are here for the wedding," I said.

Mother opened her mouth wide, but no sounds came out. Her mouth was like a fat letter *O*.

A bulb in one of the lanterns hanging from the ceiling flickered, blinking for few seconds. Then it turned off. Our booth and the one next to us went dark. The girl who was reading a book shut it, then placed it under her arm. She opened a case, taking out her glasses. They were tortoise-shell, cat-eye glasses, with a pink tint to the plastic frame. It occurred to me then that she hadn't said anything the entire time she had been there but somehow, she seemed to me like the solid center in her group of friends.

"Pastor David just paid for the tickets," my mother said. "I am here because I want to be."

"We are happy you made it. We all are," I said.

"We will be so happy in America. You'll get a great education, become anything you want to be. You don't even have to be a doctor to get rich," she said.

"We are happy here. I'm not cut out to live in a strange country," I said.

The girls were leaving. I watched the girl with the book finish her orange juice in one long gulp. The other girls reapplied lip gloss and dabbed saliva-stained fingers across one another's eyebrows.

"Do you sometimes wonder what would have happened if you didn't leave us?" I asked. My heart was filling with a strange sadness, watching that girl walk away.

"Every single fucking day," Mother answered.

"You made the wrong choice, and I want to make the right choice for my life," I said.

"Things will be so much easier for you. You will have papers already, I did not, you will have someone to care for you, I did not," she said.

"Can't I just come visit? You know, for Christmas or something?" I asked.

Mother laughed. It was a hearty, sustained laugh. She wiped the corner of her eye when she was done.

"Yes, you can visit, but I promise you, you will not ever want to come back to Lagos as soon as you arrive. This is America we are talking about," she said when she was done laughing.

A man in a green shirt pulled a stepladder into the middle of the room. Around us, church music rang from the television and speakers. If anyone but me minded Don Moen singing God is good, no one said anything. The man with the ladder stood on the second topmost rung and stretched to remove the blown bulb. The bulb cackled and came to life at that moment, stunning him.

The man on the ladder lost his balance and struggled with steadying himself. I got up immediately, as did another young man, from a booth behind me. We stood on opposite sides of the ladder, steadying it.

Once the bulb change was complete, I signaled to Mother that it was time to leave.

The streets were busier now. The sun had gone down, it was early evening. Many people getting off the buses that brought them from jobs on the island were stopping to buy stuff before getting on other buses to take them farther into the mainland.

"Do you think we can get a taxi this time?" Mother asked.

"This is rush hour, the prices will be astronomical," I answered.

"Astronomical," she repeated, laughing again. "Americans will love you. They love black men who use big words."

"If you could do it all again, would you?" I asked.

"Do what?" my mother asked.

A young girl hawking a tray of sliced pineapples and pawpaws wrapped in clear shopping bags walked up to us. "Fine auntie, please buy my fruits so I can go home. My stepmother will beat me if I don't sell them all. It's night. Please, my auntie," the girl was saying.

"Everything. Leave Lagos for America," I replied.

Mother stopped to talk with the girl who had the fruit tray. She bought most of the sliced pineapple on the tray. She let the girl keep the change.

"Now go home and get some sleep," Mother said to her.

"In America, that little darling would be taken away from her parents. Given to people who know better than to let a girl that young roam these dangerous streets selling stuff," she said to me as we watched the girl go away.

I did not really expect her to answer my question about regrets. Just like I needed to ask, she needed to not answer. She did not seem to remember who she was before she ran to America in hopes for a better life. I did not know anything but the mother she used to be. That comparing and contrasting was my burden. I did not pay the price that she did, so America was not at all beautiful to me. What is the value of a thing but the price a buyer pays for it? How can I expect someone who went to prison for a chance to live in a country not to be excited when she got that chance? I did not really hate my mother, I did not even hate America. How can you hate something you do not know? America will always be, to me, the country that stole my mother and sent back something unrecognizable in her place. I will not call that country beautiful, or its people beloved.

The bus we rode home filled with passengers in less than five minutes. When the driver tried to start the engine, it sputtered and coughed several times but failed to start. As if on cue, with no words spoken, I and every other male on the bus got out and began to push. We were seven men trotting behind a bus. As I pushed, I noticed the girl with the fruit tray emerge from behind one of the shops in the market. Her tray was full again and she was looking around the crowd like a trained scout.

I smiled to myself as she ran to a tall, light-skinned woman dressed in a black skirt suit, a lawyer's white bib hanging around her neck.

"Fine auntie, please buy my fruits, so I can go home. It's night. Please." The girl was shouting. Her voice sounded like she had been crying.

The tall lady said something I could not hear and handed the girl some money, taking none of her fruit.

The bus sputtered and came to life. One after the other, all us men ran after the moving bus, jumping in, finding our seats.

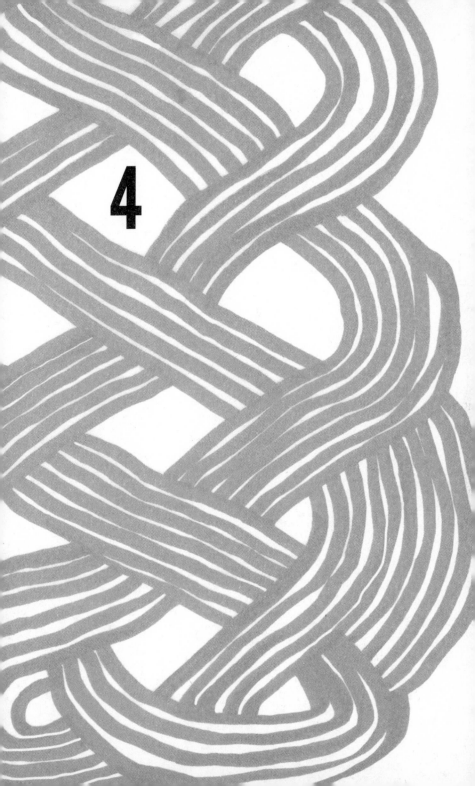

THIS OLD HOUSE

BIBIKE

2012

IN THE HOUSE where my daughter, Abike, is born, my grandmother, her great-grandmother, sits with my daughter in her arms. My grandmother's legs are stretched out straight before her. Her back is curved in a perfect half circle, bent like the handle of a teacup. She is singing the oriki to my daughter.

> *Abike for whom kings have gathered.*
> *Abike, her skin shines bright as palm oil.*
> *We ask her for meat, she gives the herd.*
> *We ask her for light, she brings the sun down.*

Sometimes my grandmother lifts my daughter's feet to her mouth, gently biting off her overgrown toenails. I tell her I have a baby kit with steady-grip nail clippers and a soft hairbrush and even a nasal aspirator. My grandmother laughs at me.

"Abike is my mother returned to the land again. I will not let you offend her with this imported nonsense," she says.

There is something about a new baby that makes older people think of all those who have passed. Each day of my fourteen-day postpartum hibernation, and many days after that, Grandmother tells me a new story about her own childhood.

"When I was a young girl, maybe just seven or eight years old, my father killed an elephant when he was out hunting by himself in Idanre Forest. Of course, no one believed him because he could not carry it back to the village.

"Then he went to Oshamolu, the native healer, and asked for a transporting spell for two beings. Oshamolu told him he could only transport two live beings at once or two dead beings, so he could not transport a dead elephant and a living hunter.

"My father then went to Father James, the white priest in town, to ask him if he could raise him from the dead, since the priests were always talking about Jesus, who raised people from the dead."

I cannot tell which parts of her story are exaggerated and which ones are real, but I love them so much that I record everything. I have a little voice recorder that records all of her stories and songs. When Abike is grown, I want her to hear it all from my grandmother's mouth. I want to cover my daughter with Grandmother's Yoruba, in the pure softness of her Ondo dialect, baptizing her with every sentence sounding like birdsong when she speaks.

The first thing you see when you walk into my grandmother's living room is the large brown rattan dual reclining daybed with white cushions. It is the kind of set you'd find on a patio in a different country; in Lagos, we keep our expensive furniture indoors. We—my twin sister, Ariyike, and I—got the set for our grandmother after she hurt herself in the kitchen. Now Grandmother spends most of her time sitting in the living room, watching television. A young woman, a daughter of an old friend, comes over three times a week to help with cooking and cleaning.

In this house we grew up in, sometimes I sit next to my grandmother in her recliner, listening to Ariyike preach the gospel of Jesus Christ on national television. It is all still surreal to me, how easily my sister slipped into this role of pastor's wife, women's leader, television minister. Everywhere I go in Lagos, her face is on posters and billboards, right next to Pastor David's, welcoming people to church. In these pictures, she is smiling. She seems comfortable and happy. It is almost as though she has prepared her whole life for this role. How is it possible that I missed that? We are twins, identical. I once believed we were exactly the same. I did not even know she really believed in Jesus.

Often, Grandmother watches Ariyike on television with me, shaking her head as she does this, complaining loud and clear.

"I really wish your Taiwo did not join those people," she says.

"It is a job like any other," I'd answer.

"No, it is not. Cooking is a job. Nursing is a job. Typing is a job. This thing, this telling people what God thinks they should do, is not a job. I have said it many times. I will say it again, but I am just an old lady and no one listens to me anymore."

Grandmother herself was a Christian once. She has told me many stories over and over. As a young girl, she was even baptized in the church. At her catechism, her name was changed from Olanike to Stella Maris. This happened in the fifties, when fewer Yoruba were going to the Catholic church. The Roman Catholics taught in English and sometimes Spanish, but the Anglican churches already had Bibles and hymnbooks in Yoruba. Grandmother went to school during the day and worked in the priest's quarters at night. She insists she was just a hard worker. She insists that she wasn't particularly clever or literary and was always nervous around new people, but that soon enough, all that reading and writing in English paid off and she was hired by A. G. Leventis in Lagos. I do not agree with her assessment of herself. She is the most intelligent person I know.

When my grandmother talks about growing up in the village, her voice is bland and steady, completely devoid of nostalgia. She does not speak ill of her village or speak of her youth with longing or wanting. Whenever I try to ask more questions about her life after she left the village for Lagos, about the grandfather I never met, she evades with Yoruba proverbs like:

"No one has to show a squirrel the way to the stream."

"No one sits by the river and argues about soap suds."

It is easy to get tired of proverbs. They contain a certain specificity of wisdom, a peculiar scale of right and wrong. Sometimes that scale is ineffective in the modern world. I am learning to create my own values. If, for example, I consider it sensible to sit by the river and argue about soap suds—which I think means that trivialities aren't worth discussing—I will very well do that.

I hope to be the kind of mother who answers all the questions my daughter has. I hope when she tries to talk with me about important stuff, she doesn't always feel like she is prying a periwinkle out of its shell.

"Let me tell you why I stopped going to church," Grandmother says to me one day, with no prior warning.

I am in the kitchen doing dishes when she wakes up from her nap. Immediately, I wipe my hands, walking to the living room, where she is seated. Abike, my baby girl, is asleep in a cot in the corner.

"Kehinde, are you hearing me?" she asks before she says anything else.

"Yes. I am here, Maami," I answer.

"Are you going anywhere today?" Grandmother asks.

"No." I said. "I will go out on Friday. I am taking Abike to get vaccinated."

GRANDMOTHER RESPONDS WITH her often repeated suspicions about vaccinations. She knows she is old, but she has seen things and the government is poisoning children with all those injections.

•

SHE SAYS SHE had a dream about her old priest and in spite of it all, it was a great dream, she was a girl again, that is, until she woke up and her legs were disappointingly wrinkly, long and skinny.

I laugh when she says this, disagreeing with her. I tell her that she has hot legs, full, fresh, and fair, that any young girl with sense would envy them. She says the world is a weird and cruel place and only the wise survive. I respond by agreeing with her and praying to Olodumare for the blessings of a wise head. It is part of the family lexicon to acknowledge with prayers Grandmother's opinion of the world. We know all the right ways to respond to her.

Her last day in church was when the priest told the story of Sodom and Gomorrah and said that God destroyed the cities because of panshaga. I laugh every time she says *panshaga* because it is the umbrella Yoruba word for sex between unmarried people, and it is funny as heck to say out loud. Grandmother interrupts my laughing to correct me. She thinks I am laughing at the idea that she was fighting for the right of young people to fornicate. Only the priests fornicated in those days, she tells me. As a young girl, she was more terrified of her parents' curse than anything a priest said.

"I went home that day and read the book of Genesis by myself. You should remember, we only had paraffin lamps and paraffin was too expensive to be using for that type of stuff," she says.

I laugh again. Abike rouses at the sound of my laughter. I pick her up.

"Do you realize that in the same chapter where angels destroy the cities, the daughters of Lot are forced to sleep with their own father and have children by him?" she asks.

"Yes, I know that, Maami," I answer.

"Why did God not destroy them and their children? Did they not do worse than the people in those cities?" Grandmother asks.

"Well, I have heard that Sodom was destroyed because of homosexuality specifically," I answer.

It is my grandmother's turn to laugh.

"Thank God those priests never said that type of stuff, the village people would have stoned them for that type of hypocrisy," she said.

"So what do you think the reason was?" I ask her when she is done laughing. Abike is waking up again. My daughter is drawn to laughter like edible termites are drawn to bright lights.

"Well, in the earlier chapters, God himself tells Abraham that the outcry against the cities is so much. It seems obvious that it was an unjust city and the people were always doing wrong to people who could do nothing but call on God." She picks up the remote and turns on the television. "Anyway, those priests said I was being heretic when I said that the next time in church, so I said goodbye to their nonsense and I have never been in a church again," she says.

"I think that you actually have to believe that the Bible is true to come to those conclusions in the first place, Maami,"

I say after a few minutes. "It is full of all these types of incompatibilities."

"That is why I believe it," Grandmother says. "It is lies that are neat and straightforward."

I imagine what opportunities would have opened up for a woman like my grandmother if she had lived a different life. I imagine her with a robe and a wig, a Justice of the Supreme Court or a professor in a university. I will never know why she did not pursue more education or get married.

"Make sure you get a priest to pray Viaticum when I am dying," Grandmother says, interrupting my thinking. *Viaticum* sticks out of her Yoruba like a strange word from an alien language.

"Maami, you will be with us for a very long time, stop that type of talk," I say.

"Amen," she says.

I pause the video player and begin singing the Yoruba prayer made famous by a local musician.

> *Mommy o, e ma pe laye.*
> *Mommy o, e ma jeun omo.*
> *Eni ba ni ko ni ri be*
> *A fo lo ju.*

> *My mother, you will live long*
> My mother, you will eat food from your children
> Anyone who refutes this
> Will go blind.

She laughs and laughs. Abike wakes up and laughs along.

In this house my grandmother built, there is a framed picture of my father at his second wedding. A young woman I have never met, her face as round as a full moon, is in a white sleeveless dress at his side, smiling directly at the camera. There is a second picture, of her twin boys on their first birthday, their heads still too big for their frames, their faces oily with party food. I wonder about the trip these pictures have made to this house.

A photographer, invited to a wedding, a birthday party, stands in the background seeking a perfect shot. Later, the couple, the parents, look at a screen then select from several shots which ones to order prints for. Next, they order copies, then mail those copies to friends and family, then they order more copies. Did my father and his new wife even stop to wonder if those photographs hurt more than they helped?

When she received them, Grandmother had her young helper buy wooden frames and hang the pictures right in the living room. When I look at those pictures, I wonder how she does not see them as a cruel testament to her abandonment, this smiling, happy, procreating photographed face.

THE MORNING MY father came back, his mother, my grandmother, had stubbed her toe on the edge of her recliner. Immediately, she clicked her fingers, circling them around her head over and over, saying in Yoruba, "My head turns all evil away. Evil will be far from me."

Later that afternoon, he was standing in the doorway

wearing all white, like the Eyo masquerade. He had the same wide, happy face in the wedding picture. He was as tall as he has always been, but it shocked me seeing him again, big-boned and happy. I was reminded instantly of how it felt as a little girl, to sit on his broad shoulders and touch the ceilings of rooms. I hoped that the boys, my brothers, Andrew and Peter, still had a chance to grow into this height and manliness despite the years of poor nutrition and hardship. I imagined them standing next to him and feeling like poor copies of a glorious original.

Grandmother screamed a long noiseless scream when she saw him. Father lay prostrate before her on the floor in the customary Yoruba greeting. I heard her inhale then hold her breath for the longest time, exhaling only after he got up off the floor.

"Why did you not send a message to let me know you were coming, Bankole?" she asked, hugging him. "We would have cleaned up, we would have made you something special to eat."

My father responded with a surprising glibness. He said he was in Lagos for a meeting that ended earlier than expected. It was a last-minute decision to stop by. Only his business partner, who was in the car outside waiting, knew he was here visiting her.

When I left the room to give them some privacy, he had not yet acknowledged my presence or my daughter's. He had taken a seat on one half of Grandmother's recliner and begun whispering to her. The turned-off television displayed their distorted reflection. From the entrance of my room, I watched him whisper. He was cuddling Grandmother with one hand. With the other, he made several frantic hand gestures.

I smelled his eager, brash male cologne. It was an interesting aquatic, synthetic smell that reminded me of resident doctors at the hospital where I worked as a teenager. There was a specific brand of ambition I had unknowingly come to attach to that smell. I did not know why, but at that moment, I was overwhelmed and terrified.

A few moments later, another man walked into the living room without knocking.

"Maami, this is the business partner I told you about," my father said, introducing the stranger to my grandmother.

"Feel free to take a look around," Father said to the visiting man.

I said nothing. I stood at the door to my room and silently hoped the man would come that way. He did not. He walked straight through the living room to the backyard.

"We are more interested in the space itself, to be honest," the male visitor said to Father. "This structure is rather old."

It was then obvious to me that this visit was not accidental. If Grandmother could tell, she did not show it. She clasped my father's hands in one hand and held them up to her face over and over again.

"Bankole, so this is your hand, Bankole, is it really you?" she repeated again and again. "Is it really you? Have you been eating well? Have you been getting enough sleep?" She placed the back of her hand on his face and neck like one would do to feel for the temperature of a sick child.

My father responded with exaggerated warmth. He kissed her forehead. He apologized that it had been so long since his last visit. He promised to bring his little boys to visit next week. His wife was pregnant again, did she know that? The doctor tells him it is another boy, isn't it all so wonderful?

The visitor looked uncomfortable with the display. He stood right by the door, running his hands along the wall above the door frame. When Grandmother embraced her son in another full hug, asking a new set of similar questions, the stranger made a loud throat-clearing sound. When that failed to get the expected attention, he knocked on the walls with his knuckles several times in quick succession.

"I am sorry," he said to me, because I was staring him down. "I just want to be sure this wall is still solid."

Father took full advantage of the opportunity to disentangle himself from Grandmother's arms. He stepped away from her, standing next to the visitor, tapping the wall with a closed fist.

"Ah! What are you talking about? This is a solid structure," he says. "Come outside, let me show you some exposed brick."

They stood together for a few minutes. The visitor insisted the walls sounded a little hollow. Father countered by pointing out they stood next to a well, that the sound he heard was a small echo from the depth of the well. As they strolled to the gate, they remarked how clean the yard was, everything swept and washed and in the right place. It was only after the gate shut and the car drove off that Grandmother moved from the middle of the living room, sitting again on her recliner.

Grandmother was restless after they left. She spent the rest of the day staring at the walls. Her face was blank, and even when she replied to a direct question, she seemed absent and confused. She would sometimes begin to ask a question or make a statement, then, in the middle of what she was saying, she would stop and apologize, telling me or whoever else she was speaking with to forget about it.

When she slept, I watched her for a couple of hours. The rise and fall of her chest was out of rhythm. She was shivering, even though the room was warm and she was wrapped in a blanket. Rapt, I did not notice when the young lady who helped with cleaning walked in.

The young lady bent low to the ground next to me, watching Grandmother for a few minutes. Getting up, she signaled to me to walk with her to the kitchen. I walked behind her to the kitchen. Her sleek black hair was secure in a tight bun. She had several raised red spots at the back of her neck.

"Sister mi, is everything all right with Grandma? Why does she cry?" she asked.

"Crying? She has not been crying," I answered.

"Yes, she has," she said, "her face is wet with tears."

I did not tell her that Grandmother had been asleep for more than two hours and that it meant she must have been crying in her sleep. Instead I asked if she could watch

Grandmother alone for a little while. *There's an errand I have to run*, I said. *There's a prescription for Grandmother's knees I need to pick up from the hospital before her doctor leaves.* She whispered a soft yes. Then she surprised me by hugging me. She was small and wiry. The hug was tight and short. I was calmed and appreciative.

But the calm did not last long. My daughter dropped her pacifier the moment I placed her in her car seat. She began to scream in uncharacteristic despair. Unexpected tears filled my eyes as I searched all over the back seat for the pacifier. I did not find it; it seemed to have been swallowed up by some dark part of my Honda Civic.

WE MADE MY daughter on a Tuesday morning in the living room of my grandmother's house. I had returned to the house three days after taking Grandmother to the hospital for knee replacement surgery, to pick up a change of clothes and a "spicy" meal. Tunde, my boyfriend, a sergeant in the army whom I met in the weekend classes I was taking at Lagos State University, had driven me because I was too sleep deprived to drive myself. Tunde, who had driven the entire way with one hand on the wheel, the other on my thigh, regaling me with pointless Lagos celebrity gossip, was the perfect antidote to all that stress. I remember thinking while we were fucking how intoxicating it felt to do something so teenager-like, many years after I stopped being a teenager myself. I remember instructing myself to do it more often, to be more relaxed and carefree.

It was in the spirit of being carefree and enjoying a cherished independence that I rejected Tunde's pregnancy-inspired marriage proposal, choosing to remain with Grandmother to raise my daughter. I was going to school. I had started my own beauty supply store. I bought a car. Every other Saturday, I took my grandmother and daughter to see the newest movies.

Why was it so easy now for all that to vanish? What chance did Grandmother have against her only child, who had decided he wanted the house for himself? It did not occur to me, as I drove all the way to see Tunde, that he was not at home. He lived in the junior barracks in Sabo, and sometimes overzealous orderlies refused to let guests in if they were not on the circulated list.

The oddest thing about all that worrying is that, although I knew in the back of my mind that I had just seen the man who left us more than fifteen years before, my mind had yet to fully comprehend it. Ariyike, my sister, brought that to the fore when I called her from Tunde's apartment.

"Bibike! What did you say? You saw our father?" she screamed. "When? Where? Today?"

Tunde's apartment was dimly lit. It smelled like cigarettes and beef stew. I placed the receiver down to open the windows, my sister still going on and on. She knew our father was still alive. The Lord had promised to preserve him. She knew a family reconciliation was imminent. That was what happened when you trusted in the Lord and made him your restorer.

"He brought some investor to look at the house. I think he means to sell it. He really upset Maami," I said finally, interrupting her.

"That old house? Someone wants to buy that thing? How much can he even get?" My sister laughed a little.

"I am not going to let him do this," I said. I was angry at my sister for laughing. She was not laughing at me, but it felt that way. I was angry that she was so far removed from all this and she did not need the house in the same way I did.

"Well, he is her only child, and she is so old she is barely functioning. That house is technically his," she said.

"So he should be allowed to disrupt her peace?" I asked.

"Don't get in the middle, Bibike, try to get on Father's good side, you need a man in your life, after all," she replied.

If Tunde's apartment had been anything like Grandmother's house, after ending the call with my twin sister, I would have at that moment gone into the backyard and walked up to the guava tree. I would have grabbed the thickest branches my arms could reach and shaken them so hard, daring them to break off. Instead, I paced the length of his living room, my fingers interlocked and cradling the back of my neck.

"I am not going to let him do this, Tunde," I said. "I swear on my grandmother's head that I will not let him do this."

There were many options open to me, Tunde observed. He was supportive and available to help, he reminded me. He could take us to the State High Courts, for example, and then Grandmother and I could swear to an oath before a judge that she did not want to move, and she wanted me to stay with her. It was all very easy and straightforward the way he explained it.

In the past, I had fought with Tunde for the way he took charge of everything, treating my whole life like a problem needing his intervention. I realized then that my daughter, Abike, was lucky to have that in her father, someone so comfortable with responsibility that he'd take on more without being asked.

WE WERE LONGER than we needed to be getting home. Tunde had asked for a few minutes to shower before going back with us, but showering required clothes coming off and he did not know how to take off his clothes around me without dancing and making a production out of it all.

It was half past eight when all three of us got back to Grandmother's house. The night was dark and humid, and so even though I could not make out the faces of most of the small crowd gathered around my house, I could smell them. It was the smell of a poorly ventilated molue bus stuck in traffic for hours. The crowd was bustling, noisy. Our living room was the nucleus of this diseased cell.

My grandmother was spread out on her daybed, her body straight like a ruler, covered with a long linen cloth. I knew she was gone before anyone said anything. Her body was lying so straight and stiff, stripped of all that mesmerizing unease she carried with her. Grandmother's body was always moving; even when she was still, her finger would twitch for no reason. You would be in another room and hear her bones crack as she stretched.

This old house, the house my grandmother died in, was built in a hurry. That explains the reappearing wall cracks and the fact that the door spaces have always been just a little too wide for regular doors. It had two different sets of builders. The first, a set of German contractors who were in Lagos to help the Nigerian federal government get ready for some international sports or arts festival. The year was 1976 and the Nigerian federal government was building five thousand houses in a hurry to accommodate visitors for this arts/sports festival being held in Lagos. This festival was an ambitious, hurried project, and by the time all the dancers, boaters, singers, thinkers, and artistes had begun to arrive from all over the world, this old house was one of the few hundred yet to be completed.

When my grandmother bought it, the house was halfway completed and abandoned. She finished up one room, the main bedroom, and moved in with her son. She spent the next five years fixing it up little by little, room by room. This is why some rooms have white ceilings while others have gray. Some rooms have those eighties' interlocking rubber tiles, and others have laminate flooring. The one bathroom has had several incarnations. At first, it was nothing but a latrine with a hole in the middle. After Bankole got out of school, he added a water closet, bathtub, and tiled the walls. When Grandmother fell in the kitchen and had surgery on her knees, my sister, Ariyike, had someone take out the old bathtub to install a walk-in cubicle with a custom-made chair. The new bath has a wide swinging door that smells like burning rubber when you take a hot shower.

It was in this new bathroom that I hid to weep. My chest had exploded into several million burning pieces.

A NEIGHBOR I do not know knocked on the door.

"Please do not cry," she said, "Maami has lived well, now she's gone to rest."

The crowd swelled around me like a sick stomach, bloated and moaning, talking in loud whispers to one another, repeating the same questions over and over like an unending chorus.

"Maami die? What happened?"

"Her son came here?"

"What did he do when he came?"

"They say he pushed her."

"No, I heard he shook her like a tray of picking beans."

"Where has he gone now?"

"Who knows where he is?"

"Who will go searching?"

My Tunde with his eager baritone uncharacteristically somber-herded the crowd away from the center toward the gate. The skin was broken, and the pus flowed freely. Our neighbors were weeping loudly and with abandon as they went home. Just like that, the spectacle of the strange death was over, and the mourning began.

In this house my grandmother built, on a short stool in the corner of her room, she has her ere ibeji shrine. There are three small wooden effigies at the center of the shrine. Their bodies are short, about four inches high. They have elongated skulls, exaggerated faces. The oldest one, the one who Grandmother washed, bathed, and sang to regularly, is female. She is dressed in a white dress, doll-sized bangles in each hand. She is Grandmother's twin, who died when they were toddlers, when Grandmother was too young to realize that there were two of them. The other two are identical, Grandmother's first children, dead within months of each other before their first birthday.

The older Yoruba believed that identical twins shared a soul before birth, that the length of their lives was nothing but a conscious uncoupling of souls. When one twin died young, they believed the living twin was in danger of dying as well.

I picked the effigies up, one after the other, wiping them with the hem of my dress. I wished Grandmother had talked to me about them. She did not practice many rituals of Yoruba traditional belief but these effigies she loved. These she bathed and dressed in hand-sewn clothes. I realized then that it was more about grieving than religion. These figures were a testament to her loss.

Tunde walked into the room as I was cleaning. It was his first time in there. If he was startled by the shrine, he did not show it.

"I have called your sister and sent emails to Peter and Andrew. An ambulance is coming to take her away," he said.

The young woman who helped with Grandmother came in with my daughter in her hands.

"Auntie, Abike won't stop crying. I don't know what to do," she said.

They were looking to me for direction, reassurance, something. I did not have it to give.

"WHAT HAPPENED HERE?" I asked her.

"Am I not dreaming?" I asked him.

They had the same look of pity when they looked at me.

The house had emptied out, leaving only a couple of people, one woman who had worked with Grandmother and another woman, the mother of the young help. They were eating puff-puffs and drinking juice out of wineglasses. I had no idea where the food came from.

"Come with me," Tunde said to me.

We walked out of the house and got in my car.

"What do you want to do?" he asked.

"I don't know," I answered.

"DO YOU THINK he may have sold the house already?" he asked.

I had not thought about it again. It was strange how little I cared about this old house now. It was Grandmother I wanted to be around, the mellow person she became in the last five years.

I missed her already. How everything my daughter did made her laugh so hard. How she hoarded the Maltesers that Andrew brought the last time he visited. How she took to wearing sneakers for the first time in her life because Peter gave her Nikes for Christmas.

"You can come live with me," Tunde said. "You know I want nothing more."

"That barracks is no place for a child," I said. "You know that."

A couple of luxury SUVs pulled up outside the gates as we talked.

"I think that is your sister and her husband," Tunde said. "You should go talk to them. Just wanted to let you know that I can go get those papers back. Grab a few friends from the barracks. We will find him in this Lagos."

My sister had arrived, but her husband was not with her. I watched from inside my car as she, together with two other women, walked into the living room, then reemerged a couple of minutes later. They seemed confused, out of place and unused to feeling that way. They were dressed in formal black attire like they thought it was already a funeral. My sister had a fascinator with a lace side piece hanging over her right eye.

"I am not ready to leave this house, Tunde," I said.

"You will not have to leave, I promise you," Tunde said.

The next morning, we were intertwined in my bed. It was still dark outside when Tunde whispered in my ears.

"I'm not leaving, I'm coming," he said.

Sometimes when we are leaving, we say *I am coming*. It is the influence of Yoruba on our spoken English—instead of goodbye, we say *till next time*, we say we will see each other again.

It is morning and it hits all over again like a fresh blow. I'm thinking about Grandmother and the death she desired. I think she wanted to die slowly, with time to send for the boys, time to hand over her shrine and trinkets and aso-ofi, time to get a priest to say prayers, to give one last admonition.

I think she died from shock—the shock of Father's brutal attack, and then the shock of her own fragility. I think she died sad and afraid.

When Tunde leaves, I pick up a broom and begin cleaning the house. I know daylight will bring with it a new set of visitors needing to be watered, fed, consoled, and listened to.

My daughter's father gets in my car and drives away. He will go to the noncommissioned officers' mess, find two or three sergeants given to drink. He will buy them bottles and bottles of beer. He will describe my father, the suspect—tall, yellow skin, balding. He will tell them what he did—an old woman shaken to her death, her property documents taken away by force. They will promise to find him, it's easy, they insist, they know most of the unscrupulous banks who buy disputed property in this part of Lagos.

Tunde tells me nothing at first. The days go by faster than a dream. We plan a wake. It is well attended. Then the internment. We get a Catholic priest. Then traditional burial rites. Andrew and Peter fly in from Chicago.

Two weeks later, the officers will find Father's house in Abuja. They will arrest him and bring him back to Lagos to answer for his actions. Father follows peacefully. He tells his wife and kids not to worry, he has done nothing wrong.

Somewhere along the Ore Highway, when the military van is stuck in traffic so bad no sirens can help, Father asks to pee in the bushes. He is given permission. A boyish officer walks with him to find a spot. Father hops off the van and limps down the road, the tar hot like coals on his feet. He follows a path through the trees, stopping at a little clearing under shade, away from the gaze of other stranded motorists. The young soldier looks away for a second—there is a Toyota HiAce bus, and the driver is playing a taped recording of a live comedy show. A young woman in a blue shirt pokes her head out a window. She is pouring water from a bottle over her head and face. The water makes a sizzling sound as it drops to the hot ground.

A short distance away, my father makes a dash for it. Four or five steps, maybe, before the young soldier notices. The young soldier calls out to him, but my father ignores him. He is running toward the center of the forest. The soldier runs after him, repeating the order to stop. The soldier shoots three quick shots, and two miss. One gets him in the underarm. It's a nick, really, a tickle. Father does not stop. The soldier shoots again. Drivers along the road are panicking and he can hear his superiors running up behind him.

This bullet goes right through his back. Father falls forward. He tries to stand again, dragging his upper body a few inches before falling again. There is a tree stump in the cleared path, and he does not see it. He trips over it. The sound his knee makes as it strikes the dry wood is a loud cracking sound. The young soldier does not know what he has heard. He thinks he is being shot at, so he shoots again, two shots to the head.

When Tunde tells me how my father died, I am sitting in the large living room of my twin sister's home. We have escaped the chaos of Grandmother's house for a few hours.

Distant relatives we barely remember have camped out, demanding ceremonial displays of justice. It had become unbearable, the unending demands, the constantly flowing suggestions of how to grieve.

My sister screams. She grabs Tunde's collar, latching on to him with childlike tenacity. It is one of his favorite T. M. Lewin shirts, but he looks at her with eyes filled with pity.

"Why? For what?" she screams. "The old house? That old woman who would have died soon anyway?"

I swallow the angry words rising from my belly. I am looking at Tunde and he still isn't angry. Even when she begins dragging him toward the flight of stairs leading to the back entrance.

"Get out of my house." She is weeping and hiccupping now. "I never want to see you here again. Do you hear me? Get out."

She comes so close to pushing him down the stairs, and still he does not resist. I get up and run between them.

"Stop that," I say. "You are hurting him."

"Get out, the two of you, take your bastard daughter, leave my house," she replies.

I do not realize I have smacked her until I hear the sound of my hand across her face.

"Shut up your stupid mouth," I say.

It is Tunde who restrains me. My sister runs down the stairs, calling for her security. Tunde and I go into the guest bedroom. Our daughter is awake but quiet in the crib, staring at her mobile with bright shiny eyes. I pick her up. Tunde picks up the baby bag.

As we go down the stairs, my sister comes back in, and she has three young men with her. They wear blue shirts over black trousers. One of them has a black beret and a policeman's baton in his hand.

"Take a good look at these people," my sister says to her staff. "Anyone who ever lets them in here again will be fired. Not just fired: arrested, sent to prison. Do you all understand me?"

"Yes," they respond, a subdued chorus.

The man with the baton looks at me, then my sister, then back at me. He takes off his beret with the batonless hand, wipes his face with it, then puts it back on.

"Hurry up, you heard Madam, leave," he says to us. He strikes the baton against the steel column of the staircase as he speaks.

"We are leaving already," I say to the security man.

We walk right by my sister. My baby reaches out to touch her nose, but she moves away. The cheek I slapped is bright red and swollen. It looks a lot worse than it really is. It will be much better in a few hours, all she needs is to run cold water over it several times. We have the exact same skin, pretty but tough. We had chicken pox for the first time as adults. The first spots showed up a few days after we turned nineteen. There must have been a thousand spots on my back alone, and we scratched with everything we could find, combs, ladles, garden hoses. Yet not one of those spots left a scar, no, not one.

BLACK SUNDAY

ARIYIKE

2015

I AM SITTING by myself in the women's ministry office. It is the Saturday before Mother's Day and the women's choir is practicing in the auditorium. They are incompetent, noisy, and restive. It is going to be a terrible service; they are doubtlessly going to embarrass us all.

I borrowed Tola, the bishop's logistics assistant, a few hours ago, but even he could not help with bringing some order to the chaos. He just sat in the seat on the other side of the table looking at me with judgment-filled eyes and saying over and over, "Just let the regular worship leader lead them. Everyone respects him."

My friend Rosetta, who is leading the women's choir, is a state governor's wife who tithes in the millions and gifts me Balenciaga and Givenchy. She is a mile and a stretch more important to the ministry than all these talentless women combined. Her husband, the state governor, is the reason the church has two private jets. The church is the reason the state governor and his family never again have to fly commercial. This is not the only reason I let Rosetta lead the women's choir. She is good for church membership growth. The younger girls adore her, the older women envy her. When she is present, all the women of this church coalesce around her like the edges of a wound.

The clank of triangles and drums and voices failing to harmonize sounds like a rowdy party in the distance. The women are succeeding in having fun, I can tell from the laughter traveling through the hallway to my little office in the corner of the building. I can tell Rosetta is being her brightest and most inspirational.

Every so often, after a new family joins our church, the wife finds her way to one of our Anointed Daughters meetings. Rosetta is there, the wife of the state governor serving, cleaning, and holding court. She draws people, makes even the most introverted make an effort to connect. Churches are built around personalities. It's hard to admit, of course, because the goal is to lift Jesus up, but it is true. Rosetta, with her ease and calm, makes people feel like they have known her all their lives. We, Pastor David and I, call Rosetta our little lighthouse.

The television in my office sits on a steel cabinet in a corner. My weekly teaching program is on air and I am watching myself. It is a recap of last year's Mother's Day service. Our network has been playing my old messages throughout the week; yesterday, it was the message I preached on the last Resurrection Sunday. All the reports from last year and the year before that are laid out on my office table. It is a pitiful pile. We are expecting fewer people for Mother's Day this year, even though we spent three times last year's budget in advertising.

There isn't much a church can do when its popularity begins to decline. Nigerian Christians are like little children. The women mostly, you'd find them with the newest, most interesting thing. These days, the most interesting thing is the prophetic, direct messages from God delivered with stunning peculiarity. Pastor David has never been that way; he is not a prophet, he is just a gifted teacher of the Word. Sadly, that counts for little these days.

Now all our programs, regardless of what we let people believe, go toward the strengthening and pampering of our loyal, committed members.

Therefore, I let Rosetta lead the choir. Even though she is tone-deaf and terrible at coordinating.

The door opens, and I am no longer sitting by myself watching myself on TV. My assistant walks in, looking more harried than usual.

"Good afternoon, Pastor Ma," my assistant says.

"Bless you, darling," I say.

"There is a young woman outside I think you should see," she says. She says "young woman" quickly, like it's a bad word, so I know this will be interesting. "Should I tell her to come back some other time, Pastor Ma?" my assistant asks as I hesitate.

"No. I will meet her in the visitors' lounge."

I have a small space next to my office, used for counseling. It's standard practice for all pastors in our ministry to have a semi-open space with doors that cannot lock from the inside to protect our ministers from false accusations and temptations—mostly temptations to tell the truth.

The young girl has angry eyes. She is young, too young for the deep frown lines spread over her forehead like ridges on a yam farm. She has a tiny baby in her hands. At first, I look at her with a smile, but she does not smile back. I understand why she is so angry. It's difficult being a young mother in Lagos. It's a thousand times worse when you are a single mother. We have a welfare program, but we only help married women. We cannot, as a church, support fornicators and adulterers with tithes and offerings. Jesus says not to cast pearls before swine. I have personally, out of my own purse, helped many single mothers. My own twin sister has two children by a man she refuses to marry, even though they carry on like the Couple of the Year, so I'm not prejudiced or unreasonable.

"Good afternoon, Pastor," she says to me.

"Good afternoon, my dear, the Lord bless you, sweetheart, you and your little—" I ask.

"Boy. It's a boy, his name is Pamilerin," she tells me.

"That's a beautiful name, God will cause you to laugh indeed just like his name says, my dear," I say.

"Amen," she answers, and now she relaxes a little. Her frown lines disappear.

I REALIZE, WITH mild shock, that I know who this is. She is one of the music ministers, a worship leader in our

University of Lagos campus church. I haven't seen her in a few months, but no one said anything about a baby. I had assumed she graduated and left the state. I am used to young girls with talent for ministry disappearing from the church. We do not do a good job of retaining females in the ministry. First of all, the leadership of the church does not think females should ascend in ministry from position to position like men do. No, our access is always tied to the men in our lives, the husbands and fathers. Second, Christian practice is very masculine. It's a religion of Father, Son, and Holy Spirit, after all. Our God is a man, His Son is a man. Therefore, all the sent are men. It is just the way things are.

"I am hoping you can help me," she says.

"Of course I will," I say. "How have you been? Are you still at the university?"

"I graduated three months ago," she says.

"Glory to God." My praise is a little louder than necessary, but it's sincere. I am so glad she got her degree regardless. As a young mother, things will be harder for her—that degree is a palliative.

"I know you can speak to Pastor David on my behalf, Ma, so he can talk to his friend. He needs to take care of Pamilerin, time is running out."

"My dear, I will talk to my husband, but I sense you are assuming I know more about this situation than I do," I say, interrupting her. "Who do you need Pastor David to speak to on your behalf?"

"Teddy," she says.

"Teddy?" I shout.

She says his name just like that. Like it is nothing for her, this little slip of a girl. She calls the state governor by his first name like just another one of her playmates.

"It's been almost a year, I thought everyone knew about it," she says.

"Knew about what?" I scream again, but she doesn't flinch. She is used to this, I realize, adults losing their cool around her.

"We met here in church. Pastor David introduced us after last Youth Conference, then Teddy invited me over for a tour of the government house," she says.

The last youth conference was in February. She must mean the conference the year before. We organize big meetings around Valentine's to keep our youth occupied. I know the governor typically speaks at these events. He is such an inspiration, he grew up poor, he is a brilliant banker-turned-politician. He is a king our young people delight to honor.

"So, what does all this have to do with me? Why haven't you gotten in touch with Teddy, as you call him?" I ask her.

She says the last time she heard from him, he gave her half a million naira for an abortion. She says she was going to go through with the abortion but then she heard the voice of the Lord loud and clear as she was sitting in the doctor's office. She says the Lord said, "Alex, you can trust me with him."

She says that's how she knew to expect a son. She says that's why she left Lagos immediately after graduating, why she now lives with her old father in Kwara. He is a retired police officer, she says; he is not rich, but they are comfortable. She has no plans to cause any trouble. She is only here because her son is sick.

"Pamilerin needs heart surgery, he has a hole in his heart, the surgery is very expensive. I have tried to contact Teddy since the week he was born but he has been ignoring all my messages," she says.

"All you little girls who think you know everything, you heard God tell you not to have an abortion. Why did you not hear God and refuse to have sex with my friend's husband? Do you have any idea what parenting is? You thought it was just getting pregnant and pushing it out. Now look at you, your first crisis, you have fallen apart. You think this is a movie? You think this is a storybook? This is real life." I do not recognize the person yelling at this girl. I do not understand this girl, why she is staring me down instead of shaking before me like a leaf in the wind. I want to hug her, but I hate her. All I see as I look at her is someone to hate. I hate what this means for Rosetta and for our church. I hate that she makes me wish she'd had an abortion even though they are illegal in Lagos and the church is very opposed to them.

"I am sorry, I am so sorry." She is crying now. All that confidence has evaporated like boiling water. I forgot for a few seconds how young she is; her initial confidence threw me. She is still barely a teenager, after all, and she is crying like one. Her makeup is melting. She drags a wipe out of her baby bag. She cleans her face with it.

I move as close to her as I can. I clasp her hands in mine. I say many soothing words. When she is composed, she apologizes for crying. She says she is sure I can understand, her son is sick and in pain, her heart is breaking, she is going crazy.

"My dear daughter," I say in the softest voice I can manage, "the Bible says the Lord killeth, the Lord maketh alive. If your child was born to live, he will. Do not be like David, crying in vain for a child of sin."

I KNOW WHAT I am doing, using Scripture for my own ends. It is impossible to spend so much time reading and teaching the Bible and be unskilled in using it as a weapon. Does not the Bible in the book of Hebrews refer to its content as a two-edged sword, cutting and dividing?

She is just a girl. She has no idea that mothering is a life-long entanglement to families, she does not know that she does not want this lifelong connection to Rosetta or to Teddy.

The girl looks at me with angry red eyes. I can tell I have surprised her. I can tell I have upset her.

"All we need is five million, the operation can be done here in Lagos. We have a doctor in the college teaching hospital, please just help me," she begs.

Now she surprises me with this pleading.

"This is a very personal matter, my dear," I reply. "It is also very sensitive. I cannot get involved. I do not even know if this is the governor's baby. You girls in the university get up to all sorts."

"I came to church to grow, to get better. I trusted all of you. I did not know that it was all a lie." She is angrier now.

She looks like the type of girl who has always been

everybody's favorite, pretty, clever, tall but not tall enough to intimidate men. She seems unaccustomed to suffering. She may have been raised middle class or lower, but she has not known real tragedy. I can tell by the way she looks now, like a balloon filled with water ready to burst.

In the glass door of the counseling room, I look at our reflection. We look like any other counseling session. It is funny how little you can tell by watching bodies move. Beyond the sliding door is my private library. After that is my assistant's cubicle. She shares a space with the youth minister. I get an idea. I suggest the youth minister to her. I tell her I am too closely involved with this thing to give godly counsel. I apologize for my words and actions. I tell her to wait for me to send for the youth pastor.

"Sometimes the godliest thing to do is to wait, my dear," I say.

"He knows," she says interrupting me. "The youth pastor knows, Pastor David knows, everyone knows. Do you think I am the first choir girl Pastor David has handed over to his politician friends? Do you think I am even the first to get pregnant? I am just the stupid girl who decided to keep it."

She must have thought she'd hit a jackpot, didn't she? She must have dreamed of all the child support, the lifestyle of ease and glamour, didn't she? She isn't sorry about what she did, about the pain she caused, she is just sad because her little meal ticket is sick.

I know what it feels like to find a way out and hold on to him. I remember what desperate feels like. I remember the intoxicating combination of fear, anger, and ambition. I can sympathize with her situation except that she's crossed the line with the "God told me to keep my baby" talk. The kind of girl to fuck a married man is the kind of girl who gets a compulsory abortion. This is Lagos, not El Dorado. There is no happily-ever-after for her here.

"You are the head of the women's ministry, you say you are here for me. For us all," she is saying to me. "Yet when Pastor David is using the choir as an escort agency for his friends, you do nothing. You did nothing, you know we went everywhere in the ministry buses, I have even been on the Life Jet."

"You seem ready to blame everyone but yourself, Alex," I reply. "You want me to feel guilt for something my husband does, something he conceals and hides from me, but you will not take responsibility for the part you played. You did not have to say yes to Teddy, you were not raped or kidnapped, little girl. You made this bed. Now lie in it."

She is stunned and silent. She is not ready for the bluntness of my words.

There is an old story Yoruba mothers tell their daughters. It begins with three men, all friends, moaning their misfortunes in marriage. The first believes he is the most unfortunate because his wife is lazy and a bad cook. The second friend says he has it worse, his wife is a day-and-night bed wetter, her condition both chronic and incurable. The third laughs at them both, insisting he would gladly trade places with either of his friends. His fate is the worst of the lot, he says, for he married a woman who lives entirely without shame.

No mother ever tells her daughter what perverse deviance

the third friend's wife performs brazenly to the consterna-
tion of her husband. No mother explains to her daughter
who these men are, or why they deserve better than the
wives they have married. This is the power of the old story:
every girl who hears it is shamed for all the things she oth-
erwise feels no shame for. Shame is female, just as merit is
male.

"You are right, Pastor Ma, I am so sorry," Alex says. The
balloon bursts and it is an avalanche of tears. She is crying
and wiping her nose.

She tells me she blames herself. She says all she feels is
guilt. Guilt has driven her crazy. She has stopped eating,
or even sleeping. She asked God to kill her instead of pun-
ishing this little innocent baby for her foolishness. She is
overwhelmed.

Even though I am trying to hide it, I feel guilty. I feel
lots of guilt. I used to believe that I was helping people here.
I used to tell myself I was making a difference and improv-
ing lives. These days, I am more accepting of the fact that I
became a Christian to help myself. I am a Christian because
I believe I am God's most important project. This is the
foundation of Christianity, it seems to me; to believe that
Jesus died to save my soul is to believe that I am important
enough, that I am deserving of the highest kind of love and
the sacrifice of an innocent.

This is my personal revolution. All my life, I never
dared to think of myself as anything special. I think often
of something my twin sister said once, about what happens
to you when you grow up as deprived as we did. She said

we got our brains locked in survival mode and we will be spending our whole adulthood dealing with that. I think she was right. Even with all this money and influence, I am still as self-serving and needy as I was when I hawked water on busy Lagos streets. But I am a Christian, so this makes it okay, God understands me and gives me His grace.

Alex is crying hard. I watch her cry. She reaches into her baby bag, grabs another wet wipe, cleans her face with it. Her cheeks are wet and shiny. She tells me she is so ashamed of the choices she has made. She realizes the fault is mostly hers. She says she just needs help, she did not create this baby alone.

The compiler of Proverbs, chapter 30, says the way of men with maidens is beyond comprehension. Is it really? It is easy to understand the appeal of youth like Alex's, all that innocence and beauty. The arrogance of power is easily explained as well. If there is any confusion, it lies in why young girls grow into women legitimizing the very systems that shame and vilify our femininity.

When Alex is done, I sit by her. I hold her hand. It is warm and dry. I tell her how sorry I am she is going through this. I tell her all mothers and babies deserve a solid system of support regardless. I apologize for not saying so earlier. I promise that the church will help even if the governor does not. She agrees to come to church for the service tomorrow, acknowledges there is a special opportunity here, its Mother's Day Sunday, we can raise a special offering for her baby's medical bills.

I am surprised that she understands. She smiles a little.

It is possible, after all, that she is more interested in getting care for her son than scandalizing the church.

When she leaves my counseling lounge, I wait a few minutes. I pray to the Lord for help. I am not sure He is listening. I walk to the auditorium; I need to see Rosetta as soon as possible. I will tell her everything I just learned. I will try to prepare her for what is coming. As I walk away from my office, toward the direction of the disconcerting sound of multiple instruments being mishandled, it occurs to me that there is something very odd about Alex's baby, Pamilerin. That baby did not move or whimper the entire time we were in the office. He just slept peacefully in his carrier like he was at home. I think about his unusual still-ness for a few seconds with a deep inexplicable dread, but I toss those feelings aside to speak with Rosetta.

My friend Rosetta is as always wearing a long dress with a single-button blazer. She is dressed a little too warmly for the Lagos heat, but her ensemble gives her a cultured put-togetherness. I have always suspected that she wears jackets and blazers all the time to hide her arms. I do not think she has anything to hide.

"You look amazing, my love, have I said that already to-day?" I hug her as I speak.

"Keke. You are too nice to me. What do you think of us?" she asks, gesturing toward the women.

"Beautiful," I say. "Absolutely beautiful."

Rosetta gathers the women together. It takes a full five minutes but soon they are together like a real choir. Then the choir begins singing a classic Yoruba hymn, "Enikan Be

To Fe Ran Wa." It is a cappella, so the rowdiness is gone. It is pleasant. Their next song, the main song, is Kim Burrell's arrangement of "My Faith Looks Up to Thee." It is a somber song, and I wish they would do away with the drums and triangles, but I say nothing. I know it is more important, for the feeling of community, to give every woman a precise responsibility.

"I need to talk with you, let's go to my office," I whisper to Rosetta as the choir sings.

She cocks her head to the side, with a puzzled, amused look, her eyes rolling like she knows what this is about, and she has already had enough of it.

The choir is singing for fun now. One of the women is playing the role of an exuberant conductor. She stands with her leg bent in a near-perfect K. She is swinging her arms back and forth as the choir sings.

I AM DREADING this conversation with Rosetta. We have talked before about her husband's philandering, and she has always been understandably protective of him. He is a man with his weaknesses like any other, all villages have their idiots, he is a brilliant and kind man who just strays. Now that I think of it, I was not really surprised to hear Alex talk about her relationship with the governor. I was neither surprised nor disappointed about my husband's role in it. What does that say of me as a woman and church leader? What type of men do we let lead God's children?

•

IN CHURCH, WE have many sayings to excuse our poor stewardship. For example, we say God does not call the qualified, he qualifies the called. We also say the church is not a place for perfect people but for perfecting people. We repeat this often enough because we hope our members can decipher the caution encoded: *Be careful around your brethren, they can be injurious.*

Beyond issuing thinly veiled warnings, there is little I can do. As the pastor's wife, I am rarely at the center of anything outside my women's ministry domain. I am invited only after the deals are signed, the guests invited, and the meeting schedule drawn. I am here for the photo opportunity and the celebratory dinner. I have become very good at invisibility, even basking in it, enjoying the protection it affords. There is, however, a dangerous dark side to this silence and the things we hide beneath it. Our Lord has promised to shine his light on every dark thing.

This is how I begin my talk with Rosetta as we sit behind closed doors in my office. I pick up my Bible and begin reading from Luke, chapter 8.

"For all that is secret will eventually be brought into the open, and everything that is concealed will be brought to light and made known to all."

"What I have learned from the Word is that Jesus did not say these words as a threat but as a promise. And it is a good promise. The promise is that God is ridding the dark of its ability to deceive His children. The promise of light is a good promise, do you understand what I am saying?"

Rosetta looks up at me puzzled, like my entering into

spiritual counselor mode is something too strange for her to comprehend.

"My dear Pastor Mrs.," Rosetta says, her tone condescending, "I am listening, but I am not sure I understand you."

I GET TO the point quickly. I tell her Alex's story. I deemphasize the solicitation to abort and the claim that their meeting in this church was orchestrated by my husband. Instead, I focus on the story's most important parts: the heartbroken, terrified mother and her unnaturally quiet little baby.

"I cannot believe that crazy girl is back in Lagos," Rosetta says. "I cannot believe she got you involved with this nonsense."

Rosetta speaks without any real emotion. I am puzzled by this. She would certainly have reacted with more fear if I had told her she had a housefly sitting on her shoulder. My friend Rosetta is short and lean. She is the kind of woman regularly mistaken for someone much younger. Her body is deceptively fragile. I know from playing tennis with her that she is strong and agile. She tells me her own version of the story. Alex as seductress, a one-night stand that results in a pregnancy.

"Teddy tries to convince her to have an abortion. He pleads, he bribes her. Do you know he bought her a car? You should know that no one told me anything at the beginning," she says.

"How long have you known about her?" I ask, interrupting her.

"Since last Christmas," she says. "So, Teddy has no choice but to arrange the abortion himself. He invites her to the guest house for what she thinks is a birthday dinner. But his assistants take her to a hospital, she is knocked out, the abortion is performed." She is speaking so casually about it. She is showing neither sadness nor remorse.

"Of course, when she comes out of it, she goes crazy," Rosetta says. "God warned her not to kill her baby, she keeps screaming, crying. They have to restrain her. She is sedated and left in the hospital for a few days."

"Is this when you learned about it? After the forced abortion?" I ask.

"Of course not," Rosetta replies with sharpness. She is impatient with me now. "You know these men, they only tell us when the whole thing explodes in their faces. I learned much later, when my friend, editor at *Weekly Trust*, told me Alex contacted the newspaper to say she had birthed the governor's child. The story did not run, of course, because she was clearly crazy with no baby."

"So what did you do then?" I ask.

"I confronted Teddy, and he told me all that had happened. I told him to get the girl some help, and as far as I know, he did."

It is almost unbearable watching the casualness with which she speaks about it all. I wonder how I missed it, this callousness. It is possible it has always been there, but I can only recognize it now because of what is happening, because Alex reminds me of the girl I used to be.

"Don't worry about her, I will tell Teddy that she is

back again. This time I will make sure she gets the help she needs," she says.

I rise from my chair and give her a quick hug.

"Don't worry about that, since we have established it's mental illness. I will get her help, you have done your best, dear. These young girls and their wahala, may God deliver us," I say.

We walk out of the office, toward the underground garages. We are talking about service tomorrow. The dress code is red or gold. We joke about all the tacky outfits we expect to see, we agree that Lagos Christian women try too hard to appear classy. *Someone needs to teach them that style is effortless*, we say.

LATER THAT EVENING at home, I sit in the large nursery Pastor David and I designed the first time I got pregnant. I have been falling asleep in here for months now, and if my husband has noticed I'd rather be here, he says nothing about it. I take off my shoes and sit on the floor. The carpeting is imported, several inches thick. If you accidentally dropped a baby in this room, the only real risk would be carpet burn.

I am praying to God for a sign, for His wisdom in this situation. Do I talk to Pastor David or do I go straight to the governor with this? Who will protect Alex if her governor is angry with her? I want to focus on her recovery, on therapy and treatment. But what about justice? What about all the other girls?

I am not one of those Christians who hears a clear,

distinct voice leading them. What I have experienced over and over is indescribable peace during a chaotic situation or inexplicable insight in the middle of confusion. That is how the Lord leads me. Today, I really wish He would talk plainly to me. I'd give anything for a burning bush, or even a still, small voice.

When I told my departed grandmother that I was going to be Pastor David's wife, she was quiet for a long time.

"Taiwo, ile-oko ile ogun, marriage is a battleground," she said. "Are you sure about this man?"

I was not sure, but I was determined.

"Yes, I am sure," I said.

"The goat and the family whose religion requires a sacrifice of goats cannot be serving the same God, do you understand me?" my grandmother asked.

"Yes, I do," I said. I was lying.

It is easy now, because she is dead, especially because of the manner of her death, to think of my grandmother with fondness, but she was really just a cantankerous, talkative old woman. Nothing was ever good enough for her. Nothing ever made her happy except nagging her grandchildren. She was tolerable only when she was telling us stories.

She told some weird stories. Most of the nightmares I had as a teenager were because of the stories she told of Olokun, goddess of the vast oceans. Olokun was believed to be the most powerful being on earth. It is said that Olokun covered the entire earth with water, trying to prevent Oludumare from creating earth's people. Oludumare had to trick her into giving permission. Grandmother's stories were her way to capture our attention and our imaginations. All those stories, all those proverbs, all they did was ingrain her in our minds. She wanted us to think regularly of her words and her wisdom.

It is three a.m. when Pastor David comes home. I am lying on the carpet, showered and shaven and pretending to be asleep. Everything he likes. He comes into the nursery fifteen minutes after I hear him unlock our front doors. He smells like okra soup and palm oil.

The women who worshipped Olokun used to be the richest, most beautiful women in Grandmother's village in Ondo. Not just Ondo, but all the villages along the Atlantic Ocean had Olokun priestesses. She gave them beauty, wealth, and honor. They were covenant protectors of her waters and life-forms. They did not eat anything from the ocean. They protected her waters from pollution, they did not bury their dead in the sea, they did not allow villagers to eat baby fish.

"Are you ovulating?" Pastor David asks, lying next to me on the carpet.

"No," I say, "I checked."

"Well, is there a difference, really?" Pastor David says. He is leaning into my knees and its hurts.

According to my grandmother, Olokun worship declined because of transatlantic slavery. Women were afraid to worship the ocean because she punished her daughters severely for desecrating her. All the mothers in the villages by the ocean wanted to be free to tell their children, "Run into the ocean if you see the white men coming. If they catch you, jump into the sea." But if you worshipped Olokun, you could not dare do that.

I had many nightmares that I was captive on a slave ship and that people were jumping to my right and left but I would not, I could not. I did not want to offend my mother's goddess.

Pastor David's breath is like steam on my neck. I wipe the invisible vapor. He does not notice. He is carrying on. I repent for all the times I wished Pastor David had a girl-friend. I repent for all the times I wished he came home every day spent, and with no interest in me.

"Pass me that little pillow, Mommy," he says to me. He calls me Mommy in faith. Someday soon, when the Lord wills it, I will get pregnant and carry it to term. I reach out to the cot and pull a little pillow that has HELLO HERO written across in it. He places it under my hips for lift.

It is easy to dismiss the truth contained in stories due to the limits of point of view. How can I accept the stories my grandmother handed down to me? None of my grand-mother's ancestors could tell why captured Yoruba children jumped or didn't jump. Those stories were lost to them as they are to me, trapped on the other side of the ocean, in the stomachs of their stolen children.

I have read about it, and I have several guesses about the captives who did not jump into the ocean. It is more likely that their chains were heavy and shackled to the ship itself. It is also likely that the ships' nets were too tall to jump over.

THIS IS WHAT I did when I was younger—approached her stories with logic, inspected them for improbabilities and inaccuracies. It was important for me to be able to logically dismiss them to stop being so afraid.

It is a common mistake, to hear a story about tragedy and disbelieve it because the telling is off. We think to ourselves, how does the storyteller know this? We are asking the wrong question. The right question is, why is the storyteller telling me this story? Because I was a child, I heard this story about a village full of mothers and the great loss they suffered and assumed it was a story about the pain of a child. Now, as a woman, I know the story is not about lost children. Children move from this plane to the next every day. It is a story about unquantifiable loss. It is a story about a lost goddess. What they lost was a god who looked like them. What they lost was the belief in an omniscient, omnipotent female spirit. Now look at this: all of us are condemned to serving these male gods and their rapacious servants.

PASTOR DAVID HAS passion. Of course, he is a minister, an evangelist. Passion is contagious, endearing. Passion does not replace integrity or courage. Passion is not a substitute for compassion.

"Mommy, did you say something?" Pastor David asks me. I must have mumbled.

"Yes," I say, "I asked if you were finished."

"Soon. I'd be faster if you keep quiet and just let me focus," he says.

It is a little funny how a man who can preach stadiums full of people into a screaming frenzy would be, in his home, as tense as a clenched fist. People tell me they leave our

Sunday services fired up, excited to take on the week. I wish there was someone I could tell that he leaves me hollow, desperate, angry, and raw.

"Have you finished outlining your sermon for tomorrow, Mommy?" Pastor David asks me. He is finished and sitting up next to me.

"A member of the choir came to see me today. Her name is Alex, she needs our help," I say instead.

"What does this have to do with the sermon?" he asks.

"Is her story true?" I ask.

"Are you going to tell me what you have prepared for God's people? Will I have to preach the women's message myself?" he asks.

"I am teaching about light and darkness, Pastor, the words of Jesus. Everything hidden will be manifested, every secret will come to light," I say, even though it is not true. I planned to teach on the faith of Ruth, who is a favorite here at the New Church.

"And what do you expect to happen after this message?" my husband asks.

"The Holy Spirit will correct, convict, cleanse," I say.

"You are just like your father, do you know that?" He gets up off the floor, standing over me like a tree. "When things get rough, you forget you are part of the church. You are looking for a scandal when there is none. You think you can bring me down? This is the church of God. This is going to last forever, do you understand that?"

"The church is only as strong as its weakest link," I say.

"That is stupid nonsense you have gotten from watching

too much TBN. Weakest link? Then the church will be per-petually weak, each day adding new broken people to the fold. The church is the incorruptible bride of the glorified Christ."

He is doing that preacher thing. That *watch me make you look stupid* thing. That *you are out of your league* thing. That *dissecting Scripture is for men* thing.

"She needs our help, Pastor," I say when he is done.

"What she needs is a deliverance minister. That girl is possessed with many sexual demons. They have driven her crazy. She has had too many men to count, she is a fractured shell of a person," he says.

"She also needs an apology, some therapy, something from us," I say.

"You should focus on your own life, your own family. I am halfway out this door and you're barely noticing," he says.

"I'm not blind, Pastor," I say.

"I think you are forgetting you are a nobody. You have nowhere to go, you are a nobody, you have nothing. What will you do if I leave you? Go and live with your sister and her boyfriend? Or in your brothers' college dorm rooms?"

In one of my earliest memories, I am running around with no clothes on. I am two or maybe three years old. I watch myself trip, fall, and I begin to cry. I stop crying as soon as I realize that nothing hurts. I can still hear crying, but it is coming from outside me, the body that fell, the body that is crying is outside me. This is the first time I realize that Bibike and I are different people, with separate bodies.

I go to her. I push her down as she tries to get up. The more she cries, the harder I laugh.

It is possible that my personality has been framed entirely by that moment, by the joy of being separate. It is possible that all my life, I have continued in this vein, intent on proving that I am different, separate from her. This is how I have convinced myself that I am important, that I am not the bonus child. It is possible that this is the reason I needed to work in entertainment, just like I needed to marry into this money and this hypervisibility.

"I am not a nobody and you are not God. You're not the one writing my story," I say to my husband.

"But I am your lord, and you will obey me like Scripture commands," he says.

I say nothing. He grabs me by the nape of my neck, pulling me up on my feet.

"Preach a great sermon tomorrow, Mommy," Pastor says. "Don't stir up trouble. Encourage God's people and look nice."

His grip is stiff around my neck, like a steel necklace.

"Yes, Pastor," I say.

IT IS A cool Sunday morning. It rained for most of Saturday night. Outside smells both fresh and musty, like a murky village river muddied by erosion. The drive to church is quiet and terrifying. Pastor David and I sit in the back of our Toyota Land Cruiser Prado.

Two men, the driver and Pastor David's assistant, sit in the front of the vehicle. There is gospel music playing.

Whenever we drive into a pothole deep enough to rattle us, Pastor David murmurs something about disrespectful Lagos roads. Whenever we drive past young people hanging out by the streets laughing, smoking, doing whatever, Pastor murmurs something about the perilous end of times.

Alex is waiting inside the lounge of Pastor David's private entrance. Her tiny baby is in one hand, still as stone, In the other hand, she holds a satchel diaper bag. It is white and yellow, pretty like a summer day. There are a few church workers milling around. One man, dressed in the black overalls issued to our camera crew, is pushing a dolly with a large speaker. Another is dragging several feet of cable wrapped around his arm. They are all busy and no one but me seems surprised to see Alex there.

The tightening in my chest is a warning, I know that now.

"Good morning, Pastors," she says to us. "Can I come with you? Pastor Ma?"

"Alex, I have spoken with Pastor about you. He will give you the answers you need," I say.

She looks at me with shock, like I just said the most incredulous thing.

"Pastor sir, I will see you in the service." I say it loud enough for everyone around to hear. "I'm headed to my office."

I do not look back to see if Alex is walking behind me or going with Pastor David. In my office, I search for the outline for my sermon. I will be teaching the story of Ruth and the dignity of her diligent labor. I find it tucked between books on my desk. I read through it, excited and relieved. The service is saved, normalcy is restored, glory to God.

I read the outline again, and I make more notes. "Ruth is one of the mothers of our faith because she learned to listen to the advice of her mother-in-law. Older Christian women have a responsibility of mentorship and guidance toward the younger girls in the church." My sermon is not revolutionary, but it is a start. We can start a spark that will someday become a fire.

The auditorium is filling with worshippers. I can hear the regular worship leader and responses:

There is power in the name of Jesus
To break every chain

I wonder where Rosetta is, where her husband is. It is possible they decided to skip church today. I am not surprised. People are predictably selfish, we are born selfish, even little babies; notice how hard they cry when they need something, screaming and demanding to have their needs met immediately. Selfishness is normal, human.

I wonder what happened to Ruth's sister Orpah.

The phone in my office rings, startling me. My assistant does not work on Sundays. I pick it up. It is Pastor David's assistant, he has heard some high-pitched screaming in the office. He thinks it's Pastor screaming. Yes, Alex is still in there. No, they are not in the counseling room. He cannot go in. He refuses to intrude.

"Can you please come here, Ma, take a look, just to make sure everything is okay?"

Pastor David is on the floor in his office, kicking his legs around. His hands are wrapped around a bleeding penis. His pants are down to his knees. The floor is littered with a bunch of bloody face tissues. He is talking to me, but I do not hear him. My eyes are fixed on Alex. She is standing in the corner with her little doll in her hands, rocking back and forth, her eyes closed like she is trying to soothe herself to sleep.

"Have you also come to take away my baby?" Alex asks. Her eyes are still shut, but her voice is calm. "Are you here to take my baby from me?"

"Call my driver to take me to the hospital, this stupid girl attacked me," Pastor David says.

I am not in a hurry to call for help. I straighten Alex's shirt. I wipe the sides of her mouth with tissue; there is semen, but no blood. I begin tidying up the room. I am also searching for her weapon of choice. I am picking up the stuff strewn all over—church bulletins, Alex's hair tie, A4 paper, a button off Alex's shirt, Scofield's reference Bible, a bloodied staple gun—there it is—several pens.

THE MORNING I married Pastor David, my mother came to me with information she had received from a "reliable" source.

"We were not the only ones who lost everything because of this church," she said.

"I know."

"You know that Pastor David was behind it all? You know that money is how he built this church? Bad money, 419 money?"

"I know."

I did not know. Of course, like any other reasonable person, I had my suspicions, but nothing had ever been confirmed.

"Please, Ariyike mi, oko mi, olowo ori mi, do not marry this man, please, I beg you, there is still time to change your mind."

Mother knelt before me, holding on to my legs like she was the child. She was crying, tears were running down her face to my feet. I stood there for many minutes saying nothing, just listening to her cry.

ALEX STAYS STILL in the corner. She is holding on tight to the little doll, like she expects me to try to take it from her. There's a sprinkle of blood on her hands, on her skirt and shoes.

"He is such a calm little boy, isn't he?" I ask.

"Yes, he is," Alex says to me. "I am so blessed."

The assistant who called me opens the door now, slowly at first, hesitating. He is just checking to see if we are all okay. He screams at the blood, at the pastor writhing on the floor, at the crazy girl in the corner and the calm pastor's wife.

I told my mother that I was marrying Pastor David as part of a well-planned revenge plot. I was going to get the money he stole from my family, and more than that, I was going to get dignity and prestige. Mother did not believe me even though I tried hard to convince her.

"Just give me five years, I'll ruin his entire life," I'd said.

IN MY FAVORITE Yoruba folktale, three children engage in idle boasts. The first one claims he can climb the tallest palm tree in the village. The second one insists he can do better: he can swim across the ocean without getting tired. The third friend boasts of catapulting a pebble all the way up to the heavens, defying the law of gravity. The tortoise, a recurring character in Yoruba stories, overhears their idle boasts and reports them to the king of the land.

The king plans a day of contest. "Now you have the opportunity, do all you have said you can do," he says to the children.

When the contest day arrives, the climber stops halfway and begs to be carried down the tall tree; the swimmer nearly drowns from exhaustion and must be lifted by boat out of the ocean. The boy with the catapult surprises them: his pebble goes up to the heavens and is never seen again. He wins money from the king and the respect and admiration of his village.

As a child, when I learned of the third child's secret, his cunning—he switched the pebble with a tiny bird—I was in awe of it. A meddling king bested by a cunning child, what a triumph.

"JESUS CHRIST! PASTOR, what happened in here? What is all this?" Pastor David's assistant is weeping and shrieking.

The assistant squats next to Pastor David and helps pull his pants up. He is weeping as he does this, asking the same pastor what happened over and over like a song stuck on a loop. Pastor David is telling him to keep quiet and take him to the hospital.

Many more people come in. *Pastor David has fainted*, I hear someone say. Together two or three people surround him like a shield, they lift him up. A different someone screams for the driver to get the Prado. I do not even like that vehicle, but I am irritated that they will get blood-stains all over the back seat and that most of the stains won't come off.

The truth is I never intended to bring down Pastor David. I married him to better my own lot. Just like I admired the third child in that story, I admire this man, somehow. He has done so many things, influenced so many lives. Even if I could, why would I, having tasted this lifestyle, want to destroy it? There is no larger life than this. This is the Kingdom.

Truth be told, it has cost me more than I imagined I was giving up. For example, it's been three years since I last spoke with my twin sister. We were once the closest sisters in all of Lagos. She is an herbalist now, having expanded her beauty supply store. Now she mixes healing potions and ori cleansing lotions for Lagos women. I am a pastor's wife, a television minister. What agreement will light have with darkness? It is for this very reason the Lord Jesus said in the Gospel according to Luke, I have come to turn your families inside out.

•

THERE ARE MANY versions of the kids-making-playful-boasts story. In one, the swimmer drowns in the ocean, his body floats for days on end, the king commands no one to touch it. In another version, the climber dies of heatstroke ascending a tall tree in the noontime. In yet another, the king has both climber and swimmer executed for failing to achieve their goals.

All versions agree, the trickster wins in the end.

ALREADY, I AM exhausted by the months that are coming. I have my eye on Alex, and she is looking up at me with bright, hopeful eyes. She is shivering and afraid. I move closer to her, wrap my arms around her, and hug her over and over.

"IT IS GOING to be okay, I promise," I say to her, lying.